VISION QUEST

Ben Reeder

For Hemlok

Ben Reeder

Vision Quest
Copyright © 2015 Ben Reeder

Cover art by Angela Gulick Design.
Published through Irrational Worlds

Other books by Ben Reeder:
The Demon's Apprentice series:
The Demon's Apprentice
Page of Swords

The Zompoc Survivor series:
Zompoc Survivor: Exodus
Zompoc Survivor: Inferno
Zompoc Survivor: Odyssey

Also from Irrational Worlds:
JM Guillen
On the Matter of the Red Hand (Judicar's Oath)
The Herald of Autumn (Tommy Maple)
EM Ervin
Wake Up Call (The Nasaru Chronicles)

Coming Soon from Irrational Worlds:
JM Guillen
Aberrant Vectors (Dossiers of Asset 108)
EM Ervin
Mother Knows Best (The Nasaru Chronicles)

For RL Hampton
You were a good man, and you made my mother's world a
beautiful place.

Acknowledgements:

As usual, this book was a team effort. Without you, Randi, none of my books would EVER get done. And where would I be without my new writing assistant Dora, eleven pounds of gray fur and purrs? In addition to the usual suspects, Monique Happy has stepped up to the plate for editing. Special thanks go to the folks at Games, Comics, Etc. for letting me set up in the back and finish the last few chapters.

This is the first actual new entry in the Demon's Apprentice series in quite some time, and there are some folks I need to offer some belated shout outs to.

One, to Becca Reynolds, for the concept of the *paramiir* and for the word itself. Second, to Summer Arnall, for Shade. Thank you for letting me take your super-hero and turn her into a teenage werewolf!

Also, I can't say thank you enough to the folks at VisionCon for making the Page of Swords second release such a success. I'm looking forward to releasing Charm School at VisionCon 2016!

Chapter 1

~ It isn't the hardship of the road, but the leave-taking that pains us most. ~ Nick Cadmus.

I didn't get a summer vacation. I got the wizard version of summer school, with long recess periods. As I stumbled into the kitchen on the last day of our trip to San Angelo, I really didn't want to see this part of it end. My dog Junkyard trotted in beside me, much more alert and happy about being awake than I was. The smell of bacon had us in its grasp, and we didn't want to miss out on our fair share. Dr. Corwyn stood at the old white stove with a pair of tongs in one hand and a plate covered in paper towels in the other.

"Good morning, Chance," he said without turning his head. There was definitely too much cheer in his voice to be human, but he was a wizard, go figure. Not only was he up and chipper, he was clean-shaven and dressed in jeans and a freshly pressed button-down blue shirt. The first rays of sunlight were coming in through the window over the sink to his right, and I swore I could hear a rooster crowing somewhere in the distance.

"Yeah, morning," I grunted as I made my way to the old-fashioned percolator and grabbed one of the thick white mugs hanging under the cabinet. While we had been here, Dr. C had been making his coffee the old-fashioned way, and I'd become a reluctant fan of the stuff. It was stronger than a pissed-off Nazirite, and it tasted pretty decent even black, but one cup was all I could ever handle. With my cup mostly full, I sat down at the table and helped myself to cream and sugar. Junkyard plopped down beside my chair, patiently waiting for anything I might 'accidentally' drop, his big dark eyes almost lost against his brindle fur. He still wore the red bandana Synreah had given him, much loved and a little faded since March.

Lucas shuffled in after I was a few sips into my morning dose of caffeine and followed the same path I had, sitting down across from me. He hadn't changed out of the sweat pants and white t-shirt he slept in, and his shoulder-length black hair was mashed up on one side of his head. I probably looked almost as bad, since my hair was longer than his and tended to tangle.

5

"Dr. C, could we at least *try* some French vanilla or something?" he asked as he poured his own cream into his cup.

"Not here," Dr. C said. "There are some things you just don't mess with." Lucas looked across the table at me and shrugged, as if to say 'I tried.' I raised my hands to look like I was commiserating, but I knew why plain cream and sugar were all Dr. Corwyn would ever let anyone put in their coffee here. Because of the Horus Gaze we had shared last October, I could relive a thousand happy memories he'd had in this place. Fifteen Christmas mornings, Thanksgivings, and Easter Sundays, thousands of meals, hundreds of nights spent playing cards or dominoes, doing homework or writing letters to friends. I turned to look into the large family room that was just off the kitchen and remember afternoons and evenings watching television in black and white, and then in color. I could remember through his eyes watching the first moon landing when he was eight. I could also remember two funerals, and how empty the house still felt after his parents died.

This house was a big part of who he was, and with the memories of his that I had in my mind, I could feel some of the fierce love for it that he did.

Mom and Dee came in from the short hallway toward the front of the house, neither looking like they were nearly as cheerful as Dr. Corwyn. Both of them were dressed, which was why Lucas and I were still in what we'd slept in. There was only one bathroom, and they had been in it when we woke up. Mom was in one of her more colorful skirts and a loose white blouse, while Dee was in knee-length jean shorts and a University of Texas t-shirt.

"Good morning, ladies," Dr. C said as Mom went for the coffee and Dee opened the refrigerator. Dee grunted something, while Mom just gave a low warning growl. Wanda came in on their heels, looking almost as bright-eyed as Dr. C sounded. For a girl with Goth style, she was disturbingly chipper in the mornings. Of course, she was equally upbeat in the afternoon. In fact, aside from being kidnapped by vampires, I'd never seen Wanda in anything less than a decent mood. She'd gone with black and red striped leggings under a black skirt, with a black button-down shirt that left an inch or so of skin showing below the hem. A pair of black knee-high boots with red panels added another three inches or so to her height.

"Morning," she said as she waited for Mom to finish getting her coffee. Dee just gave her a baleful look through the curly mop of her bangs, while Mom just gave her a raised eyebrow as she passed.

"At least she didn't say it was a *good* morning," Lucas said.

"Not yet," Wanda said as she sat down with her coffee.

"It's about to be," Dr. C said as he set the plate he'd piled with bacon next to the stack of empty plates on the table. Hands reached for plates and bacon, most at the same time. There was enough that we actually left some on the plate, and the plate of scrambled eggs came next, with hash browns, biscuits and gravy, and a stack of toast right behind it. I dutifully snuck a slice of bacon to Junkyard and grabbed another one to make up for it.

It wasn't until we were almost done that I realized how much I was going to miss this. This was what happy, almost normal people did. It was what a *family* did. Even if today and every day included the constant training, lessons, and exercises that the last two weeks had, I would prefer it to what waited for me at the end of summer. When September came, I was going to be leaving all of this behind to go to the Franklin Institute. I swallowed around the bitter lump in my throat and tried to put the thought of that out of my head. I still had a couple of months left before that happened. Today was still good.

"Chance, is the Mustang ready to make the trip back home?" Dr. C asked as we finished the last of the bacon.

"Yeah, she's got a full tank of gas, radiator's full, and all the tires are good," I said. "All we need to do is finish putting the new speakers in, but Lucas says we're almost done with that." Across the table, Lucas nodded and mumbled something around a mouthful of bacon.

"Are you sure—" Mom started to say.

"More than sure," Dr. C cut her off with a warm smile. "He saved the world, or at least New Essex. He deserves something better than an eight-track player and an AM/FM radio to listen to for the trip back home. Lucas, what about you?"

"The *Falcon*'s ready to go," Lucas said. "And the last parts we need for the Mustang should be in already."

"Good," Dr. C said. "Your proctor should be here in an hour, and our flight leaves at eleven, so we should see you boys back in New Essex tonight."

"Mom, I want to ride back with Chance," Dee asked, her voice bordering on a whine.

"Deirdre," Mom said with a little bit of iron in her voice. "Dr. Corwyn already bought your plane ticket, and Chance is going to have another person riding with him on the way back."

"I can sit in the back seat, it's really big," Dee said. Mom's face clouded and she took a deep breath. I'd seen Dee try to butt heads with Mom enough over the past few months to know that Dee was pushing her luck. Whenever Mom paused and took a deep breath, it usually meant that The Law was about to be Laid Down on Dee, and she wasn't going to like it.

Everyone jumped when the phone rang. Dr. C got up and went to the heavy beige phone on the wall by the cabinet to answer it. That phone had only rung one other time while we'd been here, and that was when the Franklin Academy had called to let us know when the proctor for my evaluation would be here. The conversation was subdued, and when he hung the receiver up, his smile had faded.

"Well, that was the Franklin Academy," he said. "Your proctor has been delayed by a tropical storm in the Gulf, so he'll be a few hours late in arriving." His voice slipped into a very formal, slightly clipped tone for the last part, as if imitating someone.

"Where the hell is he coming from, Bermuda?" Lucas asked.

"Not quite; he cut short his vacation in the Cayman Islands to bless us with his company, so I guess we're supposed to be eternally grateful for his great and noble sacrifice," Dr. C said as he sat back down.

"So, we pick him up this afternoon and follow you back a little later than we thought," I said.

"Like tomorrow morning," Dr. C said. "Early. Tomorrow morning." Lucas and I traded a look that promised Mr. Proctor a difficult night and an early wake up call.

"Even if you're going to be late getting home, we still have to leave today," Mom said. Wanda looked up and smiled, while Dee moaned about having to pack *again*. Lucas and I bolted for the bathroom. He got there first, but fortunately, he didn't take long. When we came back, Dr. C was waiting in the living room just off the dining area, a black vest on over his blue button-down shirt. He gestured to me when I came in the room.

"Chance, come with me for a moment," he said as he headed toward the back door. I followed him out to the back yard with Junkyard at my side, and he wandered over to the carefully tended section that had been his father's garden. Even though he hadn't planted anything in it, hollyhock grew against the back fence, spider plant was just beginning to bloom near a patch of St John's Wort, and wild thyme sprouted in a clump near the corner closest to the house. More than one day of my summer "vacation" had been spent pulling weeds from it and making sure that the wild growing plants were watered. He didn't say anything as he looked over it, then bent down and plucked a weed that had just poked up near the cinder blocks that ran around the edge of it. The silence stretched out for a full minute, and I stayed still and quiet. We'd spent a lot of time like this over the past two weeks, and I knew he was waiting for me to either notice something or get into the right frame of mind. A mourning dove cooed somewhere nearby, and the first cicada of the day buzzed as I stood there and waited. Junkyard, not being a part of the conversation, decided there were a few places along the fence that needed to be peed on and went to work.

"I'm leaving the LeMat with you," he finally said. "I left a couple of extra cylinders for it, and a reload for the under-barrel as well."

"That'll help," I said. "Same load as last time?"

"Incendiary spell rounds in the cylinder, yes," he said with a nod. "But the lower barrel round is different this time. A little hotter mix for a little bigger bang. Here's hoping you don't have to use it."

"Yeah," I said.

"Something's bothering you," he said.

I nodded and said, "I had the same dream last night."

"Exactly the same?" he asked as he turned to look at me.

"Not exactly. I was standing in a circle of lights, like last time, but this time ... there was someone else there. I couldn't see them clearly; they were standing just outside the circle."

"And it was silent, like the first one?" he asked. He continued off my nod. "I was wondering if this might happen."

"If what might happen?"

"Some magi get a vision early in their training, an epiphany that guides them toward something bigger. Not all magi do, though. It's very spiritual. Ever since you saw the face of the Divine in March, I figured it might happen."

"You sound worried," I said.

"Sometimes, visions … don't come easy," he finally said. "The indigenous tribes here in America figured out how to induce them through fasting and communion. In some of the European and Asian traditions, they occasionally came after hardships and trials, or at the end of a quest. You've already dealt with your fair share of trouble. I don't want to see more come your way."

"Trouble I can handle," I said, then looked back over my shoulder at the house for a moment. "Just make sure Mom and Dee make it back home safe."

"I will," he said. "Watch your back. We got lucky with that warlock in Christoval last week. I don't want you to get blindsided like that again."

"I've kicked a demon's ass," I told him. "I'm pretty sure I can handle whatever I run into."

"I hope you're right. I'm not sanguine about letting you travel alone like this."

"Not a lot of other options," I said with a shrug. "Unless you think they'll let us check the Mustang in with our bags. And we can always try to put Junkyard in a dress. Don't worry, I'll be fine, sir."

"You'd better be. I don't want to have to deal with your mother being mad at me again." He reached down and took a couple of rounded, dark stones from the cinder block at his feet. "A little bit of lore for you. There is an earth spirit who calls this garden home. I've been trying to find out from one of the Lipan *diyin* if it's one of theirs, and what to call it, but they don't trust me yet, and I'm not willing to push it. When I visit, I leave it some dried corn and drop some seeds for it to plant, and sometimes it leaves me a little something before I leave." He handed me one of the stones, and I felt it tingle against my palm.

"Gifts given at parting have a special importance, Chance. I get the feeling you and your family are welcome in my father's garden."

"Does it always give you stones?" I asked.

"Not always," he said. "Once, it left me a couple of flowers, but it seems to prefer bundles of leaves or seeds. So far, it doesn't seem to have any hang-ups about being acknowledged, so I always say thank you." He turned toward the garden and held up the stone, then inclined his head a little. *"Wado,"* he said. I copied him, using the same word, Cherokee for thank you. It was a word his mother had taught him, a small part of her heritage that he kept alive. I shook my head to clear the memories that weren't mine.

Dr. C squeezed my shoulder briefly before he turned and headed back inside. I stayed for a few moments and took in the peaceful morning. From behind me, I could hear a car door slam and an engine start as someone got ready to go to work. One of the things we had been working on was expanding my awareness, not only of what was visible, but of what ran beneath the surface. It was one of the first steps toward being able to project my consciousness outside my body, though that wasn't likely to happen for a decade or so. Across the alley, I could see movement in the house behind Dr. C's, and I felt the chaotic energy of the young couple who lived there. The house to the east had a more placid feel to it as Mrs. Jimenez, the retired teacher who lived there, went about her routine. I took a deep breath and centered myself, drawing my senses back in.

After I filled the water dish for Junkyard, I came back in to barely contained chaos as Lucas and Wanda worked on the dishes at the sink while I heard Mom's voice as she tried to keep Dee focused on one thing at a time in the master bedroom. From the dining room, I could already see Dr. Corwyn's battered leather suitcase and shaving kit by the front door. I relieved Wanda at the sink so she could go pack. By the time I dried the last dish, she was dragging her red suitcase out of what had once been Dr. Corwyn's room with her head bent over her cell phone.

"What if I forgot something?" Dee asked Mom as they emerged from the other bedroom on Wanda's heels. Dee's gaudy purple backpack was perched on her shoulders, a stuffed pony's head sticking out of the top, and she dragged her smaller suitcase along behind Mom, who was carrying her oversized duffel slung over one shoulder.

"Your brother is going to be here for at least another day," Mom said. "If you forget anything we can call him and have him bring it with him. You have Mr. Hooves, and your backpack, so you should have everything you need."

"He's *Doctor* Hooves, Mom," Dee corrected her before she gave an exasperated sigh at the failings of adults. Lucas and I chuckled at that, since Dee wasn't more than a casual fan of the show he was from. He was more social camouflage; Dee was more a fan of another Doctor, even if she didn't get everything about the show. The Doctor was cool, and so were bow ties, evidently.

We made it to the cars before Dee remembered something and dragged Dr. C back toward the gate in the chain-link fence that led into the backyard. Once he had the gate open, she practically sprinted toward the shed in the backyard and hopped up and down until he unlocked it and let her in. Moments later, she emerged carrying an eight-inch tube of brass with various shiny bits attached to it.

"I thought I said no wands," Mom said to Dr. Corwyn when he caught up.

"It's a Sonic!" Dee said before he could answer. "Chance's is a rod, Dr. Corwyn's is a wand, and mine is a Sonic Screwdriver." She waved it around, and the end lit up as it buzzed.

"It's inert," Dr. C said. "I laced it with an iron core, so it's grounded out. Just an LED and a chip to make the sound."

"And I always say they have sonics," Dee said with a triumphant smile. "Because magick isn't real," she recited.

"I'm going to regret this, but okay," Mom said.

"Not nearly as much as I think I'm going to," Dr. Corwyn said. "Dee, you aren't going to be able to take it on the plane with you. You'll have to pack it in your suitcase." She nodded, but I could tell by her expression she wasn't happy about that.

A few minutes later, Mom and Dee were in the Mustang with me, and in my rearview mirror I could see Dr. C looking uncomfortable in the passenger seat of the *Falcon* as Lucas backed out of the driveway. The Mustang rumbled to life and I backed out behind him, then followed him as he headed for the airport. The black 1967 Shelby GT model might have been old, but she still looked good, and she was still an eight-cylinder beast under the hood.

"Promise me you're going to drive the speed limit the whole way," Mom said as we took the first turn. "I don't have the money to pay for a ticket. I can barely afford to cover the insurance on this thing as it is."

"Not a mile an hour over," I said. "Or two or five or ten," I added quickly.

"Mom, can we do a scrapbook for our trip?" Dee asked from the back seat, and I thanked her for that, but quietly. As they rehashed the vacation so far, I kept one ear on the conversation, but both eyes on my surroundings. I'd been keeping a pretty low profile since my birthday in March; I hadn't pissed anyone off for at least a couple of months, and no one knew where we were outside of the Conclave. That hadn't kept a warlock from stumbling across us a few days ago, though she'd seemed as surprised as we were when she found us. Still, we'd handled her, but I'd been on edge ever since. It wasn't until we pulled into the parking lot at Mathis Field that I let my grip on the steering wheel relax. The airport itself was a public facility, and it flew an American flag, so it was automatically considered exclusively cowan territory. My shoulders unknotted a little as I shifted the Mustang out of gear and pulled on the parking brake.

Mom let me carry her duffel bag, but Dee was fiercely insistent that she could handle her own suitcase. Lucas and Wanda fell in beside me and we let the adults lead the way. As we headed across the small lot toward the doors, I couldn't help but notice the grin on Wanda's face. She'd gained a couple of inches lately, both in height and in curves, something that hadn't been lost on the local boys. Seeing her standing beside Lucas seemed to make it stand out all the more, especially how her face seemed to have gotten a little leaner.

"This summer vacation thing boring you?" I asked as we walked through the doors and into the lobby.

"I'm a city girl," she said with a little bit of the local twang.

13

"None of us are exactly the country type," Lucas added. "Except Dr. C."

"I had a good time," Wanda said. "I'm just looking forward to getting home." We trooped across the terminal toward the ticket counter on the left. The line wasn't very long, mostly men and women in uniform, with a few folks in business wear. A few minutes of shuffling forward, and Mom, Dee, Dr. C, and Wanda were checked in, their bags checked, and we had nothing to do but wait.

"Make sure you go through the list twice before you leave," Mom said. "Stop every couple of hours on the road or if you start to feel drowsy, okay?" Lucas and I nodded in unison. "Do you have enough money for gas?"

"We're good, Mom," I said. "We have enough money to drive to St. Louis if we have to." She smiled and put her hand on my arm.

"I just worry, sweetie. Make sure you give Dr. Corwyn back whatever is left when you get back home."

"Mara, it's fine," Dr. C said. "Chance can deal with anything he might run into, and don't worry about the money."

"We'll call you when we leave, and we'll check in along the way, Miss Murathy," Lucas said with a smile. Mom was about to say something else when the PA system crackled to life and announced their flight boarding. Wanda was on her feet, her phone out and finger flying across the screen before Mom could get her purse and Dee's backpack. I got enveloped in a Mom-hug, then tackled by my sister leaping from her chair into my arms. Even though her feet were still a foot off the floor, I staggered back from the impact.

"What is Mom feeding you?" I asked as I squeezed her hard. "Bricks?"

"Promise you'll come straight home?" she said as I let her down.

"You know it," I said. "No side quests along the way." That seemed to satisfy her, and she accepted her backpack from Mom. I turned to Dr. C.

"You packin'?" I asked. He pulled his vest aside to reveal the butt of his wand sticking up out of the special pocket sewn into the lining.

14

"That and a couple of touchstones," he said, which for him was more than enough to handle most armies. "Remember, Lazarus Moon is in Fort Worth, so if you need any help along the way, you can call on him."

"I'll be fine, sir," I said for the umpteenth time. He nodded and put one hand on my shoulder.

"I'm sure you will. I guess I worry a little, too. Your proctor should be here soon, so I recommend staying close by. You don't want to keep him waiting. We'll see you tomorrow, then." He turned and trotted to catch up with everyone else, leaving Lucas and me to watch them file through the security line.

"Is it just me, or is Wanda's head not in the game right now?" Lucas asked as we watched them shuffle forward.

"Kinda," I said. "She's been blowing up someone's phone all morning."

"Boyfriend?" he asked.

I shrugged. "Probably. I'm gonna wait for this proctor guy here. If you want to head back to Dr. C's place and hang out ..." I offered.

"Dude, I'm in this with you," he said. "You wait, I wait."

"You don't have to."

"In a couple of months, I won't *get* to, Chance," he said. "So we're hanging out as much as we can until then." I couldn't argue that.

Five hours later, I was beginning to think he wished I had. By then the folks in the airport's cafeteria had seen more than enough of us, and we knew the arrival and departure times of every flight for the rest of the day. It was almost three in the afternoon when the PA system called my name and asked me to pick up the courtesy phone by the ticket counter.

"Mr. Fortunato, this is the tower," the voice on the other end said when I picked up the receiver. "We've been asked by Mr. Gage to let you know he's landing in five minutes. You can meet him at Hangar B." Without waiting for me to answer, the guy on the other end hung up.

"Great," I said. "Where the hell is Hangar B?" One of the ladies behind the ticket counter looked up and smiled.

"It's down the runway a little ways. It's one of the private hangars," she said. "Ask at the operations office over there, they'll have someone take you out there."

Ten minutes later, we were bouncing along in a golf cart toward a curved building. The sound of a jet engine greeted us as the driver pulled through the open hangar doors, and I could feel the heated gust from its exhaust wash over us. Standing beside it was a blonde guy in slacks and a dress shirt and a blazer. A pile of luggage was stacked beside him, and he looked at his watch as we pulled up. I made him at eighteen or nineteen. His blonde hair was styled within an inch of its life, and his narrow face was deeply tanned.

"I've been waiting a full two minutes," the man said as we pulled to a stop in front of him. "I gave you plenty of notice of my arrival, and I do not like having my time wasted, Fortunato."

Lucas shook his head and winced at the greeting, and I got out of the golf cart.

"I've been waiting five *hours* longer than I planned on," I told him as I crossed the distance between us. "You're here to observe me in *my* life, not make me jump to make yours more convenient. You've already set me back an entire day, so don't bitch about two minutes."

He took a half-step back with a wide-eyed look on his face, then he recovered and shook his head.

"Do you even know who I am? I'm Winthrop Gage, of the Boston Gages. You will not take that tone with me, plebe. Not if you want to even set foot in the halls of the Franklin Academy. One word from me and you'll be lucky to shine the shoes of a real mage." He tilted his head back a little and actually looked down his nose at me before he gave me a sniff of disapproval.

I crossed my arms and tilted my head. "You can keep me out of the Franklin Academy?" I asked.

"With a single word," he said.

"Do it," I said. "You'd make my day."

Without a word, he pulled a phone from inside his blazer and tapped the screen. "I have Master Draeden's personal number on speed dial," he said. Moments later, he put the phone to his ear and turned away from me. "Master Draeden, Winthrop Gage. This Fortunato boy, he simply won't do. He's insolent, slovenly,

16

and he has no notion of how to treat his betters. I'm formally …
no, sir … no, sir, it isn't. I understand that, sir, but we have
standards … no, sir, I don't. No, sir, I haven't. Yes, sir, I do
recall that. And I appreciate your … yes, sir, I do. But, Master
Draeden, those are not the same. I'm a … no, sir, there is no
difference. Yes, sir. One moment." He turned and handed me the
phone, his face set in a stiff expression. "He would like to speak
to you."

"A valiant effort, Mr. Fortunato," Draeden's voice came over
the line. "But you won't be getting out of your appointment to
the Franklin Academy that easily."

"Can't blame a guy for trying," I said.

"I can, but I won't. Mr. Gage is not there to approve or
disapprove of your attendance at the Academy. He is there to
observe your character, evaluate your level of skill, and
recommend placement upon arrival. Nothing more. If you pull
anything like this again, I will personally recommend that you be
placed in preparatory classes for the rest of the summer session.
Do I make myself clear?"

"Yeah," I said.

"Put Mr. Gage back on the line then."

I handed the phone back to Gage.

"We're gonna need a bigger boat," Lucas said as he walked
up beside me. He nodded toward the pile of luggage. "They're
sending another cart for the luggage. Should be here in a few
minutes."

"Do you think he's got one of those giant hair dryers in the
trunk?" I asked.

"If he does, you can slap a tail on my butt and call me Barf."

Gage walked back toward us as he put the phone back in the
pocket in his blazer, looking like he'd swallowed a live slug.

"Well then, plebe," he said. "Let's be on our way."

"Isn't that a West Point or Annapolis term?" Lucas asked.

"The Franklin Academy predates the military colleges by
decades. *They* took many of their traditions from us. You must
be his *cowan* friend, Lucas Kale. Where is Wizard Corwyn?" he
asked.

"Flying back with my mom and my sister."

"This is highly insulting," Gage huffed. "I cut my vacation short to come all the way to this hell hole, the *least* he could do is be here to meet me."

"You're seven hours late," I said. "You're lucky we were still here to pick you up."

"I ... I'm lucky?" he sputtered. "You have some nerve, speaking to me like that. You'll show me some respect. My time is valuable, and you're lucky to have me here." By then the second cart had arrived, and the two men in coveralls were putting his bags on it.

"Whatever, Winnie," I said as I took the front seat in the cart. "Get in or walk." He got in. The ride back was quiet, not least because of the hundred-degree-plus heat. By now, Lucas and I were used to it, but Winthrop looked like he was about to melt. When we got to the cars, he pulled a handkerchief out of his pocket and wiped the sheen of sweat off his face before he started insulting the guys putting his luggage in the back of the *Falcon*.

"We're not all going to fit in that little thing," he said after Lucas and I gave the two porters a few bucks and thanked them.

"You're riding with me," I said as I went to the Mustang.

"I suppose it would be overly optimistic to hope that there was even a two-star hotel in this city," he said as he got in.

"No clue. You're staying with us at Dr. C's place."

"I am not sleeping on a couch or on some fold-out bed," he started to protest.

"Dude, chill. You'll be in the second bedroom," I told him. "Do you bitch about everything?"

"I set high standards, and I don't accept anything less than the very best from anyone." He cut the statement off as if there was more he was going to say. I let it lie and started the Mustang, then pulled out behind Lucas. With the windows down, Gage lost a little of the wilted look to him, though he never got past slightly irritated.

"Where is he going?" Gage asked when Lucas turned off to the right.

"To pick up some stuff we were supposed to grab hours ago," I said as we crossed over the Concho River. Dr. C's place was only a few blocks away by then, so the awkward silence only lasted for a couple of more minutes. Junkyard was jumping and barking at the fence by the time we pulled under the awning and turned the engine off. I got out and went to the fence to say hello.

"Sorry we took so long, buddy," I said to him as I reached over the fence and rubbed his ears. "You want some pizza tonight? Would that make it up to you?" He barked and spun in place before he came back to me and put his paws up on the fence. I smiled at the idea, since Winthrop had no idea what kind of torture he was in for later. Cheese and Junkyard made for a smelly combination, which was why I almost never let him have any. "This is Winthrop," I said, nodding toward our guest. "He's a guest, so no biting him." Junkyard leaned toward Winthrop and sniffed at him, then tilted his head and gave him a sort of huff.

"What breed of dog is that?" Gage asked.

"Best I can tell, he has some Boxer in him, some Rottweiler, and a little Pit Bull. And he's all mutt."

"I agree. Fortunately, pets aren't allowed at the Academy. Only familiars."

"He *is* my familiar," I said.

"You're joking. No, I see that you aren't. That ... bandana won't do. You'll have to get a proper collar on him."

"He won't wear one," I said. "And I won't put one on him."

Gage just gave a short laugh and said, "Your first day is going to be fun to watch. All that aside, can we get out of this infernal heat?"

I nodded and headed for the front door. The window unit was keeping the front room pretty cool, and he closed his eyes as the chilled air hit him. I headed for the door into the hallway on the right, then opened the door on my left. As hallways went, it was really more of a box, with doors on all four sides.

"This was Dr. Corwyn's room," I said as I flipped the light on. A twin bed took up the right side of the room, with a desk on the far wall next to a dresser that sat right in front of the door. Posters covered the walls, including Farrah Fawcett's iconic red swimsuit photo. "You'll be sleeping in here tonight."

"Dear Lord," Gage almost whispered. "Did I go back in time to the sixties?"

"Late seventies," I said. "If you get the urge to boogie down or play that funky music, I'll get the disco ball down from the

19

attic for you. Bathroom's the next door to the right here, and Lucas and I will be in the room across the way." I stepped back and he followed me out of the hall and through the kitchen and dining room to the family room at the back of the house.

"We might as well get started," he said as I sat down in one of the two recliners that faced the TV. "Show me the tools you've made so far."

"Seriously?" I said.

"Very seriously. Cowans have no business dealing in mage affairs, so while he's gone is the best time." He sat in the other recliner and moved the old TV Guide off the end table that sat between them. I pulled my trusty TK rod from my pocket and resisted the urge to use it on him before I laid it on the table.

"Ah, the infamous telekinesis rod. May I?" he said, gesturing at the length of red-leather-wrapped copper. I shrugged and gave him a nod. He picked it up and took a moment to inspect the quartz crystal tip, then looked at the butt end of it, which I'd replaced with a polished garnet for a little extra push. After giving it a critical inspection, he set it down, then put his thumbs and index fingers together and muttered something under his breath. When he moved his hands apart, he kept his fingertips and thumbs touching to create a glowing green sheet of magick in the space he'd just created. Then, with another movement, he pulled his hands apart a few inches and the green rectangle expanded. When he opened his hands, the rectangle stayed suspended in midair. He reached for my TK rod again and held it up in front of the floating green energy sheet.

"Infamous?" I asked as he turned the rod slowly.

"Rumor has it you used it on Wizard Chomsky's killer, and threatened Master Polter with it."

"I've never used it to kill," I said. "And the Council had taken it from me by the time Polter and I first met."

"These sigils," he said, as if I hadn't just dispelled all the rumors about me, "fae, I presume?"

"Arianh-Rod's designs, yeah," I said. "I did the actual etching, though."

"It's a wonder it hasn't blown up in your hands, then. The execution is barely tolerable. You butchered an exquisite design to the point where it is barely recognizable. Were you my

20

apprentice, I would have destroyed this thing and made you re-do everything ten times. Do you have anything else?" He handed the rod back to me with a sigh of disapproval. I pulled the retrieval ring off my right hand and laid it down in front of him, then pulled my touchstones and my amethyst pendulum from my pocket.

"That's what I have on me," I said. He picked up the touchstones, then the amethyst, finally looking the ring over.

"Barely adequate … crude and limited … nothing more than a gimmick," he said as he set the ring down. "Now the necklace." He pointed at my chest, and I instinctively put my hand over the silver pentacle Wanda had given me. The points of the outward-facing crescent moons dug into my skin slightly, a somehow reassuring sense that it was still there.

"No."

He did a double take and sat up a little straighter. His eyebrows came together and he took a breath.

"It's a gift from a friend. And it's sacred; as in touched by a Goddess sacred."

For a few seconds, he just sat there, then slowly seemed to deflate. "Very well," he said with a slow nod of his head. "What other tools have you crafted?"

"Mostly, I've been working on casting the TK spell without the rod," I said. "But, there is this …" I said as I reached for my backpack. His eyes went wide as it flickered into view. I'd replaced the ever-so-slightly-illegal *neglenom* charm with a chameleon talisman. As long as it was still, the talisman bent light around it, so that you saw what was on the other side of it almost as if it wasn't there. It still wasn't perfect; you could see the edges of the bag as a slightly blurry or warped line, but most people never even noticed that. The look on his face was worth a bit of a smirk as I opened the bag to get what I was really after: a small mirror. I had etched runes around the edge of it in green enamel paint, with matching runes on the back side.

"Is your backpack … armored?" Gage asked.

"Kinda, yeah," I said. "The original aluminum back plates got pretty banged up a few months ago, so Lucas and I replaced them with titanium. I bought the chameleon talisman, but this uses a spell of my own."

21

"What does it do?" he asked as he took the curved mirror from me. I set the backpack a couple of feet away from me and let the talisman hide it again.

"Look at it in the mirror," I said. He angled the mirror, then frowned as he turned his head to look at the place where he knew the bag was.

"The talisman is decent work," he said. "How does your spell see through it?"

"Trade secret," I said. "Those are all of the tools I made. Except for the talisman."

"You said you bought that," Gage said.

"I lied," I said.

"Franklin students do *not* lie," he said, his voice stern.

"You did when you said my work was crap," I said. "Demons are pretty demanding masters … and they lie a lot. So, I know my work is good, and I know when you're lying to me." The front door opened and Lucas called out.

"I'm baaaack!"

"I'll alert the media," I said as I got to my feet. "Let's get those speakers installed." Winthrop gaped like a fish as I walked past him.

"We're not done yet!" he said by way of protest.

"I am," I said.

In a two-bedroom house that was built in the forties, there was only one place a guy could get some privacy to meditate: the roof. The sun was almost below the horizon by the time I pulled myself up over the last rung of the ladder and set foot on the cooling tarpaper, but my car now had a working sound system, and I'd even managed to get a short run in. Even with only three people in the house, I preferred the solace of Dr. Corwyn's old retreat. Maybe spending an hour up here every evening for the past couple of weeks had conditioned my brain to see it as a quiet place. Or maybe it was because this was the only place I could talk to my girlfriend uninterrupted. Who could say? Even apprentice magi were inscrutable like that.

My phone was a cheap pay-as-you-go model that Mom could barely afford the minutes for. Texting took me forever on the little numeric keypad, and it couldn't do all the slick things

Wanda's or Lucas's phones could, but I could text and talk to Shade, and that was good enough. I slid the top up and followed the menu to the text screen, then slowly put in my message.

– Hey. U there? –

For a couple of minutes, I watched the screen. Every time there was a delay, my brain went into overdrive. Was she out with her parents? Was she laughing with a friend at her boyfriend's dumb text? Was she going to text me back and break up? It was stupid, I knew none of my terrible fears were going to actually happen, but I couldn't stop the thoughts from tumbling over each other in my head. Maybe she was just going to ignore me tonight …

– Hey, baby. Miss u. :) U coming home tonight? Want 2 c u so bad! –

I smiled as I read her message, fears forgotten and my day instantly better.

– Miss u 2. Had 2 stay 1 more day. Long story. Want 2 hear ur voice. Call? –

– Sure! 2 minutes. –

My smile got bigger and my stomach flipped as I laid the beach towel I'd draped over my shoulder down on the roof and settled on my back to wait for her to call. It took an eternity for the phone to buzz. My finger hit the answer button in a split second.

"Hey, beautiful," I said.

"Hey yourself," she breathed. "What are you doing?"

"Sitting on the roof, trying not to kill the stupid proctor from the Academy. What are you doing?"

"Sitting in the chapel we hid in last October. So, whatcha wearing?" Her tone was playful, and I couldn't help but chuckle.

"Sweat pants and a t-shirt. I'm all sweaty from working on my car."

"I like you all sweaty," she said, and I could feel my body react. "Now, ask me what I'm wearing."

"Okay, what are you wearing?"

"Same thing I was wearing that night," she said. Her voice went sultry, and I could feel the heat from it seep into my veins. Just the thought of that night still made my monkey brain sit up

23

and take notice. I swallowed and took a deep breath before I went on, imagining her in the same pink t-shirt and sweats.

"When?" I asked.

"At the beginning. If you were here, though ..." she said, then gave a soft little moan that curled my toes. "Would you stop me this time?" My right hand curled into a fist as I remembered her taking her shirt and her bra off like it was yesterday. I'd stopped her then because it hadn't felt right. We both knew how to use sex as currency, and neither of us had been able to say no until then.

"I wouldn't want to," I rasped.

"But you might?" she said. I didn't say anything for a moment, torn between what she'd said and the thought of what I *wanted* to do. She sobbed, and I sat up.

"Shade, are you okay?" I asked. Stupid question, yeah, but it was all that I could think of. "What's wrong, baby?"

"You ... you're determined to make me fall in love with you, aren't you?" she said, her voice breaking a little.

"Well, yeah," I said, feeling like I was missing half of the conversation. My thoughts were slow and clumsy, and even I didn't know exactly where they were going. "And yeah, I might still stop you. But ... not why you think."

"Then why?" she asked.

"I'm not sure. I just ... I guess I'd know what to do if I was there."

"God, why the hell aren't you here?" she almost whined, but I could hear more of her wolf in the question than a teenage girl being pouty.

"The proctor guy the Academy sent showed up like seven hours late, so we have to take off in the morning. He's a real dick, too. He's a Boston Gage, talks like his teeth are stuck together half the time."

"I already don't like him," she said, sounding more teen than wolf. "He's keeping my Chance from me. And I get cranky if you're not here to kiss me and nibble on my neck enough."

"We'll have to fix that," I said, my own voice suddenly husky again at the thought of doing just that. The sound of the screen door opening and closing reached my ears, and I heard Lucas greeting Junkyard.

"Dude!" he called out. "Pizza's here! I'm not waiting on you." Over the line, I heard Shade laughing.

"What?" I asked her.

"You're going to feed Junkyard cheese, aren't you? You know chemical warfare is against the Geneva Convention, right?"

"I'm a very bad person, I know," I said. "But he really, really deserves it."

"Damn straight he does," she agreed. "He's keeping my man away from me. When are you leaving?"

"Oh-dark-thirty," I said. "We're only stopping for gas and food."

"Get drive-through," Shade said, her voice smoldering again. "I can't wait to see you."

"I can't either. I've gotta go. I miss you."

"Miss you, too."

We hung up and I headed for the ladder. Winthrop Gage was going to regret making me late getting home.

Chapter 2

~ Our shadows are often our anchors, our reflection in negative. ~ Lazarus Moon

"I'm beginning to see the appeal of car sickness," Gage said after the first hour on the road. Lucas was leading the way, and I had Linkin Park in the CD player. "At least then I would have something else to focus on than that noise and this God-forsaken landscape." He looked a little less dapper without his blazer, and no amount of product in the world was going to keep his hair in place in a car doing seventy with the windows down. Okay, seventy-ish. Most of the time. His white shirt was unbuttoned at the top, and it was still visibly damp under his armpits. Of course, the back of my Miskatonic U. shirt was pretty much soaked with sweat, but that wasn't unusual for an eighty degree morning.

"There's a box of eight tracks in the trunk," I said as "Burn It Down" ended. "If you're looking for something a little more classic rock."

"I believe I'll pass," he said. "Perhaps we can forego the music entirely for a bit."

"Sure," I said, and hit the stop button. The Mustang's muted rumble filled the sudden silence, and I drove on, all the while envying Lucas, whom I could see through his rear window bouncing to whatever he was listening to.

"Lord, what is that smell?" Gage asked a moment later. We had topped a hill, and I could see the rows of white buildings to our left. The morning sun was just hitting them, and we were being treated to the smell of agriculture in action. Below us, I could see the road ahead, with patches of sunlight and shadow from the big, puffy columns of cumulonimbus clouds to the east.

"Fresh air and eau de pig," I said with a little more relish than the moment called for. In the rearview mirror, I saw Junkyard pop his head up. He sniffed the air for a moment, then nudged at my neck with his nose.

"What is it, big guy?" I asked as we hit the base of the hill. He gave a soft huff of a bark and put a paw on the seat.

"He probably objects to the smell even more than I do," Gage said. "Though I'm amazed he even has a nose left, given the stench he produced last night."

I ignored the comment and grabbed the walkie talkie from the middle console.

"Lucas!" I called out. There was no response, and I could see his head still bobbing in time with his music. I tried again, but he still didn't respond so I sped up a little and flashed my headlights at him. It wasn't until I honked my horn that he noticed me.

"Sorry, dude, what's up?" he asked over the radio.

"Junkyard's—" was all I got out before the world around us went dark.

"Whoa!" Lucas called back. "You didn't just play a glowing ocarina did you?"

"This isn't me," I said. "No matter what, you just keep moving till you see sunlight. You got it? Keep heading north."

"Yeah, I got it! Keep movi—" Lucas's voice disappeared in the hiss of static. His tail lights came on in front of us and the road in front of him lit up under his headlights. I let up on the gas and watched him pull away.

"Junkyard, backpack," I said as I opened the top of the center console. The LeMat was nestled inside. I reached over my shoulder and felt Junkyard's fuzzy head under my hand, so I reached down and followed his jaw until I could grab the handle of my backpack. "Good boy," I said, and he let go.

"What are you doing?" Gage demanded. He had his phone out and was busy running his finger over the surface of it. "We need to set a ward and call for help!"

"Yeah, you have fun with that," I said as I dropped the pack into his lap. "And once you figure out you don't have signal, open that up and grab my Ariakon." The car coasted to a stop, and I opened the door.

"Your what?" he asked.

"The big pistol-looking thing in the holster-looking thing," I said as I got out of the car and reached into my front pocket. The smooth, flat surface of my touchstone slid beneath my finger as I fished for what I wanted, finding the rounded surface of the stone Dr. C had given me. I pulled it out and held it in the palm of my open hand. This was different magick than I usually did, mostly because I was asking someone else to do all the heavy lifting. "Little brother, I need roots that go deep and hold strong." The stone suddenly grew heavy in my hand, and my skin tingled as something out in the darkness turned a powerful and horrible attention on me. The taint of true darkness had a different feel from what we were in the middle of. This was shadow, easily lit. We'd passed under the shadow of a cloud right before this had started, so I was guessing whatever was behind this wasn't looking to get a tan. And that could work for me. All I needed to do was ground the shadow.

"I found it!" Gage called out, his voice high-pitched and bordering on panic. "Get in the car!"

I stepped away from the Mustang and straddled the yellow line in the middle of the gray asphalt. My left side seemed to tingle more than my right, so I turned my head to face that way.

"I feel you out there," I said to whatever it was. "I drop a rock on your shadow." My hand turned slowly, and the rock slid across my palm and fell toward the ground. It seemed to drop forever, and when it hit I could feel a surge of power pulse by me. The world seemed to ripple at my feet for a moment, then it was past, and I heard the otherworldly screech of something Infernal and pissed-off.

"What did you just do?" Gage demanded as I slid back behind the steering wheel.

"Dropped an anchor on something's foot," I said, and then floored it. The Mustang fishtailed for a moment, then leaped forward with a roar of eight-cylinder glory, and I power-shifted through all four gears as I tried to catch up to Lucas. Over the engine's full-throated rumble, I heard something snarl, a sound like reality splitting down the middle. Then the smell hit. Not even Junkyard's worst emissions could compete with the stench of brimstone. People had compared it to Sulphur once, but it wasn't even close.

"What is that smell?" Gage managed to gasp.

"Brimstone," I said. "Makes rotten eggs smell kinda like Pine Fresh, doesn't it? What color is the tape on the top of the paintball gun?"

"Red, I think," Gage said. Incendiary pellets were marked with red. It would do for the moment, but I needed something a little more potent.

"Let me have it. Look in the backpack for one with white tape on it."

"What do you have it loaded with now?" he asked as he rummaged in the pack.

"Flaming hot sauce," I said as I looked out my window.

"And the white-marked hoppers?"

"Holy water and garlic," I said. Something big was moving alongside the road, keeping pace with us.

"A much better option," he answered. I pushed the gas pedal down a little further and watched as the speedometer climbed up past eighty, then ninety. Up ahead, I could see Lucas's tail lights getting brighter. As we got within a hundred yards of him, he swerved and a shadowy shape narrowly missed his back fender. I had only a second or two to maneuver before I was right on top of it, but I just straightened my arms against the wheel and ran it down. There was a screech at the moment of impact, then it was like the thing burst into a black goo that splattered against my windshield and seemed to evaporate in a few seconds. I looked at my hood, but it wasn't dented. Whatever it was had dissipated almost as soon as the front bumper had hit it.

The list of demons that could come out during the day on their own was short. The list of shadow-based demons who could defy the sun was even shorter. But only one ran with a horde of minions that had a problem with anything ferrous.

"Orlaggish," I said softly. "Servant of Nergal." As soon as the words left my mouth, I felt the tingle of magic down my arms confirm my guess. Now the field was a little closer to level. Up ahead, Lucas was swerving left and right, trying to avoid Orlaggish's shadow hounds.

"Why doesn't he just ram them like you did?" Gage asked.

"Airbags," I said as we got closer. "His front fender isn't made of steel like mine is, either. You wouldn't happen to know any combat spells, would you?"

"No," he said, sounding almost offended. "I'm not a Sentinel." We were almost even with Lucas by then, and I realized I was moving almost faster than I could improvise.

30

"What about a spell for light?" I said as we drew up beside my best friend.

"Of course I know light spells," he said. "Every idiot learns those in first yea—"

"Then cast the brightest one you can in front of us!" I said as we surged past the *Falcon*. A shadow hound hit the front bumper and disintegrated, then another as I pulled in front of Lucas.

Gage looked at me with a frown on his face, then moved his right hand in a complex gesture and uttered *"Fotizei!"* A bright ball of light appeared between his fingers. The inside of the car got blindingly bright, and I had to close my right eye with my head turned a little away.

"Can you focus that a little?" I asked as I squinted at the road. The front bumper shuddered a few times as I mowed down more hounds.

"Aktina," he said a moment later, and the inside of the Mustang stopped looking like a firefly's ass. The light narrowed and seemed to intensify. Ahead of us, a shadow hound got caught in the narrowed cone and became an expanding cloud of black vapor. *"Foteinóteros!"* Gage called out, and the beam got even brighter as I poured on the speed. More and more hounds made black blossoms against the force of his spell as we plowed through them. Only a few hit my bumper, and none of them got close to the *Falcon*. I risked a look in my rearview to make sure Lucas really was okay, and saw Orlaggish astride his steed, a six-legged monster that looked like a cross between a beetle and a horse. Of course, my luck being what it was, it ran like a horse, and it ran fast.

"We're almost to the edge!" Gage said. I tore my eyes from the demon behind us and looked ahead. Sunlight showed beyond the edge of the shadowed zone, but I could also see another shaded place on the road maybe half a mile beyond it. I wasn't sure Orlaggish was the kind to just shrivel up the second he hit sunshine. He was a creature of shadow, not darkness. The smart money was on him being stronger than the nasty little surprise I'd dropped on him and surviving until he got to the next batch of shadow. And betting against demons was never a good plan.

A hundred yards away from the edge, I gestured for Lucas to keep going, then pulled to my left and hit the brakes. The

Mustang slewed to the right and Gage's spell faltered as Lucas sped past us. I reached over and grabbed the white-marked hopper from his lap and changed the incendiary load out for it.

"Are you nuts?" he asked. "What do you think you're doing?"

"Loading the dice," I said as I turned the car around and started heading back toward Orlaggish. Shadow hounds dove to either side as we approached, parting like the Red Sea ... if the Red Sea was black, and made of Infernal hounds. Behind me, Junkyard growled, and I could see his hackles up.

"Even your mutt doesn't think this is a good idea," Gage said. Junkyard barked at him and bared his teeth.

"Don't call him a mutt," I said as I sped toward the bad guy. "And get that light spell handy again. We're gonna need it here in a second." As the distance between us closed, I started to agree with Gage; this was a bad plan. I only knew Orlaggish's name and little about him. As we kept going and he kept getting bigger, I began to realize that he was huge, easily eighty feet tall on his mount. He came to a hill, and I could still see his head and chest above it as he came closer. Then he was over it, eighty feet tall if he was an inch. Even from the top of the next hill, we were at the same height as his waist. I hit the brakes again and grabbed the Ariakon as I pulled the steering wheel to the left.

"Aim at the mount!" I said as we screeched to a halt with the passenger side facing Orlaggish. Gage lit his spell up again and pointed it straight at the mount's compound eyes. It skidded to a halt and reared back, front legs and mandibles waving even as they started smoking. In a heartbeat, I had my door open, my left foot on the ground and the paintball gun steadied on the roof of the Mustang. I pulled the trigger as fast as I could, aiming high and center. My target was at pretty much maximum range for the CO_2-powered pistol, but it was also just freakin' huge.

Seven of the holy-water-filled rounds hit it. The results were, to say the least ... explosive. Holes the size of manhole covers appeared in its body, and one of the legs was blown off by the last shot. Orlaggish leapt off of its body as it fell forward, and I tossed the paintball gun at Gage as I slid back into the seat. The back wheels spun on the asphalt as I hit the gas, and I twisted the wheel around hard. The demon got small in my rearview mirror pretty quick, and we raced toward the edge of the dark zone.

"Fasterfasterfaster!" Gage said as he turned in the seat and looked out the rear window. Junkyard was perched on the back seat with his paws against the top, barking at the thing following us.

"Working on it," I said, and shifted into third. The line between shadow and sunlight got closer, but Orlaggish didn't get any smaller in the mirror. I shifted into fourth and started to gain some ground on it, but not nearly enough. "Come on," I said as we got closer. "Get to the end ..." We hit the edge and were suddenly bathed in light. Heat washed over us and I let up on the gas. The *Falcon* was pulled off to the side of the road a couple of hundred yards ahead, and I coasted until I was even with him, then turned left across the road and opened the door. Lucas almost bounced out of his car, his face creased with worry. I grabbed the LeMat and got out.

"We're not out of the woods yet, are we?" he said as his gaze focused on the gun. I shook my head. Just then, forty feet of pissed-off demon lunged out of the shadows. Where his mount had been a mix of bug and horse, Orlaggish leaned more to the tentacley end of things from the waist up, with what looked like an octopus for a head and a pair of thick tentacles for arms. Black orbs were set above a ring of tentacles around a beaked mouth. I brought the gun up and thumbed the hammer back, then lined the sights up on one of its thick legs. The gun bucked in my hand when I pulled the trigger, and a split second later a gout of flame sprouted from the side of his leg. He let out a trumpeting roar and tried to take a step forward.

Before his off foot hit the ground, he was yanked back by an invisible force and staggered back a step. He leaned into the step and tried again, only to find himself held in place. The stone I had dropped on his shadow was holding him in place like a tether that had reached its limit. I aimed at the other leg and pulled the trigger, but no smoking wound appeared after the gun went off. I thumbed the hammer back again and pulled the trigger once more, this time with better success, blowing a hole in his knee. Smoke started to rise from his skin, and he turned his bulbous head to look back toward the darkness.

"Dude, he's gonna bolt!" Lucas cried out. I wasn't about to let that happen. I put another round in his right leg, and he fell to one knee.

"No, he isn't," I said, and shot the bent knee. More smoke rose from the exposed skin of his back, and his green skin started to blacken under the sunlight as he flopped on the ground.

"What are you doing?" Gage said from behind me. "He's trying to get away."

"You don't let demons get away," I said. "Sends the wrong message."

"Just what message is that?" he demanded.

"Don't fuck with me. It's bad for your health." Flames shot from the middle of the demon's back, and his cries became agonized screams as the sunlight did its work. One tentacle reached back toward the shadows, gripping the road's surface and trying to pull the rest of him back to the cover of darkness. Flame engulfed the slime-covered arm, and it was charred to black in seconds.

"Then at least put it out of its misery," he said. I turned and raised an eyebrow at him, then headed back for the car.

"I think misery's part of the message, Winnie," Lucas said from behind me. Gage almost made it back to the car before he threw up. But at least he was quiet once he got in.

Once I got back up to the speed limit, I pulled my phone out and hit the speed dial number for Dr. C.

"What happened?" he asked as soon as he picked up. I didn't even bother to ask how he knew. We hadn't been on the road long enough for me to be calling unless something was wrong.

"Someone sent a demon after me," I said.

"How much of a demon?" he asked.

"Upper Abyssal, servant of one of the Eleven Abominations. Shadow hunter, tough enough to Walk during the day and handle sunlight for about a minute. Think one of the bounty hunters from Empire, only about forty feet tall. Nothing I couldn't handle." I didn't mention his name, partly because I didn't want his attention on me anymore, but mostly because Dr. Corwyn wasn't likely to know who he was just by his name. The Magi were still way behind when it came to Infernal politics. Demon lore was pretty much a forbidden subject with them, and all nine

Hells worked hard to keep their business away from prying eyes. The only info that tended to get out was what they wanted people to know; just enough to make a deal, basically.

"Where are you now?"

"South of Abilene," I said. "Whoever sent him is going to think twice about trying again. I made sure he was hurting pretty damn good when I sent him back."

"Have you contacted your mother?" he asked. I bit my lip for a moment and tried to come up with an excuse that didn't involve not wanting to make her worry. "That's what I figured. That's good. Minimal contact is best. I'll let her know."

"Thanks," I told him.

"I'd tell you to head to Fort Worth to seek Master Moon's protection, but I know you won't. I'll alert the Council. Get back as soon as you possibly can."

"Yes, sir," I said. "I will. Poor Winthrop's going to need some therapy." I ended the call over Gage's half-hearted protests and pushed the pedal down a little closer to the floorboard.

"How did you know?" Gage asked after a few minutes, pausing and turning a little pale before he tried again. "How did you know how to kill that thing back there? How did you know its name?"

I glanced over at him and let out a little snort. "They didn't tell you my nickname when they told you to come watch me?" I asked.

"The demon's apprentice ... I thought that was just an affectation," he said.

"Nope. Pretty much the only thing anyone ever gets right."

"It certainly explains a few things," he said. I turned my head and gave him a full-on glare. "The rough edges," he explained.

I shook my head and pulled out a CD. "For that, you're going to listen to the same CD until we get home," I threatened. The opening notes of Satriani's Super Colossal erupted from the speakers, and I leaned back into the seat to enjoy what was left of the ride.

Chapter 3

~ Most cowans suspect the existence of the Veil, but fear too greatly the wonders and terrors they might discover beyond it to seek it with great enthusiasm. ~ Ben Franklin, Letters To a Young Mage

"Why didn't you call me when it happened?" Mom demanded. I sat there and didn't say a word, feeling like I was six all over again. "Why did I have to hear this from Dr. Corwyn?"

"I thought it was best that he limit contact," Dr. Corwyn said from where he leaned against the doorway into the kitchen. "It made it harder to track him." I nodded in agreement, but Mom's expression didn't change.

"Tell me why I'm supposed to believe that's a good thing," she said.

"You have the most powerful connection to him," Dr. C said. "If I wanted to scry for him, I would have waited for him to contact you and trace him back through the bonds between you. With him in motion, it would have been the only way to pinpoint his location."

"You had to choose between limited protection and complete invisibility," she said. She nodded and her features relaxed a little. "It makes sense, and I would probably have done the same thing. I still don't like it."

"For what it's worth … neither did I," Dr. C said. For the first time since I'd made it home, his face broke into the barest hint of a smile.

"And I'm fine, Mom," I said. "The Sentinels caught up to us in Oklahoma City and followed us home from there."

"You'll pardon your dear old mother if I don't find that exactly comforting." Her tone was only half-joking. Mom had never had much use for the Sentinels. The Conclave's combination police force and military had technically arrested me twice a few months ago, and I'd faced a death sentence from the Council for the things I'd been forced to do while I worked for Dulka. But keeping me out of a demon's hands had been their job in the first place, and Mom wasn't ready to forgive them for failing so spectacularly at that. For that matter, I didn't have a lot of warm and fuzzy feelings for most of them myself.

"I took care of the one demon on my own anyway, Mom," I said. "Dr. C left the LeMat with me for the drive home, and I had my paintball gun. And ..." I hesitated, not really wanting to say the next part out loud. "Well, Winthrop actually helped. He's what, a senior?" I asked Dr. C.

"Yes, he's an upperclassman, in his ninth year."

"That's a lot of high school," I said.

"Magick is a demanding subject. Since you mentioned it, we can't let your training suffer, especially not now. Winthrop will be evaluating your skill levels, and if he ranks you at anything less than apprentice, the rest of your summer is going to be even harder."

"Yeah, Draeden mentioned prep classes or something. So, what do I have to do to make apprentice officially?"

"Be able to scribe a spell onto a written medium and cast it, cast spells onto items that remain stable and release them later, cast spells from foci efficiently and consistently, cast a spell with a non-specific tool such as a wand, and cast at least one spell with no tools." He looked at me as he said the last part with a skeptical expression. From behind him, I could hear footsteps on the stairs, probably Gage coming down to complain about something else.

"I can already do almost all of that," I said. "I mean, I still need to get my own wand. And figure out the whole casting spells without a focus."

"Just buy a wand," Gage said as he slid past Dr. Corwyn. "Unless you can't afford one."

"No apprentice of mine buys his first wand," Dr. C said with a little heat in his voice.

"As you say, sir," Gage said with a quick bow of his head. "Might I ask how far along your apprentice is in the crafting of his wand?"

"About a day behind where he's supposed to be," Dr. C said as he gave Gage a sharp look. I could almost have chipped the ice off of his words. "But that can be remedied, if you don't mind making a couple of stops with Chance tomorrow."

"Of course not, sir," Gage said, sounding like he was anything but thrilled to tag along with me.

"That means you're going to have to go to Bjerning Depository," Dr. C said. "You've put that off for too long, and you're going to need the currency." I opened my mouth to protest, but he gave a tilt of his head that challenged me to even try. He'd already shot down every argument I'd made. Only one in a thousand trees might produce wood suitable for a proper wand, and it might take me months or even years to find one. A wand-wright like Arianh-Rod probably had what I needed on hand. And she would be able to show me the right placement for gems and metals in the piece I did choose. More importantly, her services weren't cheap, and in terms of the world behind the Veil, I was pretty much flat broke. Except for the six-thousand-plus trade points I had in bearer chits from Bjerning Depository. I took a breath in and blew it out through my lips, down to my only *real* objection. I really didn't want to go to the Underground. Dr. C straightened his head and frowned, and I understood his argument as clear as if he'd said it out loud.

Deal with it.

I let my shoulders slump and gave him a minute nod before I looked away.

"All right, I'll go," I said.

"Yes, you will," Dr. C said as he straightened and stepped away from the doorway. He pulled a small cloth pouch from his pocket and handed it to me. "Once you're done there and have your wand blank, come to my place and we'll get you started on your wand and work on your lessons. I wouldn't expect him home for dinner for the next few nights, Mara."

"I usually don't," Mom said. "At least you tell me ahead of time." Dr. C made his exit, and Mom shooed us out of the kitchen. "If Shade comes over, she's more than welcome to stay for dinner," she said. "And the door to your room stays open."

"I don't think that'll be a problem," I said as Gage headed up the stairs. I headed out the back door and pulled my phone out of my pocket.

A few minutes later, Shade was pulling up on her bike and pulling her helmet off. She didn't even bother with the gate; instead, she just put her hand on the fence and vaulted over it.

Her feet had barely touched the ground before I had her in my arms, my lips nuzzling her neck. With a soft sigh, she tilted her head to the side and pressed her body against mine. When my teeth grazed her skin, she gave a short gasp and one hand slid up behind my shoulders to hold me against her. I bit down on the smooth curve where her shoulder met her neck, and she trembled against me, her breath escaping in a moan. Her teeth found my neck a few seconds later, then we were locked in a kiss that was deep enough to drown in.

"I missed you," I said when we came up for air.

"Mm-hmmm," she said as she buried her face in my shoulder again. "Noticed that. Gods, I missed you so much." Her other hand slid up the back of my shirt, while my right hand slid up along her spine. I stopped when I felt her shoulder blades on either side of my hand … and nothing else.

"Are you …?" I asked as I pulled back to look her in the eye.

"Nope," she said with a wicked grin. She pulled back and took my hand, leading me to the bench swing by the back porch.

"You know my mom wants you to stay for dinner," I said once we were snuggled up together.

"She always does," she said. "And you're going to be trying hard not to stare."

"Oh, that's mean," I said. She made an affirmative-sounding murmur into my shoulder and laid her hand on my chest. A few seconds later, she curled her legs up beside her and wrapped her other arm around my back, then held tight, which meant my ribs creaked for a few seconds. When she breathed in deep, I put my hand on her hair and just stroked gently. Her body relaxed a little as she let out the breath, and she took a few more slow, deliberate breaths.

"What happened?" I asked her.

"Bad dream," she said. "I shouldn't have gone back out to the chapel."

"It's okay," I said. I wanted to know more, but I wasn't sure if I should ask or not. "It was just a dream, right?"

"Does it work when you tell yourself that?"

"Not really," I said. "Hell, we both need some serious therapy or something."

"Who'd believe us? You got sold to a demon and I got molested by a perv werewolf. That would get us both a one-way ticket to a padded room at Twisted Oaks."

"Didn't say we'd *get* it, I just said we *needed* it."

"You ever try to talk to Corwyn about it?" she asked.

"Yeah," I said. "He gets it a little too well from walking around in my head. Half the time it screws him up as much as me."

"At least we have each other," she said.

"That's more than enough," I said. I felt her expression change against my shoulder, and I guessed she was smiling.

"More than you deserve, too," she said.

"But not more than I can handle," I told her as I moved my hand to her side and poked a finger into her ribs. She yelped and jumped off the swing. Of course I chased her. She led me around the big oak tree and back to the swing before she turned and faced me again.

"I'm the Wolf Queen," she said with a giggle. "I'm more than any mortal man can handle!" She came at me as she finished, and I side-stepped to keep myself out of her clutches.

"I'm no mere mortal," I told her. "I'm a great and *oof!*" I managed before she pounced on me and dug her fingers into my stomach, the one place I was the most ticklish. "… powerful … wizard!" I said between laughs as I grabbed for her wrists. There was no way I was going to overpower her. If I wanted to carry the day and survive against such a powerful foe, I was going to have to cheat. I let go of one of her hands, and she immediately went for the belly again.

"Ha!" she said as I broke into a fit of laughter. "Great and powerful wizard, my sweet ass!"

I wrapped my right hand in the thick auburn hair at the back of her head and pulled. Almost immediately, her eyes closed and her mouth opened as she bent her head back and arched her shoulders into the direction I pulled her, until she was on her back in the grass.

"I know your weaknesses," I whispered to her as I rolled onto my side to look down at her. She squirmed a little, but she didn't try all that hard to get away. Once I laid my left hand on her stomach, she went still, and her eyelids snapped open. Caught between wolf and human desires, her eyes were a deep green. As long as they didn't go gold, I was still just at the edge of dangerous territory. Her breath came in short little pants, and her gaze somehow managed to be wide-eyed enough to be vulnerable and placid enough to be absolutely trusting. I leaned down and kissed her parted lips gently, then did it again. When her eyes opened after the second kiss, they were gray again.

"And you're not afraid to use them against me," she said as she put one hand against my face.

"I'm a bastard that way," I said, lifting my hand from her stomach to touch her cheek. My lips touched hers again, then I kissed the tip of her nose. "And it is a sweet ass." Our eyes locked again, and my heart pounded. Suddenly, I didn't have anything funny or romantic to say, but I wanted to say something, except for the words I was too afraid to just blurt out. I wasn't even sure if they were true.

The fateful phrase was just on the tip of my tongue when I heard the back door open. Mom's shoes scuffed on the back porch, and her voice came on its heels.

"Dinner's almost done," Mom said. "Alexis, would you like to eat with us?"

"Yeah, Mom, she's staying for dinner," I called out as we got up.

"I am?" Shade whispered with a little bit of menace in her voice. The alpha wolf in her wasn't always fond of being told what to do, and even as her *gothi*, I didn't get much leeway where that was concerned. An adviser can only get away with so much before wisdom is more wise-ass.

"Yes, you are," I said. I brushed grass off my pants and stood up. "Unless you want me to end up killing poor Winthrop."

"Oh, we can't have that," she said with a mischievous smile. "I'll do my best to distract you." As she said it she arched her back, and I failed miserably at the whole not-ogling-her-thing as her body did interesting things to her shirt.

"By the way, we're heading to the Underground tomorrow," I said as we headed for the back door. "And then we're going to the Hive. I ... want to show you ... what my world's like."

"You mean, when no one's trying to kill you," she said flatly.

"That, too," I said a little too casually and held the door open for her.

Gage skipped out on dinner, and on the rest of the evening, too. He slipped in late, waking up Mom when he rang the doorbell. He was about as quiet as a dump truck as he crept into my room and got in the bed. Junkyard and I laid there, still and quiet, until I heard his breathing slow and fall into the rhythm of sleep. A few minutes later, I closed my eyes again. He yawned and stretched at an unholy hour, and I propped myself up on one elbow. Junkyard got to his feet and headed for the door, waiting to head outside.

"You snore," I said

"What the ..?" he yelped. He rubbed his eyes, then looked more closely at the blanket I was sitting on. "Is that where you slept?"

"Yeah," I said as I got to my feet.

"You didn't have to sleep on the floor," he said. "I could have taken a couch or rented a room."

"Don't worry about it," I said as I grabbed my running shorts. "I always sleep on the floor." His mouth was still working on making words as I left the room. The next time he managed to make his mouth work was when we were in the car and pulling out of the driveway.

"Why do you sleep on the floor?" he asked.

"Because I do," I said, which was a lot nicer than what I wanted to tell him.

"Where are we going?" he asked.

"To meet my friends at the park."

"Do you involve mundanes in everything you do?" he asked.

"They're my friends," I said. "Not mundanes, not cowan or any other shitty thing you want to call them. And yeah, we do a lot of stuff together. Deal with it."

"Mun—normal people, people like Lucas … in the end, when it counts, they will turn on you." He sounded almost sad as he said it, and he shook his head like he was telling me some unfortunate truth.

"You don't know Lucas and Wanda," I said as I pulled into the parking lot for Founder's Park.

43

"I know cowans," Gage said. "They envy us as much as they fear us. We wield powers they can barely comprehend, and they destroy what they can't control or have for themselves. They'll blame you for anything that goes wrong in their lives, and they'll betray you to the first thing that offers them an easy way out."

"You," I laughed, "still don't know my friends."

"Neither do you," he said as he got out of the car. Junkyard followed me as I got out and we headed over to the bench where Lucas and Wanda were waiting. Both of them had on gray sweat pants, but Wanda's tank top was red while Lucas wore a baggy white t-shirt. As usual of late, Wanda had her head bent over her phone, and Lucas was leaning back with his arms across the top of the backrest. As soon as we got close, Wanda put her phone away and got to her feet to close the distance between us.

"I'm glad you made it home okay," she said as she wrapped me in a hug. I squeezed her close for a few seconds and felt the warmth of her press against my aura. Ever since I'd given the Goddess's gift to her, she'd felt like that, like a ray of sunlight that warmed the soul. She pulled back and turned her smile on Gage. "Hi, I'm Wanda. You must be Chance's proctor."

He took her proffered hand in his and tilted it so that her fingers were draped over his, then inclined his head slightly.

"Winthrop Gage," he said. "I'm delighted to meet you. Chance speaks highly of you."

Her smile warmed up a few notches from merely radiant to something just shy of needing welding goggles to protect my eyes.

"Come on, guys," I said. "Let's get moving. Those miles aren't gonna run themselves." I set an easy pace, just fast enough to start a burn in my legs and make me sweat. Our morning runs weren't about training for a marathon, they were mostly to build endurance and keep me in good shape. Dr. Corwyn had insisted that I start running when he first started training me, and lately, Lucas and Wanda had joined me. I didn't bother checking on Gage. Lucas and Wanda kept pace with me with ease, and Junkyard ran along beside me like it was nothing.

We rounded a curve near a wooded area, and I slowed when I felt something at the edge of my mystic senses. Wanda and Lucas slowed too, both of them looking around as if they felt

44

something off as well. Lucas had some Talent, and Wanda's communion with the Goddess on the Equinox had left her a little more perceptive to some things than normal people. It was Wanda's reaction that worried me more, since her sensitivity was more in tune with the Celestial and Infernal than to magick.

"You guys feel that?" she asked as she came to a stop. Lucas and I stopped as well and nodded. Gage jogged up behind us, then blinked as he came to a stop and scanned left and right.

"Feels … nasty," Lucas offered. "Kinda like that thing we ran into on the way home, but …"

"Weaker," Gage finished. "Much weaker, like an old summoning circle." Wanda turned toward the opening of a trail and pointed.

"That way," she said, and plunged ahead. We followed and twenty yards later came out in the middle of an old clearing. An outline of chalk sketched a rough circle near the middle, and a pile of ash marked a fire that had been lit in the center.

"I was right," Gage said as he pointed to his right. "You can see the summoner's circle of protection over there, and that must have been the portal itself in the center."

I walked over to the smaller circle and knelt down to take a closer look. What Gage had described as the summoner's circle intersected the main circle, so that part of it was inside. The ash pile was only a few steps away, and I nudged it with the toe of my sneaker. The overturned ash floated like a small cloud and revealed black squares of charred wood.

"Clearly someone summoned a demon here," Gage was saying. "There's no telling what Infernal errand they sent it upon." He stopped when he heard me laugh. "Is there something about summoning demons that you find amusing?"

"Oh, no, I'd take this very seriously," I said. "If this was a summoning circle instead of a conjure circle."

"A distinction without a difference," Gage said with a dismissive wave of his hand. "I'm clearly the senior mage here, plebe. Shut your mouth and open your ears and you might actually learn something."

"Sure," I said with a grin. "What year do they teach demon summoning?" I waited while he sputtered for an answer, then shook my head. "A conjure circle pulls a demon's presence without calling their form. The summoner's circle intersects the containment circle, and the fire creates a sort of medium for the demon's presence to take shape in. If they were trying to bring the demon's form through, the summoner's circle would be tangential, not intersecting."

"So, whoever did this was …" Wanda said.

"Consulting with a demon, not inviting them to drop by," I said. "Or at least, they were trying to. When you're successful in opening even a narrow portal like you need for a conjure, you get spiral patterns in the ash."

"This was a failed casting?" Lucas asked. "I'd hate to see what a successful conjure feels like."

"Yeah, you would," I said. "So far, there's nothing to worry about, but let's tell Dr. C and we'll look into it a little later on." I headed back to the jogging trail, still concerned that someone was trying to call up demons in my city.

I kept a relaxed pace the rest of the way. Still, running a five-mile circuit, even at an easy pace, will take the wind out of you. We were all panting by the time we made it back to the bench and slowed to a walk.

"So," Lucas said between breaths, "what are we all up to today?" He put his hands behind his head as we walked.

"I'm going shopping for a piece of wood," I deadpanned.

"Just one?" Wanda asked with a grin.

"Yes, but it's a *magick* piece of wood."

"Are you buying a wand?" Lucas asked.

"No, just the magick wood for one, like I said."

"Right, magick wood. Well, I'm going to be bored to tears at the lake with my folks. My dad's insisting on 'quality time' as a family, so we're going to go swim and frolic while Dad chars meat on a grill and calls it bar-be-que."

"Let me guess," Wanda said. "No books?"

"No books, no cell phones, just a deck of cards, a box of dominoes, and good old-fashioned, awkward-as-hell togetherness. What about you, Wanda? Please, give me something exciting to wish I was doing!"

"I … have a date," Wanda blurted after a moment of hesitation. Her face turned almost as red as her tank top as she looked over her shoulder. "I've wanted to talk to you both about this for a while, but ..."

"We kind of suspected," I said as I waved Gage back. He frowned but his steps veered away.

"Really? Because we've been really low-key about it. We've both been trying to keep it quiet. Did you go through my phone or something?" Her expression hardened as she turned to face us.

"We didn't have to," Lucas said. "Every time you get a text, you get this big smile on your face, and it's like we're not even there. I don't know about Chance, but I've been a little disappointed that you didn't even tell us who it is."

"I've just been insanely jealous because it wasn't me," I told her. "But seriously, when are you going to introduce us? I mean, we're behind the curve here. We still have to threaten him if he breaks your heart."

"And there's all that silent judging we still need to do because he's not good enough for you," Lucas added.

Wanda turned and put a hand on each of our shoulders. Her eyes flicked back and forth between us as they welled up. "Please," she said, her voice wavering.

"What's wrong, Wanda?" Lucas asked.

"Promise me you won't be upset with me," she said.

"Sure, you know I won't be," he said, his voice low and laced with concern. "Are you okay?"

She turned the full force of her attention to me.

"I won't be upset with you, whatever it is." I put my hand over hers and the first tear slid down her cheek.

"It's Giselle," she said softly. Her wide-eyed gaze went back and forth between Lucas and me, and her breathing was shallow.

"The girl Damian was mind-fucking?" I asked. Wanda nodded and then looked to Lucas, her eyes searching his face.

"You've got good taste," he said a little too casually.

"I don't ... this is important, Lucas. Please, can you take this seriously?"

"I'm sorry, Wanda," Lucas said. "I'm trying to act like this is no big thing because it's *not*. I don't care if you're dating a girl. I've got your back no matter who you date."

She turned back to me, and my heart broke a little at the worry I saw in her eyes.

47

"You're my friend," I said. "Who you date doesn't change that. You could sell your soul, and I'd help you get it back."

She took a shaky breath and wiped the back of her hand across her cheek. "Goddess," she said softly, "I didn't think I'd be this much of a wreck over this."

"Were you worried that we'd freak out or something?" Lucas asked.

"Kinda," Wanda said as her face went red again. "Giselle's folks went totally apeshit when one of her friends came out. They really don't like the whole Goth thing to begin with, and if they found out about us, they might kick her out. She's scared to tell any of her friends because she's afraid someone will tell her mom and dad."

"What about your mom?" Lucas asked.

"She'd be cool with it," Wanda said. "But I needed to know you guys were gonna be able to deal with me and Giselle being together."

"Why wouldn't we be?" I asked.

She shrugged and blushed even more. "I don't know. This is my first time coming out about this to anyone. You guys are like family to me, but ... people get weird about this."

"Well, we're about as weird as it comes," Lucas said. "And we're not kicking you out of the club or anything."

Wanda smiled at him, her eyes brimming again, and hugged him. I heard him grunt as she squeezed him tight, then she let him go and wrapped her arms around me. "Thank you soooo much for being cool about this," she said into my shoulder. When she pulled back, her eyes were red but the smile on her face was mirrored in them. "You didn't even ask to record us or for pictures or anything."

Lucas slapped his hand against his forehead and made an exasperated sound. "I *knew* I was forgetting something!" he said. "Dude, a golden opportunity, gone. You're supposed to have my back on this kind of thing. If we screw up like this again, we're going to have to turn in our man cards."

"I figure we're going to get plenty of opportunities for a live show," I said as we turned and headed back toward the cars.

Wanda put her fist into my arm, but her heart wasn't in the punch. "Jerk," she said.

"Prude," I shot back.

"See you tomorrow?" Lucas asked as we got to the lot.

"Yeah … I'll probably be most of the day taking care of this."

"And I've got that exciting bar-be-que thing," he said. "Sounds like you're the only one having a good day today, Wanda."

"You have my pity," she said as she opened the door to the *Falcon*.

"Sure we do," I said as I got into my Mustang. Junkyard hopped into the back seat and plopped down. Gage was already in the passenger seat looking less than thrilled. On the up side, his pissy silence was a lot easier to deal with than his snide comments, so I counted it as a win.

Mom and Dee were already gone when we got back, Mom to work and Dee probably at the Romanoffs'. Wanda's mom saw almost as much of my little sister as I did. I ate breakfast while Gage showered, then tried to finish my own shower before the hot water ran out. By the time I got out, I was shivering. I put on my Blue Sun t-shirt and a pair of black cargo shorts in the bathroom, then crossed the hall to my room and shoved my feet into my black sneakers. Finally, I opened the secret compartment I'd made in my closet and grabbed the satchel Biladon had given me with all the bearer chits in my name.

"I'm looking forward to seeing what passes for real culture in this city," Gage said as we pulled out of the driveway. "I've heard about the Underground and of course your Bazaar. It's not as sophisticated as Boston, I'm sure, but it's bound to have a certain rustic charm all its own." He was looking ever so sporty, with a red polo shirt bearing the Franklin Academy crest, expensive-looking khaki shorts and deck shoes.

"Oh, I'm sure," I said with an exaggerated twang. "New Essex is all manner of rustic. Quaint, too. Heck, sometimes we even get downright pastoral. And don't get too comfortable."

"Why?" he asked as I turned onto Violet Drive. The houses were getting nicer as we went, and the yards bigger.

"Because my girlfriend never rides in the back seat."

"I am not playing chaperone so you can impress some cowan girl with *our* world. The Veil is there for a reason, plebe, and you are not going to violate that. It's one of our cardinal rules. Turn this vehicle around this instant!" His voice was sharp and carried all the authority of a yippy dog. Maybe other kids found it impressive, but it fell way short of matching a pissed-off demon.

"You really didn't read my file, did you?" I asked

"I skimmed the important parts," he said defensively.

I turned my head and gave him an amused look. "Then you'd know my girlfriend isn't cowan."

"Your social life isn't important. Your skill level is. Or, in your case, the lack of same. Your over-dependence on foci and your inadequate base skills is alarming, your extensive knowledge of forbidden lore makes you a danger to everyone around you, and your focus on combative spells is a perversion of the arts arcane. Frankly, if it was up to me, you wouldn't even know the Franklin Academy existed, much less be sponsored by the head of the High Council himself."

We turned onto Shade's street as he listed my failings, and my ears burned. I fought the urge to tell him off, and mostly won.

"You know, Winnie," I said with a smile, "if it was up to me, I wouldn't send me, either. But it isn't, so shut up and get in the back seat." I pulled into her driveway as I finished. Her parents' place was a three-story pile of brick and stone with a curved driveway in front and a separate driveway for the garage in back. I'd seen the inside a couple of times, and it was just as sterile as the exterior. I pulled to a stop next to the front door and let the Mustang's engine rumble. Gage met my look for a few seconds before he opened the door and got out. The front door opened as he slid into the back seat, and Shade came out looking like a goddess in jeans and a blue tank top that had the word "Princess" in sequins across her breasts. She had on a white button-down shirt that she'd left open, and her eyes were hidden behind a pair of movie-star-sized sunglasses with a fancy gold frame. Her mother stood in the doorway behind her and waved at me.

"Morning, Mrs. Cooper," I called out. She gave me a smile in return, and I wondered if I was seeing a glimpse of what Shade might look like in twenty years. If her mom was any clue, I hoped I was around to see it. Her auburn hair was a paler shade than her daughter's, and her eyes were a darker gray. Smile lines were just starting to show around her eyes, and she took Shade's good looks and turned them regal.

"I'll be back later, Mom," Shade called out as she jogged to the passenger door and got into the seat beside me, shoving a big purse with some designer logo on it between us.

"Have fun!" her mom said and closed the door. As soon as the elder Cooper was out of sight, Shade leaned across and kissed me.

"Hello, sweetie," she purred.

"Hello, sexy," I said as my lips tingled. I put the Mustang in gear and pulled out of the driveway.

"Who's this?" she said after she buckled herself in and turned in the seat.

"Winthrop Gage," Winnie said from the back seat and offered his hand. "I'm Chance's student mentor from his new school."

"Alexis Cooper," Shade said, keeping her right hand in her lap and pulling her sunglasses down with her left. "Alpha of the Diamond Lake pack." Gage leaned back in the seat with a stricken look on his face. I snuck a look at Shade. Her eyes were full gold, with no white showing, and her canines were slightly elongated.

"You didn't tell me she was a … a …" he floundered, suddenly sounding a little less sure of himself.

"The word you're trying not to say is werewolf," I said. "I'm pretty sure it's in my file."

"Is there anything else I might have … skimmed over?" he asked.

"Plenty," I said. "Probably even more that isn't in there." I turned to Shade. "Your mom actually acknowledged my existence this morning."

"She still thinks you're part of my rebellious phase," she said as she dug in the bag and pulled out a black shirt. She reached over her head, grabbed the white shirt by the collar and pulled it over her head, then hooked her arms behind her back and fiddled with her bra. A few seconds later, she slipped her bra straps over her shoulders and pulled it out from under the front of her shirt. I tried to keep my eyes on the road as she pulled the straps of her tank top to the side and shimmied into a sports bra, then pulled the tank top off without exposing an inch of skin that any straight

51

guy or lesbian with a pulse would have hoped to see. Finally, she pulled the black t-shirt on, revealing the logo for Dogma Breath on the front. "I think she's convinced that if she acts like she approves, I'll break up with you out of spite or something." Not to be forgotten, Junkyard laid his chin on the seat and let out a little rumble. Shade leaned down and rubbed her cheek against his ear while she rubbed the side of his face with her free hand. He licked her chin and she let out a giggle, then he sat back down in the seat, apparently satisfied with the greeting.

"So, where are we going?" she asked as I headed toward downtown.

"First, we're going to the Underground," I said as we hit the zone between residential and full business district. I crossed a railroad track and turned right, heading south past the edge of the heavy industrial section of the Joplin district and into New Essex proper. Buildings got taller and taller around us until we were in Lakeside, where the oldest money in New Essex did business. I drove past the green expanse of Centennial Park, then turned right, into the parking garage of a beige stone building. I took the Mustang down to the bottom level and headed for a set of parking spots marked with Reserved signs. As I got closer, I fought down the urge to leave this parking level. *There are better places to park closer to ground level,* I heard in my head. *It's dark and secluded down here. No telling what might happen...* Like most external influences, the thoughts bounced off my mental defenses. Shade tensed beside me, but she was no stranger to mind control magick, either. I turned into one of the empty parking spots, the effects of the aversion wards suddenly let up. Technically, they were legal, but they were the absolute limit of how far you could go in influencing behavior.

"I cannot say I'm entirely fond of that effect," Gage said as the last remnants of the ward's suggestions faded.

"Right there with you on that," I said as I turned the car off and got out. Junkyard hit the pavement beside me, hit claws clicking against the concrete as I went around the car and took Shade's hand.

"So, is the Vanderbeek Building part of the Underground?" Shade asked as we headed for the large alcove that looked like it only held a single door to the stairwell.

"Not exactly," I said as we stepped into the well-lit area. About ten feet by twenty, it didn't take a genius to notice that the stairwell door was set in the far right side of the long wall. The rest just looked like bare concrete. *"Ego sum inter illustrator,"* I said. *I am among the enlightened,* or something close to that. The illusion of a blank wall shimmered and faded, leaving us facing a broad wooden door with brass fittings and a small window set in the middle at eye level. On the right side was a single brass button, set in a rectangular brass plate. A small red light in a metal cage was above the plate, and when I pressed the button, the light blazed to life. Moments later, the sound of a motor reached our ears.A minute dragged, by then another, and I could see Gage's expression start to turn a little sour, a millimeter of a dip at the corner of his mouth, and the slightest lowering of his eyebrows. A loud clanging sound came from below us just as he opened his mouth to say something, and we all jumped a little. It was enough to keep him quiet for another thirty seconds.

"Are you sure this is even the right place?" he demanded.

"I'm sure," I said.

"It doesn't sound very safe," he said.

"Nothing fun is," I said with a squeeze of Shade's hand. She smiled at me and leaned over to give me a slow, lingering kiss.

"Are you saying I'm dangerous?" she asked with a wicked little grin.

"Extremely," I said, and kissed her again. Once we pulled apart, I leaned down and grazed my teeth along the side of her neck, eliciting a satisfied little sound from deep in her throat and a smile for my efforts. Gage made a disgusted sounding little snort as Shade turned so she was facing me and nipped gently at my neck, then grinned at me with her teeth bared and her eyes a deep green.

"Could you two *please* keep your clothes on for a few minutes longer?" Gage said as a light began to shine behind the small window set in the elevator door. "The car should be here in an hour or so, and I'd hate for the two of you to have to dress in a hurry."

"I'm sure you'd be so disappointed," Shade said. "Having to watch me get dressed, that is." A creeping tide of red spread from his neck to this forehead as Shade's comment turned the tables on him. He sputtered for a moment, trying to find something to say, but the elevator door opened and saved him from further embarrassment.

Facing us was a Dwarf in a blue jacket with a broad leather belt around his middle that was covered in boxy pouches. A heavy revolver rode on his right hip, and I saw the hilt of a knife jutting from the top of his left boot. Fiery red hair flowed from beneath the matching blue hat he wore, a Dwarven style that resembled a longer version of a watch cap that had his clan insignia in brass pinned to the front. His beard was just as red but shorter, barely coming to the first button on his jacket, which, among Dwarves, marked him as fairly young and inexperienced, which could mean anything from forty to a hundred.

"Seeking passage to the Underground are ya?" he asked with one hand on the butt of the revolver. His eye fell on me, then on Shade before he turned to glance at Gage.

"I'm looking to open an account a Bjerning's," I said. "I am hight Chance Fortunato, *gothi* to the Diamond Lake Pack, apprentice to Wizard Corwin and Seeker of the Maxilla Asini. I serve no power of Hell or enemy of yours." Dwarves loved titles almost as much as they loved the stories behind them. The trick was to drop at least one that they already knew. Evidently, this guy knew something about me that he liked, because his beard split to reveal broad teeth as he smiled.

"Your name is known here, Fortunato," he said. "Be welcome in the Underground. And you, how are you known, young lady?"

"I'm…Shade," she said, a little hesitant. "Alpha of the Diamond Lake Pack."

"That's all?" the Dwarf said, his voice sounding a little disappointed. "That does you no justice, Lady Shade. Firemane, I call you. Lady of the Diamond Lake Pack. Who are you, then?"

"Wintrhop Gage the Fourth, alumnus of the Franklin Academy, heir to Winthrop Gage the Third and Proctor of the Academy by order of the Wizard's Council," Gage said confidently.

"Your name is not known here," the Dwarf said. "But your family's is, and the Academy is well known. Step in, then, and be welcome to the Underground." We stepped into the elevator car at his gesture. The car itself looked like a metal cage. The Dwarf pulled the outer door shut, then an inner door, and when he pulled the lever on the stand beside him, I could see that it really was basically a metal framework around a steel mesh platform. Junkyard sat next to me and leaned against my leg.

"My name is Brad by the way," the Dwarf said, suddenly dropping the Dwarvish accent and sounding almost exactly like someone I would hear on TV. Everyone turned to look at him, and I wondered if my own expression was as dumbfounded as Shade's. Seeing our faces, he let out a deep, booming laugh that seemed to shake the car. "Nay, pay no heed to my jest. I am Brand Firebeard, of Clan Hengist, alemakers to kings. Now, mind your lunch, lady and gentlemen. The view changes soon, and you'd best brace yourself for it."

"What view?" I asked. A metallic *clang* sounded, and I saw the concrete walls suddenly replaced by iron, then another *clang* sounded, and the walls fell away. I looked up to see the iron doors closing above us, with another set dropping open to let us pass. At each corner, a steel shaft ran down the sides of the car, with iron filigree work connecting the shafts to each other at regular intervals.

"That view, lad," Brand said with a wave of his hand.

Below us lay the Underground. We had to be at least three hundred feet up. The cavern was huge, narrow at one end, widening out to encompass the buildings, then narrowing again before the floor rose as if it was going to meet the ceiling. But it never got there. A huge oval opening gave us a view of a second chamber, this one less historic looking, and much more Dwarven. The sides were steeper and closer together, and most of the buildings were carved directly from the living stone. Quonset huts were arranged in neat rows below us in an almost perfect grid, with larger buildings that wouldn't have looked out of place on a World War II era military base set up in the middle of the whole thing, bisected by what I first took to be a railroad track. It looked like a normal city at night, with lights shining in every window and street lights guiding the way. Even the railroad track looked like it had been laid in the Forties. Then I spotted the third rail in the middle. The railroad track disappeared into a tunnel that ran below the larger opening at the far end. Junkyard, never one to miss a good view, put his front paws on the railing and looked out over the subterranean city alongside me. On the opposite side of the track, another elevator like ours was ascending, and I could see the tall, impossibly narrow framework that supported it from the outside.

"You're in luck," Brand said and pointed to the narrow end of the cavern. A light appeared in the tunnel that the tracks emerged from. "You're just in time to see the Silver Phoenix arrive." I looked to the tunnel, expecting to see and hear a train. A horn sounded that reminded me more of a semi than a locomotive, sending a wall of sound ahead of it that seemed to say in no uncertain term that something *big* was coming. What emerged from the tunnel wasn't so much a train as a jet on rails. The first car, what I figured *had* to be the locomotive, was a silver cylinder that tapered down at the front. The whole front end was dominated by a huge air intake for a giant turbine engine. Unlike normal trains, this one had a glassed in cockpit at the front that reminded me more of Dr. C's pictures of the old B-29 bombers, basically a smooth surface with the windscreens set flush to the metal. This one curved up from the front and ran back in a widening rectangle. A single line of glass panes ran back from the cockpit for the length of the engine. I caught all of that in a single instant as it rocketed out of the tunnel, pulling shiny steel cars with windows that ran along the sides and tops of each car. Another row of windows ran along the sides of the car, and I noticed that the doors sat high and in the middle. Then the Phoenix came to a stop. For a moment, I wondered how people were supposed to get off the train. My question was answered as the entire trained dropped three feet in a smooth descent. Beside me, Junkyard let out a short bark.

"Yeah, that *is* cool, buddy," I said.

"What's that over there?" Shade asked, pointing to a series of flickering lights that ran along one edge of the cavern.

"Degenerates and scum," Gage said. "Nothing more."

"Hate to rain on your picnic, lad," Brand said, "but that's just some poor folk. Can't afford to buy a place in town, but they're not well suited to living on the cowan side of the Veil. Them as don't have natural Glamoury, like the fae and such, or honest folk fallen on hard times. Seems there's more and more of that nowadays, bad as things are."

"That's utter nonsense," Gage said. "My family's business is doing better than ever. They're just too lazy to work hard enough to make a decent life for themselves. I'm interested in the new construction over on that far wall, though."

"That'd be a bunch of lazy degenerates building their own homes out of the cavern wall," Brand said with a straight face. "Bought their own tools, and got licensed proper. Slow going that. Doing most of it by hand." Gage turned to glare down at the rest of the small city below us.

"Why does it look like an Army base?" Shade asked.

"Because it was," Brand said with a laugh that seemed to come from somewhere south of his knees. "Did you ever hear of Project Bright Halo?"

"Oh!" Shade said with a smile. "We talked about that in American History one day when we had a substitute teacher. It was one of the super-secret projects during the Cold War, some kind of bunker to keep the government going if the Russians ever attacked us."

"Exactly so," Brand said. "The Underground used to just be the far chamber, then the cowan government came down, built their little town, and left. The Conclave made sure they forgot where the put it a few months later."

"How did you keep them from discovering you?" I asked. "Warding runes?"

"Damn big ones," Brand said. He pointed toward a smooth spot halfway up the opening in the other wall. "See there, that bare patch? That is where we had to chisel the rock away to dispel the runes." By that point, we were almost level with the top of the tallest buildings. Below us I could see the slightly elevated platform where, in theory, we would be stopping. A small kiosk was set next to it, with a small light glowing atop it. Brand moved the handle forward, and our descent slowed, then we came to a stop as the car came level with the platform.

"Welcome to the Underground," the Dwarf said as he pulled the inner door open. The outer door slid to the side on its own, and we stepped out onto the platform.

"Great," Shade muttered. "Now what?"

"An excellent question," Gage said. "Surely you know where Bjernings is, yes?" He sounded far too satisfied with himself to me, and I resisted the urge to smack him.

"Of course I do," I said as I headed for the board marked "Information" near the edge of the platform. "After all, it's my first time here. I instantly know where everything is."

"The Franklin Academy does not accept excuses for ignorance," he said. The cadence of his voice was measured and precise, like something that had been drilled into him. "Your attitude is as much part of my evaluation as your…ignorance…" he trailed off as I pulled a map from one of the wooden holders.

"I wasn't being *that* sarcastic," I said as I unfolded the map. "Now I know where everything is."

"Should I sing the map song?" Shade asked.

"The what?" I asked.

"From the kids' show," she explained.

"I think I know that one," I said.

"What idiot wouldn't get that reference?" Gage asked. I didn't bother to answer him as I headed toward the narrowed end of the first chamber. According to the map, Bjerning Depository was in the next chamber and on the left. We headed for the edge of the open area furthest from the tracks. That put us on Scriveners' Way, which looked like it was home to more than scribes. Granted, it had its share of book shops and stationery stores, but in a magickal town, quills and inks were specific enough to warrant separate specialty shops as well. Helvig's Elder Tongues specialized in scribing and interpreting runic alphabets according to its sign, while Set In Stone seemed to be devoted the secrets of Babylonian and Persian cuneiform.

A mix of beings was on the street with us, some covered in baggy clothes, others barely covered at all. On this side of the Veil, fairies and pixies didn't seem to bother to conceal themselves. A couple of sprites flew past as well, their dragonfly wings almost transparent. Fairies jeered at the larger fae as they passed by, but the sprites just kept their heads forward and flew on.

"What's up with that?" Shade asked. "Those bigger ones looked like they could boot the fairies into next week."

"A few decades ago, the sprites joined the Unseiligh Court in supporting Heidler's Damonkrieg, what the cowan know as the Second World War," Gage said. "After the war, they offered their freedom as a people as recompense for their crimes."

"So they're…"

"Slaves," I said. "To pretty much anyone who wants them. If they're not bound to someone, they have to go *find* someone to own them."

"That's bullshit," she said. I nodded.

"The word in the Nine Hells was that they just accepted Unsealigh protection," I added. "And that the dark fae offered them up as a scapegoat."

"A likely enough story," Gage sneered. "They're bound to it until the war passes from living memory, either way."

"That's at least another decade or so," Shade said, her voice rising. "And what if Chance is right? What if they were tricked or something?" Gage stopped and looked at her with narrowed eyes.

"That's not for the likes of you to question," he said with a hard tone. "The Council doesn't allow that kind of mistake to be made." He turned and stalked off a few paces, then gestured to me to join him. I put a hand on Shade's arm and shook my head before I crossed the distance to him.

"Keep your woman in line, plebe," he said once I got close. "I won't warn you again."

"Keep *her* in…," I sputtered. "She's *well* within her rights to rip your throat out right now. You don't dress down an alpha unless you've *earned* that privilege. And even then, you never do it in public."

"I don't care if she's the damn queen of all werewolves," he hissed at me. "She will keep a civil tone in my presence, or in the presence of any mage. And she will *not* question the wisdom of the Council in public."

"You want to keep her in line?" I asked. "You do it yourself. And then you go explain to the Council why you've got two pissed off packs at their door howling for your blood. Assuming you survive pissing her off in the first place."

"I would have nothing to fear," he said. I laughed in his face.

"I've got news for you, Winnie," I said with a tight grin. "The Conclave isn't as all powerful as they want you to think. How else do you think a demon was able to keep me as a slave for eight years?"

"Everyone knows you went willingly," he said.

I shoved him hard enough to put him on his ass, then went and grabbed him by the front of his shirt.

"Go back," I said, my voice harsh in my own throat. He looked up at me with wide eyes as he tried to scramble away from me. "Go get a hotel room and don't come anywhere near me until you read my goddamn file."

"You know Master Draeden will automatically put you in remedial courses if I do that," he said.

"Then don't speak," I said. "Don't talk to me, about me, or near me. Just observe, and do it from as far away as you can."

"Master Draeden will hear about this," he said.

"You can bet on it." I took a lot more satisfaction in the wide eyed expression he gave me than I should have. Still, I'm not a complete asshole. Maybe ninety five percent there, but not so far that I was beyond pulling him to his feet. Besides, we were getting a little more attention than I would have liked. People were crowding at windows and doors of the nearby Quonset huts, and over the heads of the crowd, I could see a couple of silver ankh-topped *paramiir* staves bobbing our way. I gave Gage a sharp look as the Sentinels showed up. Naturally, they went to his side first, one facing him, the other keeping his eyes on Shade and me. Both of them wore the blue cloaks of their office, but were dressed in slacks and white button down shirts under that. Both had haircuts that would have cost them more than my mom made in a week, the one talking to Gage dark haired with a narrow face, and the one keeping an eye on me with brown locks and a jaw you could chisel granite from. They carried paintball guns in holsters that sat high on their right hip, with a black nylon pouch on the opposite side for other tools. Junkyard pressed against me as Shade took my hand.

"He's telling them it was nothing, no big deal," Shade whispered from beside me. I looked over at him to see him shaking his head and smiling. "No details, just a…slight misunderstanding. Heading to Bjernings to open an account...little bastard's vouching for us." After a moment, the Sentinel talking to Gage nodded to his partner, who came our way.

"What's your business in the Underground today, Fortunato?" he demanded, his square chin thrust out at me like a weapon.

"I'm opening an account at Bjerning's Depository," I said with a gesture toward the satchel. He held out his hand, and I handed the leather case over. When he opened the flap and looked inside, his eyes went wide for a moment and he looked at me.

"Where did you get all of this?" he asked.

"I have an account with Biladon Garnet, in the Hive. There's a receipt for what's in there minus about a hundred and fifty trade ounces or so that he had on hand." I let out a sigh as he took a couple of steps away and summoned his partner over. Of course it looked odd for a sixteen year old kid to have bearer chits for more than six thousand trade credits on him. Even in the Underground, there were folks who didn't see that much wealth in a life time. Add in a guy with my reputation, and things went from a little odd to downright shady looking. Having a receipt for the whole thing seemed to be helping about as much as a knife at a gunfight. It took another ten minutes before they decided I might not have just robbed someone. The other Sentinel took the satchel from his partner and came over to me. His expression was hard to read behind his mirrored sunglasses.

"This transaction took place in October," he said. "Why did you wait eight months to open an account?"

"It's been a busy year," I said. His eyes narrowed at that. Anyone who knew anything about me knew I'd done quite a lot since I'd escaped from Dulka. In addition to killing a rogue werewolf and vampire with aspirations to demonhood, I'd also found the Maxilla Asini, a boss level weapon that could kill demons. Plus, I'd earned a reputation as the go-to guy for minor magickal problems among the fringes of cowan society that was aware of the Veil. They might not know what went on behind it, but they knew things existed on the other side, usually because they were the innocent bystanders who caught a spell from a dabbler or a stray hex. Most of the Sentinels didn't like me because of that, even though they usually turned down cowans who asked them for help.

"I'm giving you an hour," he said as he pressed the satchel against my chest. "After that, I expect you to be a long way from here." He shoved me back a step as he finished. I took a slow breath to calm myself. As much as I wanted to smart off to him, I'd seen Sentinels lay waste to an army of vampires all too recently, and I really didn't want to be on the wrong side of a *paramiir* in any of its three forms. I nodded instead and took a step back. Shade's mouth was a tight line and her eyes were a dark green as she glared at the Sentinels. But she'd seen them fight, too, so she kept her distance and her silence. Gage came our way, but I turned my back on him and headed toward the narrowed end of the cave.

The cobbled walkway wound through more shops and eventually came out close to the wall, where the cobblestones ended and Missouri limestone took over again as it led to a wide tunnel in the rock. Inside the darker confines of the tunnel, a series of chambers had been hollowed out, most by nature but some by the denizens of the Underground. Most of them offered some sort of food, some of it already dead and cooked, the rest … not so much of either. A thousand smells hit my nose, from savory to the sickly sweet smell of decay as we walked through the tunnel. On our right, a trio of grunged-up fairies had hollowed out a smaller chamber just at eye level on most humanoids and were offering fae wines and cakes. Between their tattered wings and patched clothes, plus selling fae goods for sale, I figured them for outcast. Actually selling fae food was below most fairies. Junkyard held his nose high as we went, his head weaving left and right. Even Shade's nostrils were flaring, and I wondered what Gage and I were missing.

Both Shade and Junkyard sneezed as we cleared the opening to the next chamber. "I know, right?" she said to him as they both shook their heads. He made a warbling noise that bordered on a whine, and she laughed.

"Am I going to have to worry about you two talking behind my back?" I asked her.

"I'm not that kind of bitch, baby," she said before she kissed me. It was my turn to laugh.

Up ahead, Bjerning's was easy to see. It towered over the other buildings, even though it was set into the wall to give it a flat front. Four thick columns ran across the front, and a pair of huge brass-colored doors stood open. Each column was in the shape of a Dwarven statue holding the upper level on its massive fists. We walked up the five broad steps to the doorway, passing dozens of people going about their business. A pair of bearded Dwarves stood at the doorway in heavy black tunics with broad black belts on their waists. On the left side, one had a heavy bladed ax with a short handle, while the other carried a thick-bladed short sword. But on the right side, both carried a massive revolver. In the broad, three-fingered hands of a Dwarf, it might look normal, but I doubted any mortal would be able to hold one steady, much less stay on their feet if they pulled the trigger. Judging by the length of their beards, I would have put them both at under a hundred, though the honor beads woven into their facial hair spoke of more than a couple of fights. And in spite of the hustle of beings going in and out of the building, I was pretty damn certain that they noticed everyone.

Inside, the place was a marvel of Dwarven bureaucracy. There were benches for customers, but I had never seen a Dwarf sit while he or she was working, so the desks were all a little taller than average, with a raised area in front of them for chairs. No one was sitting on the benches, and almost as soon as we stepped into the waiting area, a red-headed Dwarf in a dark green tunic waved us over to his desk. Dwarven bureaucracy was, like most things they did, actually efficient.

We stepped up onto the platform and I stopped to let Shade choose a seat first. She sank gracefully into the seat on the right, so I took the one in the middle, leaving Gage to the leftmost chair. Junkyard sank to his haunches on my right. The desk was neat, with a pair of metal pens in a holder on either side of a brass plate that read "M. Firebeard, Account Manager" in black, etched letters. His craggy features barely moved as his eyes flicked down to a card placed on his desk.

"Good afternoon," he said woodenly. "How may I help you?" I didn't stop my smile at his forced politeness. When I'd dealt with Dwarves before, our conversations usually started with "What do you want?" It wasn't that they were rude, they just didn't believe in wasting time on what they called useless social fripperies.

"I'd like to open an account," I said as I lifted the satchel and set it on the desk. His gaze lingered on the satchel for a moment, then went back to the card on his desk.

"We'd be happy to assist you with an account," he recited. "What is your name, sir?"

"Chance Fortunato," I said. I waited for the usual reactions, but all I got was a tilt of the head.

"Heard of you," he said after a beat. "Good work beating the Count." I did a double take at that. A single compliment from a Dwarf would have been gushing fanboy squee from anyone else.

"Uh … Thank you," I said after a few seconds. On my left, Gage squirmed, obviously wanting to say something. Firebeard was looking through the satchel and, after a moment, stood and left the desk.

"What's he …?" Gage started to ask, but I held a hand up. Dwarves didn't do anything without a good reason. A few seconds later, Firebeard came back with a human in a blue double-breasted suit with gold buttons. Without a word, the Dwarf took his seat again and pulled a form from one of his desk drawers.

"Good morning," the man said as he came around the desk and offered his hand to Gage. "I'm Andrew Salvatore. I understand you wanted to open an account with us today." Everything had been addressed to Gage, and Shade and I might as well not have been there. Gage sputtered for a moment while I stood up.

"I want to open an account," I said. "Is there a problem?"

"No, of course not," Salvatore said smoothly as he offered his hand to me. "Having a human liaison is just standard procedure for any account with a balance higher than two thousand ounces. Dwarves tend to lack the social skills our more affluent clients desire, if you take my meaning." His smile had only faltered for a split second, but something about him just grated on my nerves. Maybe it was the casual dismissal of the people he worked for, or maybe it was how I'd been invisible to him until he found out that I was his potential client.

"Actually, Mr. Firebeard's social skills are just fine," I said. "I think I prefer to work with him." Salvatore's smile faltered, while Firebeard kept his head down and his pen moving.

"Well, if you insist," the man said, his tone a bit cooler. "Is everything in order for Mr. ..." he stopped as he read the name. "Fortunato?" Firebeard nodded and kept writing. Salvatore reached down and picked up the receipt Biladon had written out for me. "If you'll excuse me. Just a few formalities involved with an account this size. I'll return shortly." I watched him scuttle off with an uneasy feeling rising in my gut. Beside me, Junkyard tilted his head as he looked at me, like I was missing something.

"Sign here," Firebeard said as he slid a form across his desk. I gave him a skeptical look and read over the form. Working for a demon had made me cautious about putting my name to anything I hadn't read or didn't understand. I'd wormed my way out of a few tight spots by getting other people to agree to things too quickly, too. But this was a standard agreement to hold my assets. I reached the end and signed it. Firebeard stamped it and slid it into a drawer, then excused himself stiffly and headed to the back.

"Where's he going?" Shade muttered.

"Most likely to get a key for the sub-vault Fortunato is being issued," Gage said. "Makes it so he can get access to funds at any of the Bjerning offices."

A couple of minutes later, Salvatore hustled back up to the desk with another man in a dark green robe behind him. Gage leaned back in his chair with something that looked like a suppressed smile bending his mouth slightly. The green-robed man was older, with wisps of gray hair and a tuft of white clinging for dear life to his narrow chin, trying desperately to be a goatee.

"Elllsworth Chaffee," the older man said, his thin beard wiggling with each clipped syllable. "Mr. Salvatore tells me that you have attempted to circumvent mandatory reporting procedures regarding your account." Gage leaned forward, any amusement gone from his face.

"What reporting?" I asked. "No one said anything about reporting anything."

"Any account over two thousand ounces must be reported to the main office," Chaffee said. "Mr. Salvatore says you have refused to allow him to perform his duties as liaison, which includes filing that report. Therefore, we cannot allow you to conduct business with us, Mr. Fortunato. I'll have security see you to the—" He stopped as Firebeard laid a heavy brass key on the desk.

"What are you doing?" he asked, his deep voice rumbling like thunder.

"I'm sorry, Mr. Firebeard, but we won't be doing business with Mr. Fortunato," Salvatore said with a wave of his hand. Chaffee reached for the satchel, only to find his wrist caught in Firebeard's massive hand.

"Yes, we will," he said.

"He refused a human liaison," Chaffee repeated. "There are notifications to be made ..."

"I did them," Firebeard said.

"But the liaison—"

"Isn't necessary," Firebeard said. "Go away, before I decide *you* aren't necessary." The two humans exchanged a glance, then beat a quick retreat. Firebeard shook his head and handed me the key and a sheet of parchment. "Your account is open. The key will only work for you. The directions for use are there. Read them. And ... I'm sorry for the trouble." He offered me his hand, and I took it.

Shaking hands with a Dwarf was like shaking hands with a mountain. His grip was firm without being crushing, but I knew I wouldn't get my hand back until he was ready to let go. With most humans, I got nothing; with mildly talented people like Lucas, I would usually feel a tingle of magick. With Firebeard, it was more of an insistent heat, like lava under his skin.

"It was no trouble at all," I said, hoping I wasn't stepping on toes I didn't want to. "I hope I didn't cause you any problems." Every time I had tried to apologize to a Dwarf about something, they had made like whatever had happened wasn't an issue. I hoped it would work now. He nodded and the barest hint of a smile escaped from under his moustache as he leaned forward.

"Some call you the demon's apprentice," he said softly. "We raise our glass to the boy who escaped." With that, he let go of my hand and straightened. I tilted my head to him and stepped back off the platform. Junkyard and Shade came with me on my left, and Gage followed a little more slowly.

"So, where are we going now?" Shade asked as we emerged from Bjerning's.

"Back to more familiar ground," I said as I started back the way we came.

"The Hive?" she asked. I nodded.

"Arianh-Rod is the only wandwright I trust."

"Is that absolutely … necessary?" Gage asked.

"Yes," I said. "Ari is more likely to have something that works for me than anyone here." I detoured a little to my right and came out on Wandwright Way after the tunnel.

"But there are plenty of reputable wand makers right here," he said, some of the condescension creeping back into his voice. "Names you could say with pride, like Luccio or Portiferro. True masters of their craft."

"They all have the same five woods," I said, pointing to a display in one window. "Elm, oak, holly, cedar, and ash. And there, dare I say it? Apple and cherry listed as 'exotic'!"

"This one has birch wood," Shade said. "It's an exclusive offering."

"All very solid choices," Gage said.

"All very boring choices," I countered. "I've tried them, I got nothing from any of them. Ari usually keeps a better selection of woods on hand. And she's better."

"These are some of the leading names in the business!" Gage protested as I turned left and slipped between two shops.

"Shut up and keep up," I said as we headed for the platform. Junkyard let out a short bark as we broke into a jog.

"You don't understand," Gage said as he caught up to us at the platform. "I'm a Gage. I can't be seen in a place like the Hive. It would ruin my reputation. My family would disown me if I embarrassed them like that."

"Don't worry," I said. "I've got your identity covered."

Chapter 4

~ Magic is easy. People? People are hard. Why do you THINK wizards prefer remote towers? ~ Killian Moon, monster hunter

"When you said you had my identity covered," Gage said as he donned the ornate mask, "I didn't think you meant it so literally." With the thin cloth cloak draped over his shoulders and the golden mask covering most of his face, no one would know who he really was unless he introduced himself. Knowing Gage, that was still a possibility.

"Are you sure you don't want your own disguises?" Synreah asked in her most sultry tone. Gage took a deep breath as her voice caressed his libido. Today she wore a cream-colored cloak that somehow managed to part at the clasp and reveal the silver lamé corset that was straining to hold her plentiful charms. As it was, she still showed an acre of red-tinted skin above the bustline. One silver-gloved hand was resting at the top of her cleavage, while the other tucked the silver-filled bag I'd given her into a pouch at her side. Her translucent silver skirt rode low on her hips, stopping a few inches short of the silver boots that clung to her legs from mid-thigh to toes. My fashion sense was as stunted as my knowledge of pop culture, so if she was breaking any rules with her outfit, I wouldn't have known. However, I'm as male as anyone, so even if I did know, I wouldn't have cared.

"I'm already known in the Hive," I said with a smile. "And it's time Shade was, too."

"I'm disappointed you haven't already introduced us," Synreah purred at me. "She looks delicious."

Shade's gaze went to the half-succubus and tried to narrow into a glare. Her harsh look turned into a double take when Synreah winked at her and gave her a seductive smile.

"Down, girl," I said. "I couldn't afford your rates and we don't have the time." I leaned in close before I continued. "And I'm not sure even you could handle an alpha werewolf."

"I can be a real bitch," Shade said with an open-lipped smile.

"In all the best ways," Synreah countered. "Never fear, alpha bitch. Your honor is never in any danger from me." Somehow, she made the word bitch sound like a compliment, but Shade still wasn't convinced.

"Is it my honor I have to worry about?" she asked with a little too much sugar in her tone. Synreah threw her head back and laughed at that.

"Yes," she said with a grim smile. "Even though he's as welcome in my bed as anyone, you and I both know that even all of this," she caressed herself with her fingertips from breasts to hips, "isn't enough to lure him into it. So, relax and enjoy the ride, sweetie. If I ever offer anything to your mage, it will be something worth far more than the pleasures of my body."

Beside me, Gage moved uncomfortably, his eyes shifting as if he couldn't keep himself from staring when she knelt and greeted Junkyard like an old friend, running her hands down his flanks and letting him lick her cheeks.

"So," Gage asked while Junkyard barked and turned around in place in front of Synreah, "we should get going."

"Yes, we should," Synreah said. "I'm happy to be your guide again."

"Usual rates?" I asked.

"Oh, no, honey, this trip is on me."

"You wish," Shade said.

"Feverishly," Synreah sighed.

"Won't your ... Master be mad at you?"

Her grin turned feral and she leaned close to me. "Not unless the dead rise. My late, much lamented Master perished in an unfortunate fire a month or so ago. I'll miss the guidance of his firm and merciful hand."

"I'm certain you will. My condolences." We gave each other a knowing look and I smiled. "We're heading to Arianh-Rod's shop for a wand blank."

She nodded and led the way into the Hive. The crowd swirled around us as we went, and Shade took my hand. Junkyard trotted along beside me, while Gage did his best to follow us without looking like he was actually with us. Shade's eyes were everywhere, trying to take in every stall, shop and cart amid the crumbling ruins of older buildings. And there was a lot to see.

Gems, spices, herbs, and clothes vied with scrolls, potions, and talismans for the attention of the potential buyer. The stench of too many people in too small a place was barely masked by the smell of smoke, cooking meats, and pungent oils. Merchants called out for customers, offering their wares at the top of their voices to compete with the murmur of the crowd. We wound our way among as many different species of magickal beings as I'd ever seen in one place, both walking on two legs and flying.

"Is there a single species of scum not represented here?" Gage asked with a grimace.

"No demons, and no High Fae," I said.

"No demons? I'm surprised at that."

"No one likes demons," I said. "Humans are the only race stupid enough to make deals with them."

"What about her?" Shade asked, pointing at Synreah sashaying ahead of us.

"She's a cambion," I said. "She's not full demon."

"Why does that matter?" Shade asked.

"It means she has a soul." Behind me, I heard Gage scoff at the idea, but Shade's face clouded. Ahead of us, the wedge-shaped building that held Arianh-Rod's shop towered above the rest of the Hive, all three stories intact. There were taller buildings around it, but nothing with more than two stories above ground that were completely enclosed. Even in higher levels, people could be seen, mostly squats of those who didn't want to live in either the mundane world or under the control of the powers behind the Veil. If it hadn't been for my mom, one of those places might have been mine.

The sweet scent of worked wood greeted us as we came through the door to Ari's, and the noise of the crowd died behind us when it clicked shut. The semi-circular display at the back of the room looked only half-full, and only the wall on the right held staves. The left-hand wall was now home to a series of display cases and racks that held smaller rods. Footsteps sounded on the wood floor, and Ari herself emerged from behind the thick blue curtain that separated the workshop from the display room.

Where before, she'd had an inch or so on me, I was now the one standing taller. Her pale blonde hair was streaked with blue through her bangs, and her violet eyes were bloodshot and tired-looking. Her eyes fell on Gage first, and she frowned slightly. Then they swept across the rest of us, and a smile spread across her narrow face.

"Chance, me lad," she said in her soft brogue. "I'm nae sure whether I want to bless ya or curse ya."

"Thank you, and I'm sorry?" I offered to cover all my bases. "What did I do?"

"E'er since ye kilt that rogue vampire, it's ever' other day that I get someone in a mask through tha' door askin' after a blastin' rod like yours. Or a wand or a stave. I swear, my trade's doubled since the Equinox, an' more than half are droppin' yer name, lad."

"My name?" I asked, incredulous.

"Why him?" Gage demanded.

"Think where ya are, boy," she said. "D'ye think Master Draeden's name carries half the clout here as the demon's apprentice?" She laughed and leaned on the display case. "Damn fools, all of 'em. They think it has to be somethin' about the wand."

"It isn't?" Gage said.

"Nae, lad, most likely not," Ari said. I turned to look at Gage, then pulled the wand and set it down on the case in front of her.

"There's one way to find out for sure," I said. "Check my work."

She looked at me, then picked the wand up to look it over. "Good, tight wrap," she said, and then held it up and gazed at it with a slightly unfocused expression. "Decent sigil work … nice, smooth fill with the *chrism*. A few minor deviations here and there. Nae bad, overall."

"If one of your apprentices handed you this, would it be good enough?"

"Nae, lad," Ari laughed. "Not one of *my* apprentices. But if I was a mage, an' my apprentice handed me this, I'd say it was acceptable work. Especially if it was his first rod." I turned to Gage and gave him a smug look. He pursed his lips a little and made a little sound of discontent. "So, what brings ya back through my door today?" Ari asked.

"I need a wand blank."

Her grin was quick, and more than a little feral. "I'm goin' to be able to retire b'fore the year's done," she said as she headed for the back.

Half an hour later, I'd run my hands over nearly every piece of wood she had in the shop, including a piece of African ironwood.

"Does this ever happen to anyone else?" I asked.

"Nae, lad," Ari said as her brow knotted up. "Well, if ya were a cowan, aye. But we both know ye're nae one a'them. Mayhap we should try bringing the mage to the wand, instead of t'other way 'round."

I shrugged and reached into my pocket for my amethyst pendulum. It was worth a shot. Once I had it set and swinging, I closed my eyes and focused on what I wanted. The right piece of wood for my own wand. I felt the chain start to swing back and forth slowly, so I opened my eyes to watch it. There was nothing behind me, so I assumed whatever it was swinging toward was further back in the shop. I stepped around the counter and followed the pendulum's swing back behind the curtain. The rear of the shop seemed disappointingly normal to me, filled with woodworking tools, sawdust, and not much more. Wooden cabinets with small drawers sat on each workbench, and a barrel of scrap wood was set at the far end of the room. The pendulum swung faster, leading me toward the far end of the room, and I followed it with a sinking feeling in my gut with every step I took toward the discard barrel.

As I got to the end of the bench, though, the amethyst started to drift right, and I held still until it settled into a stable swing again, this time pointing to a bundle of wood in a metal pail that sat next to the barrel. Without a second thought, I tucked the pendulum in my pocket and grabbed the pail, then upended it on the work bench. I tossed the pail aside and ran my hands over the scattered pieces of wood until I felt my palm get warm. For a moment, I held my hand in place and tried to zero in on where the heat was coming from. Then I lowered my hand until I felt a piece of wood under my palm. The gentle heat seemed to radiate from the piece under my fingertips, so I plucked it out of the pile and held it up.

"Sweet gods," Ari said with a barely contained smile. "That's all junk wood, stuff nae anyone wants. I let my apprentices use that for practice work."

"What it is?" I asked her.

"Hawthorne," Ari said with a twist of her mouth. "Ya picked a feckin' wood of death and the fae."

"It figures," Gage said with a shake of his head.

"Does it have *any* redeeming qualities?" I asked.

"Oh, aye," Ari said. "If ye're lookin' ta hide yer magick, hawthorne is excellent fer that. It's also well-suited to fending off the darker magicks. It tends to glow around other spells and dweomers."

"It's an evil wood," Gage said. "Choose another piece."

"Bugger off, ya git," Ari said. "Wood isn't good or bad, it's just wood. It may be an ill-omened piece of wood, but it rings true to him, certain as all Nine Hells. You dunnae get to tell him what ta choose. Nae in *my* shop."

"My apologies, Mistress Arianh-rod," Gage said with the faintest semblance of respect.

"Ye'll be needin' ta have that cored and roughed ere it's a decent blank," Ari said as she took the piece of hawthorne from me. "Plus whatever gems you want for the pommel and the tip, and whatever else ye'll be wanting to add to it. And junk wood or nae, dunnae get it in yer head that I'll be lettin' it go fer cheap, boy."

"Wouldn't dream of it," I said with a slow smile. She shooed us back out into the shop and told us to come back in an hour. Shade grabbed my hand as we hit the street and we all huddled together.

"Where to next?" Synreah asked. "Maybe a bauble for your girl? Or a tattoo?"

"No!" Shade said. "No tats."

Synreah cocked her head to one side and gave Shade a long look, the feral grin on her face slowly fading to something I hadn't seen before. "Show me," she said after a moment. I felt the tremor run through Shade before she shook her head, her denial and involuntary reaction both catching me by surprise.

74

"What's wrong, Shade?" I asked. She closed her eyes and turned away from me, mouthing a single "No" as she shook her head.

"Oh, child," Synreah said with a catch in her voice. "Oh, sweet child." She reached out and put one hand on Shade's cheek. Their eyes locked for a moment, then Shade bared her teeth, her eyes flashing to gold as a growl rumbled deep in her chest.

"What's going on?" I asked as I held Shade.

"Your girl's been marked," Synreah said. "Branded as someone's property."

"Shade, is that true?" I asked. She looked at me, then away, eyes suddenly gray, suddenly human.

"I'm sorry," she said. "I should have told you, but ..."

Wh—" I started to ask, then stopped myself. There were still a thousand things I hadn't told anyone about being Dulka's slave. I *knew* why. "It's okay, Shade," I said instead. "I get it."

"You two need help," Synreah said.

"Big time," I said. "But who would believe us? Who could even handle our kind of fucked up?"

"I can," she answered. In my arms, Shade turned to look at her while I gaped a little myself.

"You?" I said. "Don't take this the wrong way, but I don't think either of us is ready for the kind of therapy you usually give your clients."

"No, Chance," Synreah said with a smile. "I may be a prostitute, but I'm a cambion by birth. I get human nature better than humans do. Why do you think we're so good at manipulating you?"

"Hardly a glowing recommendation of your services," Gage said.

"What else do you think a human therapist does but manipulate people into acting healthy?" Synreah asked with a laugh. "No one else knows what you've both been through like I do. And no human is going to keep your secrets like I will."

Shade turned to me. "I don't know ..." she said.

"We don't have to decide anything right now," I said. "But she's right. She knows what we've been through. And we can trust her."

Shade nodded, then turned to Synreah. "We'll talk about it," she said.

"Very well," Synreah said. "In the meantime, do you want to get rid of it?"

"You can do that?" Shade asked, suddenly sixteen again.

"I can't," Synreah told her. "But I know someone who can. Interested?" The words were barely out of her mouth before Shade was saying yes.

Synreah led us through more of the maze that was the Hive, until we reached a shop that was set between two relatively intact walls and a roof that came three-quarters of the way to the front. Inside, we could see a handful of lamps that kept the place well-lit. Two old-style exam chairs were set up with a pair of stools next to them. Out front was a painted wooden sign that said "Dragonblood's Ink" over a tattooed dragon holding a tattoo gun.

"Syn!" one of the artists called out as we walked up. An easy seven feet tall, he was heavily muscled and bald as a cue ball. And green. Even though he had six inches on her height-wise, when he bounded out and grabbed Synreah in a bear hug, he seemed somehow smaller than she was.

"Ash, it's great to see you," she said as she put one hand on his arm, then turned to us. "This is my friend Chance, and this is Shade. She needs some ink removed."

"Removed?" Ash said, his face creasing into a frown. "Why?" Up close, I could see a fine sheen of scales covering his face, and the vertical reptilian slit to his dark red eyes.

"She didn't ask for it," Synreah said.

He turned to Shade and looked her over, then raised one smooth eyebrow. "Hard to imagine anyone making you do a damn thing you didn't want to," he said to her. "But if you want it gone, it's gone."

Shade nodded, then turned to me. "Can you do me a favor?" she asked. "Can you … go somewhere else until he's done?"

"Sure," I said. "You don't want me with you while he … you know?"

"No," she said and shook her head. "I don't want you to see his … I don't want you to ever see it on me. I don't even like looking at it."

"Yeah, okay," I said. "You know I'll do whatever you need me to."

Synreah stepped up behind her and took my arm as she led me away.

"She has to take herself back," she said as we walked away. "I did the same thing after I got my freedom back. Go get the other things you need for your wand. We'll meet you back at Ari's when she's done."

Junkyard barked his approval of that plan, so I motioned for Gage to follow me.

"Don't you have to be eighteen to get a tattoo?" Gage asked as we pushed through the crowd.

"Not here," I said as I headed for a gem seller. "All you need is the silver."

Shopping with Gage was nowhere near as much fun as shopping with Synreah. It was quicker, but more expensive. As soon as a merchant's eye fell on his cloak and jeweled mask, prices had a bad habit of doubling. I had to haggle hard to get them down to merely exorbitant. By the time we made it back to Ari's, I was exhausted, and out two hundred trade ounces. But seeing Shade's smile as we walked back toward Ari's shop felt like the first warm day of spring. Synreah said something that made her laugh, and I would have sworn that the sun had just come out.

"You look like you just ate a canary," I said as she put her arms around my waist.

"Something like that," she said before she kissed me and left my lips tingling. "I won't be wearing a bikini for a few days."

"Inside, you two," Synreah said. "Or you're going to put someone into insulin shock." We led the way in to find Ari behind the counter looking almost as pleased with herself as Shade. My wand blank was on the counter in front of her, and as I crossed the room, I could see that it was smooth and straight, with the bark removed and no signs of the grain being broken. Ari held it out to me when I got to the counter, and I slowly turned it in my hands. The grain made a beautiful pattern all the way around and along its length, and it fairly vibrated against my fingertips. It tapered slightly, and both ends were slightly concaved to accept a stone. A narrow band had been carved a few inches from the base to mark the wand's handle, and I knew the second I let it slide into my grasp that it would fit my hand perfectly.

"Yeah, that's sweet," I said as I turned my hand slowly. "How much?"

"Three hundred," Ari said. I'd been prepared to pay more than that, but it was still a low starting price.

"Done."

Gage's jaw could have bounced off the floor, and Synreah gave a quick little snicker before she got control of herself. I laid a trade bar on the counter next to the wand, and both were gathered up in the same smooth movement. She slipped the wand into a long leather pouch, then laid that in a box that she closed slowly and presented to me with a flourish.

"Always a pleasure doin' business to ya," Ari said. "Now, if ye'll excuse me, I have ta see about findin' a third apprentice to start trainin' up."

"Of course," I said. "And I have a wand to make."

Shade fairly skipped beside me as we made our way out of the Hive. I couldn't resist her infectious smile, and I ended up buying her a new bracelet and a bolero jacket. The bracelet was a thick metal cuff that was enchanted to stay bright and shiny without cleaning, a benefit the gnomish jeweler claimed would also affect any other jewelry she was wearing at the time. The jacket was the bigger steal, though, since it was enchanted to meld her clothes into her wolf form when she changed.

Synreah pulled me back at the iron gate that led onto the street and put both hands on my shoulders.

"You need to either keep that girl next to you as much as possible or get her as far away from you as you can," she said. "There's a bounty on you for live capture that's big enough to tempt half the Hive."

"That would explain a few things," I said. "I'm surprised no one tried to collect on it today."

"Two reasons for that," she said softly. "One, people here know you; they know what you're capable of, both good and bad. Two, and the biggest thing that bothers most of us: It's an Infernal bounty."

"Do you think it's Dulka?" I asked.

"No one knows. It was offered through an empty suit. Word is, the pay is good."

"How good?" I asked.

"Fifty thousand."

My eyes went big at that. "No way that's Dulka," I said. "He's barely got more than a tenth of that."

"Doesn't matter who it is, you just be careful. And if you need my help," she said as she slipped something around my wrist, "just call my name." I held my arm up to look at what she'd put on me.

A pewter band went three-quarters of the way around my wrist, with a pair of dragon's heads facing each other across the gap. A small tag dangled from a thread, the word "disseptum" written on it in neat, rounded script. I pulled the tag off and tucked it into my pocket before I looked back to her, half-expecting to see her back as she left. Instead, she was kneeling next to Junkyard, accepting slobbery kisses on her cheeks as she wrapped a yellow bandana around his neck to go with the red one she'd originally given him. His tail whipped back and forth as she cooed at him and ran her hands down his sleek coat. When she stood, he came to me and turned around once before he reared up and put his paws on my chest.

"Looking good," I said. He leaned his head forward and licked my cheek before he dropped back down on all fours. Synreah had backed up a few steps and gave me a dainty little wave before she turned and disappeared back into the depths of the Hive.

"What was that all about?" Shade asked as I caught up to her.

"Evidently, there's a bounty out on my head."

"What is it with you and people wanting to kill you?" she asked.

"Oh, they want me alive this time."

"Well, *that's* a relief," Shade said.

Somehow, I wasn't so sure a live bounty was any better.

"A live bounty isn't any better," Dr. Corwyn said. He looked up from the collection of materials I'd bought for my wand and peered at me over his glasses with raised eyebrows. "Though it is something of a change of pace. It would help if we knew *who* was fronting the silver for it, but you said it was an empty suit?"

"Yeah, standard for Infernal contracts."

"What's an empty suit?" Gage asked.

"A front company under an assumed name that no one's ever heard of before. The owner makes a deposit at a trusted depository, also under an assumed name, and the company offers the contract and names an agent to report to for payment on completion. No one ever sees or hears from the company owner again, and the company closes up shop. The most anyone ever sees is a guy in the shadows in a suit who doesn't exist. An empty suit."

"What I don't get is why they're offering so much for me," I said. "I mean, yeah, I'm flattered, but who has that kind of money?"

"My family does," Gage said with a hint of pride in his voice.

"Your family has hundreds of thousands of ounces in silver, yes," Dr. C. said, "but fifty thousand for a bounty is still a substantial amount."

"Who have I pissed off that has that kind of money?" I asked.

"Thraxus," Dr. C said after a moment. "But he's not that stupid. Offering that bounty would implicate him in Etienne's plot. I'll do some digging. You go practice and start working on your wand."

No matter what happened in my life, that never seemed to change. I stood up and gathered my stuff, then headed upstairs to the sanctum. Practice, lessons, and busy work. When I was Dulka's pet warlock, it was practice, and work. Now that I was free, more of the same.

"You know, other kids get to have summer vacations," I said to Gage as we climbed the stairs. "But not mages. No, I get to go out to the middle of Texas and practice my spells and astral projection. My friends are at bar-be-cues or on dates today, but noooo, not me. I get to take my girlfriend to a Dwarven bank and then go to the Veiled world's version of the ghetto to buy a wand. Other kids, they worry about getting sunburned or not having the latest piece of tech. Me, I have a massive bounty on my head from Hell."

"And lucky me," Gage said, "I get to listen to you bitch about it."

"Don't you ever just wish your life was normal?" I asked him.

"No," he said after a moment. "But today, I wish yours was."

For two hours, I worked on casting my telekinesis spell without a wand. It was even more boring than it sounded. Then I started working on my wand, which at this stage meant creating the metal core. I had gone with silver and copper, since they were both receptive metals, and yet both good for conducting magickal energy. A dual core meant more work, but it seemed like the way to go since I was already behind in other ways. It meant an hour of slowly twisting the cores together, making sure they were evenly wound and that they kept a sort of round cross-section to fit into the wand's core.

I had just finished snipping the wound wires when my cell phone rang. Since only a handful of people had my number, I pulled it from my pocket. The caller ID read "M. Romanoff." If Wanda's mom was calling me, it had to be important.

"Chance, you've got to come home now," Miss Romanoff said frantically as soon as I had the phone to my ear. "The police are here, and they're arresting your mom!"

Chapter 5

~ No one looks for subtlety when you beat them over the head with a club. ~ Jacob Cavendish, Master mage & adviser to President Roosevelt

I hit the brakes and slid to a stop at the curb, still a house away from home. Five police cars were parked in front of the house, and Wanda's mom's minivan was parked across the street. And of course, people were out on their lawns, watching the cops put my mom in the back seat of one of the cruisers. I was out of the car and running toward her in a split second, but not before a thick set of arms wrapped themselves around me and sent me sprawling. I scrambled back and got to my feet to find myself facing Tad Zucherman.

"Back off, Fortunato," he snapped at me.

"I want to talk to my mom," I said as I took a step forward. His right hand shot forward and caught me in the chest, shoving me backward and off my feet. I hit the ground and rolled backward so that I came to a crouch almost instantly. He took a step toward me with two cops advancing behind him, both with hands on their Tasers.

Something small and fierce hit him about waist high with a high-pitched scream, sending him staggering to one side. The cops drew their Tasers, but kept them pointed at the ground as the small attacker registered for everyone. It was my sister.

"Leave him alone!" Dee yelled as she grappled with Tad. That she had even managed to stagger him was impressive enough, but with her momentum spent, there was no way she was any kind of threat to him. He reached down and grabbed her arm, then flung her to the ground in front of him. She hit and rolled with a pained cry, coming to rest inches away from me. Manhandling me was one thing, but laying a hand on my sister was asking for an ass kicking no matter who you were. I came to my feet slowly, and Dee rose right beside me. Junkyard bounded up and planted his feet beside me, front legs apart, hackles up, and a growl rumbling from deep in his chest.

Zucherman took a step back, and the two cops brought their Tasers up. Another joined them, his pistol out but pointed at the ground.

83

"Stand down, all of you!" a third voice interjected. I looked to my right to see Detective Collins making his way between two patrol cars. He wore a pair of jeans and a blue Polo shirt with his badge hanging around his neck. I reached out and put a hand on Dee's shoulder and stepped in front of Junkyard.

"Back off, Collins," Zucherman said. "These kids are under arrest for assault."

"Bullshit," Collins said. "You're supposed to be the kid's case officer, not a damn linebacker. You press charges against him, I'll press charges for assaulting a minor against you. That shit means an automatic review board."

Tad looked at him, then shook his head and stepped back. "Fine, you take care of him, then." Tad and the other two New Essex PD officers backed away as Collins came to my side. His dark brown skin was beaded with sweat, and his usually smooth flattop hair cut was a little ragged around the edges.

"What are you doing here?" I asked after I sent Junkyard back to the car with a quick word of praise. "Last I knew, you were on Major Crimes."

"I am," he said. "But my phone's been blowing up since someone raided the address of one of my CI's."

"Do you know what they're arresting Mom for?" Dee piped up. Collins looked down at her, then at me, and I gave him a nod.

"They think your mom has some things she's not supposed to have," he said.

"Like what?" I asked.

"Mescaline."

My eyes went wide at that. As far as illegal drugs went, it was the one thing that almost made sense for her to have. A naturally occurring hallucinogenic, it was used by a lot of well-meaning pagans for psychedelic trips in their search for enlightenment. And if anyone *could* get their hands on any, it would be a master herbalist who worked in a New Age store. Hells below, if anyone could *grow* it, it would have been my mom. The problem was, if there was anyone who objected to urban white people treating Native American culture like a tourist attraction or an exotic way to get high, it was also my mother. She was the last person who would have sold or even given any kind of mescaline to anyone.

"Mom would never have anything to do with that," I said. "You should hear her go off on people appropriating cultures."

"I know, kid," he said as he put a hand on my shoulder. "I'll see what's going on, but first, your mom has to get someone to take care of you and your sister." He headed for the cruiser Mom was sitting in, leaving me with Dee. The words sank through the layers of denial in my brain, hammering home the reality of the situation. Mom was going to jail tonight, and all I could do was watch it happen.

I took Dee's hand and led her back to the Mustang. We sat perched on the hood, watching our world fall apart. I felt like my soul had been scooped out as I watched the cops going through the garage and talking to Mom. Dee sat there beside me, for once quiet and still, her arms wrapped around my right arm. Even Junkyard seemed subdued, looking over the back seat at us with big puppy dog eyes. Eventually, Tad walked back toward us, a smile on his face that promised nothing pleasant for us.

"You're going to be going to a foster family tonight," he started off.

"Mom will want us to stay with Dr. Corwyn," I said listlessly, not surprised that Tad was so eager to throw me to the system.

"Well, he isn't here, and that clock started almost half an hour ago. So unless he gets here in the next thirty—" He stopped as another vehicle pulled in behind us and illuminated him with its headlights.

"You were saying?" I asked as he shielded his eyes with his hand.

"Turn those goddamn lights," he said, then stopped as the lights went dark, "off." The door of the Range Rover opened and Dr. C stepped out. He'd changed into a blazer and slacks with a gray shirt, and had the air of a man used to being in charge. Even from here, I could almost feel the force of his personality slapping against Zucherman's usual bluster.

"Who the hell are you?" he called out.

"Tad Zucherman, with Social Services. Who the hell are you?"

"*Doctor* Trevor Corwyn. Stop your bluster, *Mister* Zucherman, and go get me a real law enforcement officer so I can take custody of these two kids you people are traumatizing."

Tad spent a moment with his mouth hanging open before he turned on his heel and stalked off. As soon as his back was turned, Dr. C came over to us.

"How are you holding up?" he asked me as he put a hand on my shoulder.

"I … I dunno," I finally managed.

"All right," he said. "Just stay put and think about getting you and your sister packed for a few days at my place."

"What?" I said while my brain struggled to catch up.

"Essentials. Socks, underwear, clothes, favorite stuffed animal. And don't forget her Sonic." He squeezed my shoulder before he turned to the NEPD officer that was coming up. They spoke for a few moments, then the officer nodded and waved Detective Collins over. They conferred for a few seconds, then Collins nodded and came over to us.

"We've got ten minutes to get you two kids packed," he said. "Let's go, clock's ticking." I trotted past him, the list of what we needed already completed in my head. I took the stairs two at a time and went straight to Dee's room.

"Suitcase," I said as I pointed.

"I don't want to go," Dee said from behind me. I stopped and turned, completely gobsmacked.

"Dee, we can't stay," I said. "Mom's not going to be here."

"Dr. Corwyn can stay with us," she countered. I ran my hand down my face as I tried to figure out how to get her to come on her own. I wasn't Mom, I didn't have the Mom voice or the power of the Stern Look. So it was time to make things less horrible.

"Remember when you and Mom had to go hide a few months ago?" She nodded, her face troubled. "Well, this time, you're coming with me on one of my adventures."

"Like the Doctor?" she asked.

"Yeah, kinda like that, only I don't have a blue box. But I do have adventures, and I do need someone to watch my back. I'd hoped that someone would be you this time."

"You know those shows aren't real," she said to me with one eye narrowed.

"And you know magick *is* real," I said. "I really do have adventures, and I really do want you with me for this one."

"Okay," she finally said. "I'll need my backpack, too."

We packed fast, rolling things up instead of trying to fold them. I grabbed the next three books on her summer reading challenge list and made sure she had her Sonic. That left only one decision.

"Doctor Hooves or Pyewacket?" I asked, holding up her two favorite stuffed animals.

"Pyewacket," she said without missing a beat. "I want Dr. Hooves here to protect my room."

I tossed her the floppy black cat and set the pony on her bed facing the room. My stuff was easier to pack, but I needed my laptop. I looked at the stack of library books on my desk longingly for a moment, then decided to grab a couple on the off chance I'd actually have time of my own at some point.

By the time we made it back downstairs, the car with Mom in it was gone. Collins and Dr. C were talking to Tad, and evidently they had him on the ropes, because he had his hands up and was shaking his head. We stalked across the yard toward him, and he took a step back as he caught sight of us.

"Where's my mom?" Dee bellowed at the top of her lungs. I caught the glint of light off something glass or metal, and noticed a news van down the street a little. A cameraman was focusing on us, and I stopped my hand halfway to Dee's shoulder. It must have been a slow news day if we were worth even a cameraman. "Where is she?"

Tad shook his head and stammered for a moment.

"We thought it would be better to send her to the station while you two were inside," one of the cops said to me. "We didn't want a scene." Dee started crying, almost as if on cue, but I knew these tears were genuine.

"Yeah? How'd that work out for you?" I asked as I knelt and took her in my arms.

"I didn't get to tell her bye or I love you or promise I'd be good or anything!" she bawled into my shoulder.

"We'll see her soon," I said softly. "And you'll get to tell her all of that then. Who knows? By then, that whole being good part might even be true."

She pulled back from me and gave me a tear-dampened frown. "I am good!" she protested. "You're the bad one." She scrubbed a fist across her cheeks and sniffled.

"Whatever," I said. "Come on. Let's get out of here." Dr. C had already grabbed Dee's stuff, so I hefted my duffel bag onto my shoulder and followed him. Once my Mustang was loaded up, he got in his Range Rover and led the way back to his place.

The ride to Dr. C's place was quiet, and somehow, Dee stayed quiet and subdued long enough to get her stuff up to the room we were sharing. When we came down the stairs, the smell of garlic hit our noses. We followed the smell to the kitchen, where we found Dr. C heating a pot of spaghetti noodles.

"I hope Italian is okay," he said as he dipped a spoon with long projections along the edge into the pot and pulled out long strands of spaghetti. I shrugged and gave a half-assed nod.

"Where's Gage?" I asked.

"Reporting to the Conclave," he answered. "He's also getting his lawyers to send a representative to go get his stuff from your place. Believe me, we're going to be seeing more than we want of him after tomorrow morning. For tonight, let's get the table set. Silverware is by the sink, stands are in the drawer at the end of the counter."

"Stands?" I asked.

"Yes, you know my rules about reading at the table."

"No, sir, I don't."

"Well, now you do. Only with a book stand. Now, get to it."

I pointed Dee to the silverware drawer while I got three bookstands from the end drawer and set them up. By the time we got back downstairs from getting our books, food was on the table. We read through dinner, occasionally sneaking glances at each other over the tops of our books.

"Detective Collins is going to be looking into your mother's case," Dr. C finally said. "She'll have a bail hearing on Monday morning. I'll try to schedule a visit for the two of you tomorrow. In the meantime, Chance, I need you to get in touch with your … lawyer. See what he can do."

"Vortigern isn't the kind of lawyer you call," I said. "Mom might have had his number, but I don't happen to have a scroll of 'summon lawyer' on me."

"Then perhaps she'll contact him. Either way, there's nothing more we can do tonight. So, Dee, why don't you take your book into the library and read until bed time, which I'm told by a reliable source is eight-thirty for the moment. Chance, if you'll set up the chess board in the front room, I'll take care of the dishes."

"The chess board?" I said. "You expect me to be on my game *now*?"

"Yes, I do," he said calmly. "Especially now." Before I could say anything else, he got up and took our plates. Dee, never one to argue with either time to read or an extra half-hour before bed time, took her book and headed for the library while I went to the front room and pulled the chess set out from its spot on the shelf. The heavy wooden box opened out so that the chess board itself was revealed as the inside. When I laid it down with the chess board facing up, there were two shallow drawers that held the pieces on each end, with a narrow play clock folded down on one side. I set the pieces up and held out a pawn of each color.

"I'll play white tonight," Dr. C said when he came into the room a few minutes later. He played his first move, a pawn out two spaces. I moved a pawn to counter it, but only one space. Playing against Dr. Corwyn was hard, but I had the advantage of knowing how he thought. Of course, he also knew how I thought, so over the past few months it had been like learning the game all over for both of us, though at first, my grasp of chess was pretty much how the pieces moved. By now, though, we were both playing four or five moves ahead.

"The first question of the night is who?" he said after he moved his bishop into play. "Who would want to frame your mother? Who benefits from this move?"

"I've been wondering that myself. It's a short list. I can only think of three people who might be able to pull it off. My father, Dulka, and Thraxus or one of his flunkeys. No one mourned King's loss, and none of the lesser vampires dare make a move openly against me for Etienne's death, since Thraxus sanctioned it."

"One of the advantages of having an opponent who is willing to break the rules to get what he wants," Dr. C said as he took one of my pawns. "But this doesn't sound like his style. Not scary enough; not a big enough reminder of his power. So, that leaves your father and Dulka."

"And this does sound like them," I said, moving a knight to take one of his rooks.

"If your father is involved, he's going to make a play for custody of you and your sister," he said as he moved his queen's knight into a vulnerable position. I considered taking it, but it was still covered by his pawns, and it would take a couple of moves to get my bishop in position for the kill. I moved the bishop anyway, letting him see me appear to fall for the trap.

"If he does, we'll deal with it," I said. "We still need to get money to bail Mom out Monday." He moved another pawn, opening his king's bishop to move.

"That's why he's going to make his move soon," he said a few moves later. "He knows you'll be distracted by this. In fact, I wouldn't put it past him to have framed your mother for just that purpose." I moved the pawn in front of my queen's rook, and he wasted no time in moving his other knight out into play. "This isn't a matter of if, Chance. It's a matter of when and how. You have to think ahead of him if you're going to beat him." I saw an opening in his play, one that had to look like a mistake. I moved my queen's pawn out two spaces and waited. He countered with his queen's pawn.

"Do we have to deal with this right now?" I asked a few moves later, now shy two pawns and a knight.

"Yes," he said as he made his move. "You either plan for it, or react to it, but either way, you don't get to choose what he's going to do. What you *do* get to choose is your response. The farther ahead of him you are, the more likely you are to turn things to your advantage. More importantly, if your father is behind this, you need to start asking yourself *why.*" I moved my queen out, ending up with her one space from a direct shot at his king. He moved a pawn to block the diagonal attack, so I moved my queen across the board.

"Check," I said. He moved his bishop to block, and I moved my rook into place.

"You should have taken care of your queen," he said as he took the piece. I moved my bishop out to take his.

"My queen was bait, sir," I said. "I think that's mate."

"Not yet," he said, "but it will be in two moves. Nice sacrifice play."

"Thank you, sir. I think I know how to deal with my father."

"Well, I hope it isn't by sacrificing your queen," he said.

"No, sir. I won't be sacrificing my queen. But it's going to be pretty risky."

"When are things ever safe where we're concerned?" he asked.

"True, but that's the trick. I know my father. He'll take risks; he does it all the time. But he'll take a sure bet over a risky one every time. It's why he's not any higher up the food chain than he already is."

"And why he isn't in prison yet. Okay, what do you have in mind?"

Chapter 6
~ I just want what's best for my kid. ~ Every parent ever.

I hated it when Dr. Corwyn was right. My father showed up at his place the next morning. I woke up to the sound of a horn honking out front and a fist pounding on the front door, alternating with rapid ringing of the doorbell. When I tried to get up, I found my right arm pinned to the floor. Sometime during the night, Dee had crawled out of bed and snuggled up next to me. Junkyard was curled up next to her, and she had both arms wrapped around him like a giant teddy mutt, with Pyewacket draped over his flank. I yawned as I tried to retrieve my arm from under her limp form. Junkyard raised his head and looked over his shoulder at me. He let out a little groan as if to point out the futility of expecting him to move while Dee had him in her clutches, then laid his head back down.

"Good dog … you get a cutie mark," Dee murmured as my hand came free. I could hear Dr. C's feet on the stairs, his own voice muffled by the doorway, but his tone promising dire consequences. I grabbed my TK wand off the dresser and the Ariakon from its holster on the back of the door and padded after him.

"… release the children now, and I'll see to it that no charges are filed against you," a familiar voice said.

"You're pretty slick, Mr. um … Cassavetes," Dr. C said. "Coming by early, trying to catch me right after I wake up, sounding all official, making threats. But you see, I have this thing in my study called documentation that says I'm the children's temporary guardian. And documentation trumps bullshit any day. So, here's my threat. Show me something official, and I'll see to it you don't get shot for trespassing. Otherwise, I'll tell the cops you tried to force your way in."

"And I'll back him up a hundred percent," I said from over his shoulder. "Help, help, I'm being oppressed," I said in a monotone.

"Chance," Cassavetes said, his tone placating, Dr. Corwyn suddenly forgotten. "Wouldn't you rather stay with family during this trying time?"

"I am staying with family," I said slowly. "My sister's here."

"But your father," he said, gesturing to the long black limo idling in front of the house.

"Sold me to a demon," I said. "He's not family."

The back door of the limo opened and my father emerged, looking almost dignified in khakis and a gray polo shirt. There was more gray in his hair, and it looked like he'd lost a few chins somewhere along the way.

"He's very influential," Cassavetes said as the old man walked up to the porch. "He could get these charges against your mother dropped. All you'd have to do is come back home."

"I'd rather live in a foster home."

"Mike, go back to the car," my father said. Cassavetes nodded and left. "Chance, are you turning down my generosity?"

"If you were being generous," Dr. Corwyn said softly, "you would have already gotten the charges against Mara dropped. This is extortion."

My father's face darkened, and his right hand went to his hip. "This is between me and my son," he said. "It's none of your business, *maláka.*"

"We already had this conversation," I growled. "You don't get to call me that, remember?"

"The law says different, *son.* You'd better wise up and come home before things get worse for you."

"Threats," Dr. C said with menacing softness. "You actually think that is going to work?"

"I told you to stay out of my family's business, little man," my father said. "He belongs with me, not with some boy-loving stranger."

Dr. Corwyn did the scariest thing I'd ever seen him do in the face of the old man's insult.

He smiled.

"Chance may be your offspring," Dr. C said as he stepped out onto the porch, "but he's *my* apprentice. So think about who you're talking to, and exactly where you're standing, Stavros Fortunato. Because I do not tolerate threats, and I do not suffer warlocks lightly. I would be within my rights to kill you where you stand. The only things keeping you alive right now … are witnesses."

Suddenly, the old man realized exactly who he was talking to, and a sheen of sweat broke out on his forehead. But there was still ice in his veins. To his credit, he didn't bolt right away.

"Don't be so sure of your power, mage," he said. "And hope I don't catch *you* without witnesses around." He turned to me and leveled one thick finger at me. "You better wise up fast, boy. You know there's a price for crossing me. I hope you're ready to pay it." With that, he turned and walked back to the limo.

"He's too confident," Dr. C said as we watched the black car move off. "If you ever reconsider putting a kill order out on him, I'm not sure I'd try too hard to talk you out of it."

I nodded, and wondered if I would regret not taking the Council up on the offer. After completing my Ordeal, the Council had been forced to reconsider my case. Since my father had been the one to put me in the position to be accused, all of the crimes I'd committed were now also on his shoulders, and I was considered to be the wronged party in the whole mess. That also meant that it was up to me to call for justice. The Council had offered to send the Hands of Death after him. Actually, Cross and T-Bone had volunteered to go hunt him down and give him a slow, messy death and the Council had just endorsed it after the fact. But I hadn't taken them up on the offer.

"Killing him now would still give Dulka what he wants," I said. "And the old man knows what's waiting for him when he dies. I want him to spend a long time thinking about that."

"It's probably the better decision," he said as he turned and came back inside. "Let's just hope we all survive our own merciful natures."

By midday Monday, I had grown to dread the sound of the judge's gavel. I guess if it comes right after the words "Bail set at thirty thousand dollars," the sound can sour on you pretty quick. Now I sat in another judge's chambers, waiting with Dr. Corwyn and a man with a permanent suntan and the hands of a construction worker rather than a lawyer. Evidently, the last time he'd bought any dress clothes had been the eighties; either that, or I'd missed the trend back toward pastels, baggy slacks, and wide collars. I tried not to squirm or fidget, but unless Kyle Vortigern showed up, I was pretty sure I'd end up at my father's place by the end of the day. I hoped Judge Wells (according to the name plate on her desk) took her time showing up.

If I hadn't been wondering where in the Nine Hells Vortigern was for the past fifteen minutes, I would have sworn just thinking about him had summoned him when the door opened and he stepped into the judge's office.

"You'll pardon the delay," he said with his usual cool tone. "But Judge Walters wanted to speak to me. Since these two cases are related, he's ordered me to recuse myself from one of them."

"Which one of them are you bowin' out of?" the older man asked. His voice was rough and throaty, with an accent that screamed Texas to my now practiced ear.

"Chance here has convinced me of the wisdom of representing his mother while you handle the custody case, Mister ...?"

"Fred Reed," the older man said with a smile.

"Now, there were some details I thought you might find interesting," Vortigern said as they hunched together.

"Where in the Nine Hells did you dig him up?" I asked Dr. C in a whisper.

"Port Aransas," Dr. C said. "He was a friend of my father's and he's probably forgotten more about law than most lawyers ever know."

"I just hope he remembers the right parts."

"He will," Dr. C said with conviction. "Between him in the courtroom and Vortigern's advice, things will go our way."

The door opened as he finished, and my father and Cassavetes were led in, with Judge Wells on their heels. Her Honor was a sharp-featured woman with red hair streaked with gray. She looked to Vortigern and frowned as Dr. C and Reed stood, with me a beat behind in following their example.

"Please tell me I'm hallucinating, Kyle," she said with a clear voice, "and that you're not really here."

"You're hallucinating, your Honor," Vortigern said smoothly. "I never consulted on this case, and I was never here. It must be the stress." He smiled with all the charm of a pit viper as he finished.

"Your Honor, I must protest this in the strongest terms possible," Cassavetes said. "Mr. Vortigern—"

"Recused himself from this case, Counselor," Judge Wells said. "Which doesn't preclude consultation with his client's new representation. Now, sit down, all of you." Everyone planted butt in seat in a hurry. As soon as she sat down behind her desk, Cassavetes opened his mouth. Her hand came up and she silenced him with a glare.

"Before any of you open your mouth again, I want to hear from the person who will be affected the most by this decision," she said. "Not you," she added when my father started to say something, then she pointed one slender finger at me. "You."

"Yes, ma'am?" I said.

"Who do you want to live with?"

"My mom," I said without hesitating.

"And if that wasn't possible, would you want to live with your father?"

"No, ma'am. I'd prefer to stay with Dr. Corwyn or someone else." Cassavetes and my father erupted in pure outrage at that, and the judge silenced them with a look I wished to the High Heavens I could master. Reed took the opportunity to slide a thin folder across her desk, which she picked up and glanced at before she spoke again.

"Your concerns are duly noted, gentlemen," she said dismissively, then turned to Dr. Corwyn. "And how exactly do you fit into the boy's life, Mr. ... Corwyn?" I cringed as she left off the title. I watched his face as he fought the urge to correct her, but when he spoke, his voice was calm.

"I am ... well, I *was* his science teacher last year, and I've become his mentor in the school district's AP science program. I also sponsored him for a scholarship and placement at the Franklin Academy, which he'll be attending next year." The judge looked over the file in her hand for a moment, then looked at Dr. C with a gaze that seemed to be looking a lot deeper than the surface.

"And the numerous police and sheriff's department case numbers Mr. Cassavetes has appended to the case file. Perhaps you'd care to explain those."

"Of course, your Honor. I'm a consultant with both departments, specializing in occult cases. Symbology, psychology, and history, mostly. I hold a Masters in Western Esotericism."

Wells leaned back in her chair and gave Dr. C another long look before she spoke again, this time turning her attention back to me.

"Where do you think your sister would rather live, young man?"

"Her choice would be the same as mine," I told her. "We've talked about this a lot over the past couple of days."

She nodded and turned to face my father. "So, Mr. Fortunato, you're asking for custody of both children," the judge said. "Except that only one of them is legally your offspring. You are not listed as the father on the birth certificate for Deirdre Murathy that Mr. Reed handed me. Until such time as you are able to prove your paternity, my judgment is that you technically have no parental rights to exercise over her."

It was hard to keep a straight face as I watched my father's face turn bright red while he fought to keep his temper in check. But, just as his forehead was bordering on a dark purple, Cassavetes leaned forward and smiled.

"Then perhaps we should concentrate on amending the custody ruling in the divorce decree," he said, moments before I figured the old man's control would slip, the sound of Cassavetes's voice making my ears feel slightly oily. "We know that the boy's extensive juvenile record was a deciding factor in granting his mother sole custody last year, but in the last eight months, Chance has been arrested once, and has been a suspect in at least four cases. So we can clearly see that his mother and this man Corwyn haven't had any positive effect on him."

"I don't know where Mr. Casaverde is getting his information from," Reed broke in, his gruff voice filling the room, "but he needs to do a better job. But, given his client's *business associations,* I can see why he might have missed this. I'm afraid it's something only your Honor will be able to review." He handed the judge a large sealed envelope. She opened it and drew out a thicker folder. Almost immediately, her gaze went to my father and Cassavetes, then back to me. "As you can see there, he's making a serious effort to … what's that phrase? Oh, yeah. He's trying to 'be the change,' you might say." Then I realized what he had handed to her. It had to be the Essex County Sherriff's department's file on me as a confidential informant.

"I don't see how this makes him any safer in Corwyn's care than in his father's," the judge said. "But your point regarding his character is well made, though I'm not sure who to credit with his newfound morals."

"Maybe it's who's *not* around," I said.

"I can't fault that line of reasoning either," Wells said, silencing the new round of protests from Cassavetes. "For now, the children will remain in the custody of Dr. Trevor Corwyn as per the current TO," she said. Her attention turned to my father. "File your motion to amend the divorce agreement."

"I'll have it done within the hour," Cassavetes said. He pulled a sheaf of papers from his briefcase and held it up like a weapon.

"I don't care if you break a land speed record, Mike," the judge said. "Just get your ass out of my office. We're done here." She actually stood up and offered Mr. Reed her hand, which he shook enthusiastically for a second or two before he ushered us out of the office.

"That two-bit shyster came prepared," Reed grumbled once the door shut behind us. Across the hallway, Cassavetes was seated on one of the wooden benches, busily sorting through the papers he had brandished earlier.

"He's not incompetent," I said as Shade wrapped her arms around my shoulders from behind me. I turned and kissed her cheek, conscious of how under-dressed I was by comparison to her rose-colored silk blouse and skirt. White hose and heels that made her about my height made her look regal, especially with her red hair swept up and off her neck. My white dress shirt and black cargo pants weren't even close, especially with my sleeves rolled up. "He's just corrupt."

"Yeah," Reed said as we headed for the door. "But he ain't the one that worries me. It's that old man a' yours. No tellin' what he's liable to do to get his way."

"We'll handle that when it happens," Dr. C said with a glance back at me.

Suddenly, Shade sprang forward and grabbed Dr. C and Reed each by a shoulder, bringing them both to a stop. At their surprised looks, she pointed at the corner ahead.

"Chance's father is on the phone with someone," she said as low as she dared. "He's coming this way." We all went to the wall and the old man walked past a heartbeat later, his right hand to his ear, blocking our view of his face. But there was no mistaking his voice.

"… little son of a bitch kid of mine still thinks he can just do what he wants. Tell our friend that he's on. Yeah, the whole thing. All right … call me when it's done." He hung up and brought the phone down in time to see us. When he turned, Reed stepped in front of Shade and Dr. C, but the old man's attention was all on me.

"I told you, there's a price to pay for defying me, boy," he said as he put his finger in the middle of my chest and pushed me back. "You think you're man enough to handle pissing me off?"

I looked down at his hand and then up at him. "I've killed things a lot nastier than you," I said. "And I already kicked your pet demon's ass. So, you take your hand off of me before I change your nickname to 'Lefty,' because I already know you're not man enough to handle pissing *me* off."

He scoffed, but he also pulled his hand back. "Big words from a little boy," he said.

Shade came forward with her teeth bared, but stopped when I put my arm out.

"Keep your bitch on a leash," he sneered. "Or I'll do it for you." Still, he turned and headed for Cassavetes like a man with a purpose.

"I haven't even been around your father for a minute," Shade growled, "and I already want to kill him."

"Now you know where I get it from," I said.

"The people who want to kill you are all assholes," she said as her eyes faded from green to gray. I couldn't argue with that. Besides, most of the people who really wanted to kill me were already dead.

"Let's get back home, then," Dr. C said, suddenly sounding brisk and chipper. "You still have things to do."

I rolled my eyes.

"You didn't do *that* bad," Shade reassured me a few hours later as she held an ice pack to my shoulder blade while we sat at the kitchen table. "Up until the sparring part." We sat at the kitchen table while Dr. C and Mr. Reed talked over beer in the backyard. Dee's laughter pealed through the air as she threw a Frisbee for Junkyard to chase. He still only caught it about half the time, but every leap earned praise from Dee.

"I'd rather go up against Cross," I said.

"So would I," Shade said with a purr.

"Hey, let's not injure the ego, too," I said.

"Sorry," she lied. "He's just nice to watch. At least he pulls his punches." I felt her shift as she moved behind me, and I could just imagine her free hand going to her right eye. She'd been joining in with the self-defense training since school had let out, most likely because it *had* included sparring with Cross most times. Dr. C, on the other hand, rarely joined in when we sparred. The fighting style the Sentinels used relied a lot on physics and anatomy to do maximum damage with as little effort as possible, as fast as possible. Cross was good enough to handle Shade at her best and still pull his punches. Dr. C wasn't quite on his level, but he could still keep up with her if he brought his "A" game to the circle. In spite of his best efforts, there was the rare bruise or sprain. Today it had been a pulled muscle in my shoulder for me. For Shade, who he didn't dare pull his punches with, it had been a black eye.

"First rule of sparring," I reminded her.

"Sparring hurts," she said. "If you can't handle a little pain, stay out of the circle."

"And you told him not to pull his punches," I said.

"True," she said, and I could hear the smile in her voice. "It's been ten minutes. Is it numb yet?"

"I don't know," I said. "I can't feel anything there." That earned me an ice pack to the back of the head before we headed for the library.

"So, tell me more about this little business venture you mentioned," she said as I sat down and opened my laptop.

"It was a front for what I did for Dulka," I said as I logged into an old email account. A message was waiting for me, the first layer of my assault on my old boss's infrastructure. "Sort of a magick supply and prefab spell thing. Some stuff, like protection spells and money charms, even some of the more benign attraction spells, we'd just sell as amulets. But for the real complex stuff like hexes and love spells, we sold this sort of do-it-yourself kit. Supplies, diagrams and instructions for the circle, chants, you name it. Sometimes, it would even work like it was supposed to, if someone with some real Talent got ahold of it. We set up a deal with a company in Hong Kong to manufacture the amulets and stuff, and we had a different set-up through another distributer for the cast-your-own-spell kits. We set it up to pretty much run itself. The manufacturer and distributor got their own cut from each sale, and we got the rest." I followed the link to the next email account, one layer closer to my goal.

"Wouldn't he have just changed the passwords when you left?"

"Yeah, but that's the beauty of password recovery," I said. "He would have changed pretty much everything, passwords for checking accounts, Pay-Pro, email accounts, you name it. But what he didn't do was change the part he didn't know about."

"And what was that?"

"I set up an email account for password recovery two or three accounts removed," I said as I opened an email. "And all of his accounts led to it eventually."

"Were you planning to rip him off all along?" she asked with a wicked smile. I reset the password for another email account, then logged in to it.

"Yup," I said. "Originally, I was planning on setting up a squat down in the Hive, then taking this whole set-up over to make some extra money on the side." Several messages were waiting for me to respond to, all of them leading back to the accounts I needed access to.

"Why didn't you?"

"I dunno," I shrugged. "Lots of little reasons, I guess. I kind of like being legit. And … well, I didn't mind pissing Dulka off when it was just me, but once I ended up with my mom and Dee, things changed. Just wasn't … worth it. Okay, this is interesting …"

"What's that? Is this guy asking for advice?" Shade asked as she shoulder surfed.

"Yeah," I said as I read through the email. "He wants to know how to tell if a spirit is in this world or the next." I expanded the thread, and found that it had been going on for a couple of weeks. That was disturbing, because it meant that either Dulka was replying on his own, or he had himself a new helper. I went back and looked at the times on the replies. Every three days, and the last one had been yesterday, which meant I still had a couple of days before my hack job was discovered. I went through and reset the passwords I needed, then deleted the incriminating emails. I forwarded the Pay-Pro message to another email and deleted the record of it, then went into the spam folder and started copying and pasting emails like crazy to give the impression the email had been hacked by a spammer.

"So, I still don't get how you're going to get money from a Pay-Pro account."

"That part is going to take some work. For that, I need to make or borrow a checking account. That'll take some time and some cash that I can't borrow from Dr. C. And an identity."

"I can help with that," Shade said. She looked down and bit her lip when I looked over at her.

"Really?" I said, smiling in spite of myself. A slow grin spread across her face as she nodded.

"You'll have to ditch your friend," she said, nodding toward the backyard where we'd last seen Gage. "Sneak out tonight and meet me at the camp."

A few minutes after midnight, my cell phone buzzed in my hand, waking me up from the light doze I'd let myself fall into. Junkyard raised his head as I moved, then he was on his feet and waiting by the door.

"I need you to stay here, boy," I said softly as I slipped my jeans on, but he just wagged his tail hard enough to make his butt wiggle. I grabbed my shoes and opened the door and he padded down the hallway toward the stairs. By the time I caught up to him, he was at the back door in the kitchen, looking over his shoulder expectantly at me. As soon as I opened that door, he was out, down the steps and waiting by the gate, still looking back at me as if he was the one leading me to my car. I put my shoes on and followed him to the driver's side door of the Mustang.

"You think you're going with me?" I asked him as he sat down. His opened his mouth and let out a little groan that rose at the end. Then he let out a little bark. "Okay, okay, get in," I told him as I opened the door. He clambered across to the passenger seat and sat down. I reached in, took the car out of gear and stuck my keys in the ignition. Then I started pushing, until I was about thirty yards down the road. I hopped in as the car kept rolling and turned the ignition over, and she started. From there, I headed for the freeway and turned her nose north.

Eventually, I turned off the road at the faded sign for Camp Crystal Pines. The gate was open, so I pulled in and followed the curving gravel road down until it opened into a parking lot by the camp's lodge. The power was on here, and the orange light of the sodium streetlight made a broad circle of illumination near the entrance to the lodge.

Junkyard followed me out and immediately claimed the lamppost in the name of all canine-kind before trotting back to me. There were lights on inside, and I could see another car parked near the edge of the lot, well outside the lit area. Memories of the last time I'd been here flitted across the edge of my thoughts. Off to my left was the amphitheater where I'd fought Dominic King into submission before I ended up having to kill him.

I shook my head and pushed the memory out of my thoughts. The door opened and I stepped inside to a room that looked very different than the last time I'd seen it. The liquor bottles and beer cans were gone, and so were the gratuitous T&A posters. The person-sized hole I'd made in the far wall was covered by a sheet of plywood, and I could see tufts of pink insulation sticking out along the edges. The video gaming system was still there, and one of the couches had been moved in front of it. They'd also found a bulletin board somewhere and set it up at the end of a dinner table. Mismatched chairs were clustered around it. Shade was sitting at the far end of the table from the bulletin board, with a skinny little man whose face seemed to be mostly nose and eyes.

"No, it's okay," Shade was saying as the guy froze halfway out of his chair. "This is the guy I was telling you about." She came over to me and led me to the table.

"You're not a cop, right?" he asked, almost like it was a reflex.

"Are you?" I challenged. "Cuz we brought you to where *we* do business."

"I ain't no fuckin' cop," he said defensively.

"Both of you," Shade said sternly. "Put 'em back in your pants. We've got a deal to do, unless you don't want to spend my money."

"Naw, I'm good," Nose Guy said. "Wolf lady here says you need an ID."

"I need an *identity*," I said. "One that's good for financials."

"That'll cost you extra," Nose said. "Three grand." I let my head tilt to the right and looked at him with my best "Are you stupid?" expression.

"One grand, and be thankful Shade here doesn't rip your throat out for trying to stiff me right in front of her," I said.

"I can't just make up a whole identity from nothing," Nose protested.

"No, you can't. That's why you're going to go to that list of stolen identities that you bought for half of what I'm offering you and pull a random male name that's in his mid-twenties for me." He frowned as he thought it over for a moment.

"Okay, fine. One thousand, up front."

"Half up front, just like always," Shade said. "The rest when you deliver." He nodded and Shade counted out five bills under the table, then slid them across to him. He took them, made a show of counting them and holding them up to the light, then stuffed them in his pocket and got up.

"Okay, color me curious," I said after the door closed and the sound of his car had faded.

"Dominic had us working a protection racket," she said after a few seconds. "Once we were free, we tried to stop, but a clutch of vampires started to hunt our old territory. Some of our former … *clients* … decided that paying us to keep the vamps out was the lesser of two evils. Some of them actually like us."

"And Mister Schnozz?"

"He used to keep us in fake IDs."

"Used to?" I asked.

"We used them to get booze," she said. "Without King …" she trailed off. "Getting drunk off our asses isn't as important as it used to be."

"What about the other options?" I asked.

"Not in my pack," she said. "We're clean until we graduate." Her gaze was steady, and while she wasn't being hostile, I knew that she wasn't going to tolerate any challenge to that.

"I'm good with that," I said.

"It's just as well, because we don't bring in nearly as much as we used to," she said. "That thousand for your ID just about broke us."

"I'll pay you back, I promise," I said. "It may take a—" My phone rang in my pocket, and I pulled it out with a sense of dread, expecting to see Dr. Corwyn's name on the caller ID. Instead, Lucas's number showed up.

"Hey, what's up?" I said as I hit the answer button. "You okay?"

"Yeah, I'm fine," Lucas sighed. "My dad's gonna kill me, but I'm okay. But I need a big favor."

"You got it," I said. "Anything you need."

"I need a ride home."

I didn't say anything for a second. Lucas *never* needed a ride. Anywhere.

"Okay," I said slowly once I got my jaw off the floor. "How … what happened?"

"I got into an accident coming home from gaming," he said. "Lady came out of nowhere and hit me from behind at a stop light."

"But you're okay, right?" I said. "How bad is the Falcon?"

I dunno," he said, his voice as close to tears as I'd ever heard him. "I just know I'm not driving her home tonight. I wouldn't bother you this late, but there's no answer at home. My tech-impaired parents probably didn't turn their ringers back on after we came home from the lake."

"No, it's all good," I said, suddenly grateful to have a good reason to sneak out. "I'll … we'll be there in a little while. Just text me the address where you are."

When I looked up, Shade had already grabbed her purse and backpack.

"You can drop me off at home after we drop him off," she said.

Half an hour later, we were pulling in to the parking lot of the building Lucas had texted me the address for. The Falcon, her back end crumpled and one rear wheel skewed sideways, was already loaded onto the back of a flatbed tow truck. An NEPD cruiser with its lights flashing was parked behind the other car, a white Ford station wagon with the right front quarter panel and hood looking like an accordion that had seen better days. Lucas was talking to a woman in scrubs by the other car.

"I probably shouldn't have even been driving," the woman was saying tearfully. "I'd just pulled a double shift and I know that's no excuse, but I must have dozed off or something." Her scrubs bore the logo for St. Michael's Hospital on them, and so did the ID around her neck. Nema was the only part of her name printed large enough to make out. Given what my father had said, though, I wasn't willing to take chances that she wasn't one of his. Junkyard, on the other hand, trotted up to her and sniffed her hand, then licked her knuckles before sitting down and looking up at her with those big brown puppy dog eyes of his.

"It's okay, ma'am," Lucas said as Nema looked down at Junkyard. "We're both insured, and we're both okay. I guess that's the most important part." He was putting on a brave face, but I could tell by the tightness around his eyes that it was hard for him. Nema offered him a teary smile and nodded, then knelt to pet Junkyard.

"Dude, sorry about your car," I said. He shrugged.

"I can probably fix her," he said as we took a couple of steps away. "Hell, I can't even be mad about it. She works in the NICU over at St. Michaels. That's like automatic sainthood right there. And the cop said if she hadn't hit me, she would have plowed into the train that was going by." Another car pulled up and a big guy in BDUs got out. The nurse was in his arms in a flash, and then he was looking down at her like I imagined I looked at Shade sometimes.

107

"Looks like you're hoofing it for a while," I said as I patted my leg to get Junkyard to come back to me. His head swiveled around and he trotted to my side.

"Lucky for me, my best friend just got this sweet vintage ride," Lucas said.

"You ready to get out of here?" I asked.

"Yeah, the tow truck's gonna bring the car home, and I already talked to the cop and got her insurance info, so I'm good."

We started to turn toward my car when someone called out. The soldier was jogging toward us with one hand up, so we waited.

"I'm really sorry about your car," he said breathlessly. "You've been really cool to my wife, and I just wanted to say thank you for that. I can't tell you how much it means to her right now. If you run into any trouble getting your car taken care of, if there's anything I can do to help out, you call us, okay?" He handed all three of us a business card and stepped back, then turned and went to his wife.

"Well, I suppose that could have gone a lot worse," Lucas said as we headed for the Mustang. All I could manage was a weary "Yeah," in response. We caught Lucas up on what we'd been up to in an effort to help take his mind off the wreck, but I could tell he wasn't really listening. When he didn't even ask about the fake identity, I knew we'd probably have to go over everything again later.

We pulled up in front of his house and I got out to let him climb out of the back seat. We said our goodbyes and he turned and started up the walk. He hadn't gone two steps before Junkyard jumped out the window and ran in front of him, then turned and barked at the house. I stepped up in front of Lucas and grabbed Junkyard so I could pull him out of the way.

"Junkyard, what's wrong with you?" I asked as Lucas went around him and hustled toward the front door.

"Chance!" Shade called from the car. I turned to look at her and saw a look of fear on her face. "Stop him! Get him away from the house!" She was halfway out my window, one arm outstretched, her eyes gleaming gold in the moonlight.

108

Time seemed to slow down as I reached into my pocket and grabbed my TK rod. Lucas's hand was on the doorknob as I let go of Junkyard and put my right hand out. He turned and looked at me, his brow creased.

"Vello!" I yelled as I swept my hand back to my body and felt the magick flow through my arm. Suddenly, Lucas was flying through the air toward me, and I saw Shade step up beside me. She caught Lucas and pivoted to crouch behind me in one smooth motion. I had a split second to react as something flashed behind the windows, and I put my hand back out. Magick coursed down my arm as I formed a command word in my thoughts.

"Obe—" was all I got out before the house exploded.

Chapter 7

~ Don't waste time escalating. Hit your victim as hard as you can, as soon as you can. Opening with overwhelming force makes them give up faster and keeps them under control longer.
~ Infernal saying.

I came to with my ears ringing and my body hurting. The world was white, and at first I thought I was suffering from the backlash of a failed spell. My eyes blinked and I suddenly realized I was looking into the core of a raging firestorm. Where Lucas's house used to be was a column of flame that reached into the sky. The heat of it seared my face and arms as I stared at it in disbelief. Behind me, I could hear someone screaming in agony, and I turned to see Shade holding Lucas back as he struggled to get to the house. Tears fell down my own cheeks as the enormity of what had just happened hit me. My best friend had just watched his family die. I crawled to Shade's side and put my arms around him as well, and together we pushed him further away from the blaze.

"Junkyard!" I called out as we made it to the Mustang. I heard a bark from my left, and felt a furry shoulder bump against mine. Lucas's screams were still incoherent as he kept fighting us, but one look into that raging furnace had been enough to tell me that nothing could have survived that. Still, I looked again, and saw something I'd missed the first time. The fire was starting to spin into a vortex, and at its core was a column of purple flame. My mystic senses buzzed as I felt a familiar presence in the flames, and I could swear I heard Dulka's mocking laugh. Bitter, helpless rage started to well up, but it was drowned by the sound of Lucas's screams turning to helpless wails of grief. I crushed him to me as sobs racked his body, my own tears flowing unchecked.

"I'm sorry, Lucas," I wept. "I'm sorry." I could feel Shade's shoulders shake as she fought her own battle with her tears. In the distance, I heard the low wail of sirens, too little help, coming far too late. Hands descended on us in the heat and pulled us into motion, taking us away from the worst of the heat. Lucas was pulled away from me, his face stricken as he looked back at the fire that consumed his family. I looked back over my shoulder to see a group of people pushing my car further down the street. As the Mustang rolled away, I could see wisps of smoke rising from the blackened grass of the front yard, and a cone of green that spread from the imprint of my knees in the lawn. Someone was patting my right shoulder with a purpose, and I looked down to see smoke curling up from a smoldering hole in my shirt.

"Are you okay?" someone was yelling at me, though I could barely hear them over the constant ringing in my head. I nodded and let them pull me out of the street as the flashing red strobes of the firetrucks and ambulances heralded their arrival. From across the street, I could see the sides of the houses flanking the explosion were caved in, and people were leading pajama-clad residents out. I let them lead me to the back of an ambulance and sit me down next to Lucas and Shade. All we could do was put our arms around his shoulders and offer him our silent sympathy.

"You kids are lucky to be alive," a soot-covered firefighter said to me in the gray light. I just nodded. Beside me, Lucas just stared straight ahead, all of his tears shed for the moment. The fireman stepped in front of Lucas, forcing him to focus on him. "Son, the police are going to need to know if you have any family you can stay with." Lucas blinked at him, his gaze still focused on something only he could see.

"My grandfather," he said slowly. "Hans Mitternacht." He reached into his pocket and pulled out his cell phone, his movements slow. The firefighter gently took it from him and headed over to the fire chief's truck. Shade and I ended up with a cop each taking our statements, which were pretty brief. They told us to go home, then made it more of an order once it was obvious we weren't.

I dropped Shade off a block away from her house, then headed back to Dr. C's place as clouds started to build up overhead. For a moment, I sat out front, trying to keep my head together. I knew what I needed to do. It was one of the things I said I should plan for. But the price … I'd never expected it to be this high.

Finally, I got out and walked in the front door, letting the screen door slam behind me and leaving the front door wide open. Thunder rumbled outside and seemed to follow me in, reflecting my mood.

"In the library, Chance," Dr. C said, his voice stern. "Now." I ignored him and stomped up the stairs with Junkyard at my side. Dee wasn't in the room, and I let out a sigh of relief. Junkyard hopped up on the bed while I went to the closet and grabbed my duffel bag.

"Did you think I hadn't learned from the last time you stayed with me?" Dr. C said from the doorway as I finished throwing my shirts into the duffel bag.

"He blew up Lucas's house," I said as I grabbed more clothes from my dresser. I shoved the bundle of clothing into the duffel and stood there for a moment. "He killed my best friend's family right in front of him. Right in front of me. They died because I had to piss the old man off and because I thought I knew what the hell I was doing."

Dr. Corwyn's hand fell on my shoulder a moment later and he turned me to face him.

"Chance, don't do this to yourself," he said, his voice firm. "This wasn't your fault. You *know* that."

"He said," I started, then choked on the lump in my throat. I swallowed it back down and went on. "He said there would be a price. I thought I could handle it. I thought this was between him and me. I'm gonna lose my best friend because I was a fucking idiot."

"Was Lucas hurt?" he asked.

I shook my head. "No. I *saved* him. But his family died because of me. He's going to hate me for that. And I deserve it."

"What are you going to do?"

"What I should have done all along … give the old man what he wants." I zipped the duffel closed and pushed past Dr. C, nearly running down Gage in the hallway.

"What's happening?" he asked sleepily.

"Nothing," I said. "Go back to the Caymans. Enjoy the rest of your summer vacation." I brushed past him and headed down the stairs, Dr. C's voice calling out behind me. I kept going until I got to the bottom of the stairs.

Dee stood by the door, her backpack and suitcase waiting. Every ounce of eight-year-old determination was blazing in her eyes, and I knew that somehow she had known what I was going to do before I even walked in the door.

"No," I told her.

"He wants me, too," she said. Her lower lip started to tremble. "I saw what he did. I dreamed it. And I don't want him to hurt your friends anymore! Or mine, or Mom's or anyone! If we're together, we can look out for each other."

I went and knelt in front of her, then grabbed her in a tight hug.

"Doesn't work that way, sis," I said as we pulled apart. "Mom made it so his name isn't on your birth certificate. He can't claim you're his. Technically, he's ... well, he's—"

"Technically he's a dick," she said.

"Dee!" I blurted. "If Mom was here—"

"She'd say the same thing," Dee said. I turned and looked over my shoulder at Dr. C for support, but he just put his hands up and shook his head.

"I'm with her," he said. "He's a dick. But your brother's right, Deirdre. The law says he can't make you come live with him, and you can't go live with him, either."

Her eyes fell back on me, and her face crumpled into an unhappy pout. "I don't want you to go."

"I don't want to go," I said. "But I have to, so he doesn't hurt anyone else." Behind me, Dr. C let out a growl of frustration, then he put a hand on my shoulder.

"If you're going to go," he said, "at least go prepared. Let's finish your wand, and take a few basic precautions. I still don't like it, but I can at least make sure I don't hate the idea."

"The Council isn't going to like this, either," Gage said.

"They don't need to like it," Dr. C said as he brushed past him and headed for the back stairway.

"They just have to deal with it," I said as I followed.

"What?" Gage sputtered. "What do you mean?"

Ahead of me, Dr. C stopped in the doorway to the back stairs and turned toward Gage. "Go *tell* them!" he said, then he was taking the steps at a run.

It was a little past noon when we finally pulled up at my father's house in the northern side of the Pittsburgh district. This was where the real money in New Essex lived, at least if it had been made after Viet Nam was a thing, and on the less-developed north side, you had to be able to afford some really low tax brackets to even have a P.O. box. For Stavros "the Spartan" Fortunato, it was the next best thing to actually being legit. The iron gate opened before Dr. C's Range Rover even got to the intercom, so he drove on in. Behind us, I could see a blue Crown Vic slide past, its lights on and windshield wipers on in the steady rain. Better late than never, I figured. If the Sentinels were around, odds were good I wouldn't have to worry so much about dealing with Dulka directly. Dr. C pulled up along the curving driveway, and the house came into view. On first impression, it was big, white and ugly. The front had what looked like an oversized awning that came out from the house like the front of a hotel or a gas station. Turrets or towers stuck out all over the front, and a five-car garage angled away from the rest of the house with, you guessed it, *another* rounded turret rising from the far end. It even came with its own gargoyle, tastelessly decorated in a cheap suit with sunglasses and a bulge under the left arm.

The door opened as we came to a stop, and my father came out with another goon on his heels. I got out as the old man walked toward me with a smile on his face and his arms open.

"Welcome home, son," he said, just a little too smug for my taste.

I punched him as hard as I could.

As greetings went, it went over about as well as I expected it would. The goon on porch duty tackled me and the one behind my father drew his gun as the old man stumbled back and fell on his ass. Dr. C was coming around the front of the truck, and the gun-toting goon moved to aim at him while Dee jumped out the back door of the Range Rover and landed at my side.

"Gentlemen," my father said as he got to his feet. "Stand down. Put the gun away ... let my son up." The goon on me stood and planted himself in front of Dr. C as my father came up to me and grabbed me by the shoulders. "If anyone is going to hit him," he said as he drew his hand back, "it's going to be me."

His hand started to swing forward, and then he went flying backward a couple of feet and hit the ground again. The goons and Dr. C were looking too wide-eyed to have a clue what had just happened, so I figured everyone else was just as surprised as I was. Then Dee stepped forward, her little Sonic Screwdriver emitting a light that no LED ever could.

"You leave him alone," she hissed.

I stood up beside her.

"Magick is strong in my family," I said, barely keeping a hysterical giggle out of my voice as I paraphrased a line from Return of the Jedi. "My mother has it. I have it … and my sister has it. So think twice about fucking with us."

"You disrespect me in my own home," my father said as he struggled to his feet. "And you think I'm going to let that pass unanswered?"

"I do," I said. "You had that coming and you know it."

"Then go on, tell me that's for so-and-so or whatever macho bullshit you had in mind. Let's get this over with." He rolled his eyes and shook his head before he smirked at me and held his hands out expectantly.

"That was just hello," I said as I turned my back on him and grabbed my duffel bag from the back seat. "You've already got the threats and macho bullshit covered." I gestured to Dee, and she came over and wrapped her arms around my waist in a fierce hug. I gave her a thumbs up then pointed at the passenger seat, and she went for it.

Dr. C went to go around the goon in front of him, and the guy made the mistake of trying to lay hands on him. Dr. C's left hand jabbed forward, index and middle finger together, and there was a sound like electricity arcing. The goon seemed to jump back a foot before he hit the ground and twitched a little.

"Here's the deal," Dr. C said conversationally as he walked up to the old man. "The Sentinels and *both* Hands of Death are going to be watching this place. If a demon shows up here, or if Chance goes anywhere close to a demon … Hell, Stavros, if you even *think* of a demon's name within a hundred yards of my apprentice, an excruciating death will be the least of your worries."

"I think we have an understanding," my father said smoothly.

"That's disappointing," Dr. C shot back. "But, hope springs eternal. You may screw this up yet."

116

Dr. C turned to me and held his hand out, and I took it.

"Good luck, son," he said.

"Thank you, sir." I turned away to keep myself from saying anything else and picked up my duffle bag. The Range Rover pulled out from under the awning and turned down the driveway as I walked up the steps. The door opened when I was a couple of steps away and I was treated to Jeremy's pleasant smile for a moment as he inclined his head.

"Welcome, Master Chance," he said. "Shall I take your bag?"

I went to hand it to him, and my father grabbed it before he could lay a finger on it.

"Not so fast, boy," he snarled. "Give me your focuses. All of them." It was my turn to smirk at him.

"No," I said. "I'm here on my terms, not yours. You don't—" The first punch came low and fast, and I puked on the floor at his feet as my diaphragm spasmed. He kicked me in the ribs and I slid a few feet across the floor. I came to a stop at the feet of another goon. I looked up and saw a face I recognized.

"Hey, Nico," I groaned as he reached down and pulled me up by my shoulders.

"Hey, kid," Nico said. "Nothin' personal."

"Just doing your job," I said before the old man planted his fist in my ribs. Breathing was going to be a chore for the next few days. I sagged in Nico's grip, and the old man pulled my head up by a fistful of my hair.

"Fine," I moaned. "Take the damn focuses."

"You should have said that the first time," the old man said as he pounded my ribs again. "Then I wouldn't have to do this."

After a few more shots to the body, he stuck his hands in my pockets and took my TK rod and my touchstones, then proceeded to strip any jewelry off of me. With a nod at Nico, he stepped back and Nico let go of me. I staggered forward and fell to one knee. Before I could get my feet under me again, frigid water and ice cubes rained down on me. I gasped in shock as the heavy cubes pelted my back and head, then looked up at my father with pure hate in my eyes.

"Nico," my father said as he stepped away from the spreading pool of water, "make sure he changes clothes and take him up to his room. Jeremy, clean this mess up." The old man left with a chuckling goon at his back, and Nico took me by the arm.

"Come on, kid," he said. I shivered as I stumbled along beside him, unable to do anything else between the beating and the shock of the cold water. I settled for dripping on his shoes and pants. He'd never get a crease in *those* slacks again. He led me up the stairs and off to the right, down a long hallway, then turned left into a bathroom the size of Mom's house. With unexpected gentleness, he led me to the toilet and sat me down, then went to the door and closed it in front of himself before he grabbed a couple of thick towels and came back to me.

"C'mon kid," he said. "Let's get you dried off and into some dry clothes." I slowly peeled out of my shirt and shorts, then took my briefs off. He handed me a stack of clothes from the counter and gathered up my wet things. "You go and put those on," he said as he took the wet clothes to the door and tossed them out into the hallway.

"Tighty-whiteys?" I said through chattering teeth as I held the offending item up.

"Ain't my job to buy your shit," Nico said from the door. "You want better stuff, ask the old man." He paused for a moment, then turned to look at me. "Nicely."

"I don't do nice with him," I said while I started getting dressed.

"Look, I know ya don't like the old guy," he said after I got my pants on, "but you gotta show him respect. If you did like you were s'posed ta do, none of this would've happened."

"Yes it would," I said as I pulled the shirt over my head. For a moment, it was all I could do to take shallow breaths as I fought the pain that came with putting my arms above my shoulders. "If it wasn't this, he'd find something else." There were no socks or shoes, so I got up barefoot and shuffled toward the door. Nico kept his hand on my arm as he led me to my room.

As jail cells went, it was a pretty nice one. Big bed, widescreen TV, stereo system with more CDs than I could ever listen to, and a computer with dual screens that looked like a gamer's wet dream. Of course, where my father was concerned, everything was a trap. If he'd given me a computer, he had a

118

way to monitor it. I grabbed the remote and turned the TV on, then laid down on the bed to chill out until the next torture he decided to inflict on me.

Between dozing and watching reruns of B movies on TV, the time passed pretty quickly. Around six, I heard a noise from downstairs that reminded me of a donkey braying. A few minutes later, the door opened and Nico stuck his head inside.

"Boss wants you to come downstairs for dinner," he rumbled. "He says you gotta be nice."

"I'm the epitome of good manners," I said. "Should I wear a tie for the evening meal?"

"Yeah, whatever," Nico said. "What you got on is good." He gestured for me to come with him, and I followed him out the door and down to the dining room. The cherry-wood table was big enough to seat ten people, and the old man was seated at the far end. There were two places set on either side of his, with more pieces of silverware and glassware than I knew what to do with. Jeremy waited on my father, offering him a bottle of white wine. He nodded as I sat down on his left, and Jeremy poured some into his glass. He made a show of smelling it and taking a small taste, then gave an approving nod.

"Want some?" my father said as he held his glass up.

I shrugged. "Sure, why not."

"Tonight's selection is a 2008 Domaine Marcel Deiss Pinot Blanc," Jeremy said. "It complements the flavor of sea food … and takes the edge off the company." As if announcing said company, the sound of high heels on marble preceded a tall woman's arrival. Breasts the size of volleyballs stretched a pale pink designer top to its limits, and a pair of tight white leggings disappeared into a pair of matching ankle boots. Her hair was a metallic-looking blonde that she had styled into submission, and only her mouth and eyelids moved as she attempted a smile.

"You must be Chance!" she squealed as she clattered across the room, her hands out. I tried not to flinch as she grabbed my shoulders with fingers tipped with two-inch-long pink nails. For a moment, she looked at me, then pulled me into a hug that threatened to suffocate me in silicone. Then she went around behind my father and took the seat directly across from me.

"Yes, ma'am, I am," I said after a few seconds.

"I'm Kara," she said as she grabbed the glass of wine Jeremy poured. "Oh, heavens, Jeremy, this is the 2009 Domaine Marcel. You know I hate that year. I don't know why you let him buy that crap, Stavros. Jeremy, go open a bottle of the 2008 for me, please." Jeremy nodded without correcting her, then looked to my father. Meanwhile, Kara kept on talking.

"So, you'll never guess who I ran into today but that gold-digging little slut Jeanine Tugo," she started.

"Darling, shut up," my father said. It was like shutting a light switch off.

"Yes, dear," she said, and she put her hands in her lap, eyes forward, the verbal font shut off.

"I see *that* hasn't changed," I said. "How long have you had this one?"

"About a month. They behave a little better now." We stopped talking as salad was served. That was interesting. It meant Dulka had a new apprentice, familiar, whatever you wanted to call it. If they were a willing familiar, he could cast spells through them, but it meant he still had to do the bulk of the work. It was faster and easier, but it meant they couldn't do as much independently as I used to be able to.

"Well, I'm done mind-raping people for you," I said between bites of the salad. "You're still on your own there."

"Can't a father just want to be a part of his son's life?" he asked.

"We need to review that conversation we had last October," I said. "You don't get to call me that anymore."

"I think our conversation from a few hours ago makes my position clear on that," he said. His eyes were cold when he smiled at me. "In case it doesn't, I'll clarify. I'll call you what I want in my house, and you'll treat me the way I demand to be treated. If you don't, I'll beat the shit out of you until you do. Am I making myself clear?"

I bit back the threats and rants I wanted to unleash on him, and after a moment, I smiled at him.

"Perfectly."

"I'm going to wipe that smile off your face soon enough," he said with a pointed look at Kara. The look of concern that crossed my face was genuine. He'd been unconscious for most of my fight with Dulka, but I thought he'd been awake when I told my old boss that he hadn't been in my head for years. Would he connect that to mind control magick? For the moment, I figured he wouldn't, but if he put the pieces together, I was deeply screwed. I looked down at my now empty plate and set my fork down. I wasn't sure I could let Dulka lay his compulsions on me and remove them later. I'd done it once, but the trick was going to be in keeping my defenses in place without making the spell bounce off of them.

"Darling, eat," the old man said, bringing me out of my thoughts. Kara looked surprised, then picked up her fork and started on her salad. I choked my food down, grateful for the slight buzz the wine gave me. True to Jeremy's promise, it took the edge off the company. Once dinner was done, I was escorted back to my room and left to my own devices.

Instead of sleeping or watching TV, I sat with my back against the bed and let myself slip into a light meditative trance. Most of magick was having your head in the right place, and without any of my focuses, I *really* needed to figure out how to cast something on my own. After several deep breaths, I visualized roots extending from the base of my spine down into the earth, and branches that arced up and over my head to droop back down toward the ground. Once I could feel the slight tingle of energy along my spine, I made the effort to draw it through me. Suddenly I was like a live wire, with power pulsing through my body. It was slow but powerful, more like a steamroller than a race car. Like I did with a touchstone, I imagined a matrix to store some of the energy. Once I had it stable, I syphoned power into it, slowly charging it like a battery.

Once it was full, I set it aside and repeated the process. With the second one done, I had a choice to make. I could leave them attached to myself, or I could attach them to something else. It gave me the ability to turn almost anything into a sort of touchstone, provided I had the time and the right conditions. As I set the second matrix, I was vaguely aware of someone coming into the room. I envisioned severing the two matrices as firm, unfamiliar lips pressed against mine. My eyes opened to the sight of a familiar face pulling away from mine, and the smell of ozone in the air.

121

"Now *that* was a kiss," the girl said as she pulled my face up to look at her.

"Lucinda?" I asked as the construct of roots and branches shattered in my head.

"In the oh, so delectable flesh," she said. She stepped back and ran her hands down the side of her body, outlining the curve of her hips as she struck a pose in front of me. She'd dyed the ends of her blonde hair a bright red, and had done her makeup heavy. I blinked as I got to my feet. If she'd been dressed to kill the last time I'd seen her, she was almost dressed for sex this time. A tiny purple t-shirt covered her from shoulders to augmented breasts and stopped there. It didn't even do that good of a job of covering her boobs, and the word "SLUT" left very little to the imagination about her intent. Her belly button sparkled with a piercing, and a pair of micro shorts tried their best to keep as little as possible covered around her hips. Fishnets ran down her legs where they joined forces with a pair of pink and clear plastic stripper heels to shape her legs. With the platform heels she was an inch taller than me, but she was still dwarfed by the guy behind her.

While Lucinda did her best to be a walking wet dream, Riker McCain was clearly on the Incredible Hulk workout. The last time I'd seen him, he'd been a pretty big guy, but now he was at least six inches taller and a foot wider. His shoulders sloped down into arms the size of me, on either side of a chest that sported pecs that were only a little bigger than Lucinda's breasts. His neck had been taken over by his deltoids, and his hips narrowed almost absurdly before his thighs started. He was big, but, at a second glance, he wasn't ripped.

"So you're Dulka's new bitch," I said. Riker glowered at me, and one meaty paw curled into a fist.

"Damn straight, and you have no idea what you're missing, sweetie," Lucinda said. She turned and draped herself against Riker, running her hand down his chest. "I even get my own toys."

"That's nice," I said. "You always wanted to get laid," I said to Riker. "If I'd known you just wanted to be someone's boy toy, I would have introduced you to each other sooner." He growled at me as Lucinda peeled herself away from him and came back over to me. She put one finger against my chest, and I could see her gold-enameled talons put Kara's to shame.

"Now for the fun part," she purred. "Strip."

"I already went through this," I told her. "I'm not taking my clothes off just so you two can get your thrills." Riker took a step forward, but Lucinda laughed and leaned forward to cup my crotch in her right hand.

"As much as you'd enjoy letting me ride this," she said with a light squeeze, "that's not on the agenda. We need to make sure you don't have any spells inscribed on you."

I uttered an expletive as I stripped the shirt off and undid my shorts. It felt weird undressing in front of someone else, but the thought of Shade doing it for King got me through it. She could do it, knowing something worse than getting stared at was going to happen. I couldn't do anything less.

"Well, you've hunked up a little," Lucinda said as she came up to me and ran one finger down my arm. "Have you been hitting the gym?" She walked around behind me, and I heard the little catch in her breath as she saw the roadmap of scar tissue on my back. Her fingertips slid across my shoulder blades, catching on the thick ridges of old wounds. Compared to Riker, I was more like Bruce Lee standing next to Arnold Schwarzenegger, lean and better defined but still nowhere near as big.

"Not exactly," I said as she came back around in front of me, her eyes glued to the marks on my chest. "See, no spells. Happy now?"

"Oh, I'm just getting started, baby," she said. "You know what comes next?" She put her arms around my neck, then jumped up so her legs were wrapped around my hips, her crotch pressing against my groin. "You if you're good."

"You know I don't do casual sex," I said as I picked her up and pushed her away. She squealed in delight as her feet hit the ground.

"Oh, manhandle me, baby," she said. "I like it rough."

"Go do your toy and come back so we can get this over with." She led McCain out of the room by the hand and paused just long enough to leer at me over her shoulder before the door closed behind them. But, if I thought I had gotten away free and clear, a few minutes later I was proven wrong as I heard them start to go at it hot and heavy in the next room. I grabbed the earphones for the stereo. It certainly explained a lot. Sex magick was popular among the demonic set, partly because it raised so much energy, and partly because it could so easily be twisted to Infernal purposes, since humans attached so many negative emotions to sex. Jealousy, shame, and greed were all close to the surface when you brought sex into the picture. All Dulka had to do was give her a focus to use as a lens for the spell, and she would provide the energy.

Half an hour later, a sweaty Lucinda walked back into the room. Even without opening my mystic senses, I could feel the power radiating from her skin.

"You sure you don't want to do this the fun way?" she asked, her voice slightly distorted by the magick coursing through her body. "Because I've got some serious mojo going on right now."

"I figured you'd had enough by now," I said as she walked up to me.

"Honey, I *never* get enough." She leaned in close and whispered, *"Vocem meam voluntatem,"* in the heartbeat before she kissed me. There was a jolt that ran through me as the spell took hold, and I could feel it settle around my shoulders and run up the side of my face. I went stiff as I fought the urge to resist it, and felt enough of my will stay under my own control that I could retain the ability to break it when I needed to. Maybe.

"Now, as much as I want to ride you like a pony," Lucinda said, "Daddy has some other things in mind for you. You're going to be a good boy. No sneaking out, and no talking to your friends. You prefer it here. And you'll do what your dad says. Acknowledge."

"I will do as I'm told," I said.

"Good boy. When your father calls you son, you will obey him. Got it?"

"I get it."

"Let's go show Daddy what a good girl I am, then."

I followed, for the moment, my will, like my choices, not my own. She led me downstairs to my father's study. Nico opened the door to let us in, and I took a moment to check the lay of the land. Not much had changed in the nine months or so since I'd last seen the place. The same portrait of my father hung over the fireplace on the left side of the room, one that made him look less like a bloated fish and more like the man I remembered as a child. The same painting hung on the right of the fireplace, too. It was a still life, fruit and dishes on a table by some important artist. It was also camouflage. If he hadn't changed the painting, then the safe that used to be hidden behind it was probably still there. The carpet was new, some maroon paisley pattern that was probably supposed to make a statement about how much money he had. My eyes went to the right side of his desk. The same trash can was still there, a round wire thing in black that also happened to be big enough to cover the floor safe below it.

"It's done, Mr. Fortunato," Lucinda said with a smile. "He'll be a good boy now."

"Let's see," he said.

"Say hi to your dad, Chance," she said, and I felt the compulsions stir.

"Hi, Dad," I said.

He nodded and smiled, and I promised myself I'd make him suffer for that.

"Good work," he said. "I'll take control now."

"Chance, when your father calls you son, you will do whatever he says. You'll obey him now, too."

"Okay," I agreed.

"Now, first things first, son," he said. "You're going to get in touch with that school you were going to and tell them you're not going."

"Going to the Franklin Academy is mandatory, sir," I said.

"That's not my problem," he said. "Deal with it. Second, no more of that little redhead. Break up with her. Same goes for your other friend, Wendy or whatever her name is. I don't even want you going to your other friend's funeral. As far as you're concerned, that bullshit never happened, and you're back where you belong. You don't want to go back to that other life." I felt the compulsions working, but there was a conflict, since one of the things he had told me to do wasn't going to happen. I could see Lucinda frown as she sensed the turmoil it was causing.

"Something's wrong," she said. "You've given him an order that doesn't make sense." He got up from behind the desk and strode toward Lucinda. Eight years of being in her shoes told me what was about to happen, but I wasn't supposed to be able to warn her. His left hand was closed into a fist, but he hit her with the back of his hand and sent her sprawling.

"Stupid little bitch!" he yelled. "Can't you even cast a simple mind control spell right? Even this stupid little shit got that right, and he was a fuck up from day one!"

"It isn't the spell," Lucinda sobbed. "He can't make sense of one of the orders you gave him for some reason. Just ask him what's wrong." The old man took a step forward and kicked her in the stomach before he turned to me.

"What the hell is wrong with you?" he snapped.

"Lucas is still alive, sir," I said. "There is no funeral to go to."

"He wasn't in the house when it blew up?" the old man asked.

"No, sir. He got home late." I waited for a second, then added, "I can refuse to go to his parents' service, if you prefer."

True to his nature, he gave me a sidelong look and stepped up close to me. "Why are you offering to skip their funeral?" he asked softly.

"Because it would make you look bad and hurt your custody case to have you isolate me and not show up in public. Dr. Corwyn would probably make the case for physical abuse, which would prompt an investigation."

"Goddamn it!" he spat. "You had this planned from the beginning, didn't you?"

"Dr. Corwyn and his lawyer have several contingency plans based on things I told them you would do," I said.

His face turned red, and his lips became a tight line. "Damn it," he hissed. "You two, get the hell out of my face. I need to talk to Mike." I turned and walked to the door and Lucinda came after me. She walked hunched over, with one hand around her stomach and the other cupping her cheek.

"It helps if you don't make it sound like he was the one who did something wrong," I said after we got a few steps away. "He doesn't hit as hard when you take the blame for a mistake." We walked along for a few more steps.

"But he still hits," she said.

I nodded. "Yeah," I said. "He still hits."

Chapter 8
~ Never accept an opponent's surrender at face value. ~
Often overlooked Infernal advice.

It was Friday night. Poker night for the old man, though he spent a good chunk of the evening 'out' pretty much every night, and girls' night out for Kara. The memorial service for Lucas's parents was the next day, and I was determined to go. But I still needed the compulsions in place, even while I defied them. So, as the sun began to set, I sat down with my back against the wall and closed my eyes. Slowly, I allowed myself to see the spell that Lucinda had wrapped around my aura. Instead of breaking it, I needed to turn it down for a while. What I was attempting to do was more like hitting the mute button instead of the off button. With slow, precise movements, I brought my fingertips to the glyphs that were stretched along my aura, and slowly pulled them away bit by bit.

"Compulsis resido," I whispered, and they went from bright red to transparent. Nine months ago, I hadn't been capable of such fine control, but now … Dulka was in for a big surprise.

Now that I was ostensibly under control, there wasn't a guard on my room, and I had run of the mansion. I headed downstairs and, like clockwork, Jeremy appeared as I hit the main staircase.

"Master Chance, how may I assist you?" he said.

"Do you still have what I gave you last October?" I asked. He looked around for a moment, then nodded.

"It is my most cherished gift, sir. I have not squandered it." My eyes went a little misty as I remembered him saying the same thing when I'd lifted the compulsions on him. I went down the steps to him and put my hand on his shoulder.

"Can I ask you to use it for me?" I asked.

"You may ask anything of me, sir, and it is yours."

"It means betraying my father," I said.

"Then you needn't ask. I volunteer."

"I need access to his study. And the combinations to his safes … and his bank accounts." I looked at him and held my breath, waiting for him to balk, but he nodded and turned on his heel.

"This way, sir."

Moments later, I was at the old man's desk, with my hand on the heart of his empire. The notebook I was looking at detailed who he paid for what illegal things, and how they were listed in his books under otherwise legitimate expenses. Names, contact numbers, emails, even addresses for a few folks, and people he could get to them through. He also had a series of fake email addresses he did business through, including the one he'd used to frame Mom. I hit a couple of websites I had researched earlier that day, and once I had what I needed downloaded, I pulled up the email accounts he had referenced in the notebook and made sure the emails I needed were still in the sent box. Once I was sure of that, I made a visit to all of his bank accounts, secret and known.

By that point, I had visited and verified everything the cops would need to put him away. Then it was time to get personal. I went to the Pay-Pro account and entered the temporary password to make a permanent change, then accessed the account and transferred all $4,683.00 to one of the smaller, local accounts my father used for petty cash. Finally, I forwarded a few emails and asked Jeremy to scan the notebook for me and print it out later that night. As much as I had gotten done, though, I still had no idea *why* I was there.

"Will there be anything else, sir?" he asked as I handed him the notebook.

"The keys to the Jag, if you have 'em," I said facetiously.

"Mr. Fortunato no longer owns the Jaguar," he said in his precise accent. "Miss Kara had an unfortunate accident in it. I can, however, call you a taxi if you wish."

"I do wish," I told him. "But first, I need to get to my stuff."

Mitternacht's Books was closed by the time the taxi dropped me off. I walked past the entrance to the store and pushed open the door that led to the stairwell on the corner of the building. There might as well have been a million steps going to the third floor, but I didn't count. I just plodded my way up, my heart feeling like it weighed a ton in my chest and getting heavier with every step. I didn't want to face Lucas, didn't want to take the responsibility for his parents' deaths. But I knew I had to. If he was like me, he was probably blaming himself for surviving. I reached the third floor and stared at the door for a couple of minutes, working up the nerve to knock.

"Come in already," a heavily accented voice said from the other side of the door. I laid my hand on the knob and opened the door. Inside, I finally understood why people said some places needed a woman's touch. The front room was done in dark paneling, where the wall wasn't covered by a bookshelf. What little blank space on the walls that was covered barely counted, because it was a world map. Thickly cushioned leather chairs bracketed a small fireplace on the front wall, and a heavy couch occupied the center of the room. The rich smell of pipe smoke permeated the whole room, and the glass in the light fixtures was yellowed with age. Two doorways led deeper into the rest of the apartment, one showing tiled floor and the other giving few clues.

"I could hear you stomping up the stairs from all the way down at the bottom," Mr. Mitternacht said from one of the chairs by the fireplace. Looking like Santa on SlimQuik, Hans Mitternacht was one of those men who made people who were born in the U.S. long for the "old country."

"The three girls, they are already here." He pointed to the doorway across the room. "In the second bedroom, third door down. Go, help him mourn." I nodded and went through the doorway to find myself in a hall. I heard voices on the other side of the door Hans had indicated, and knocked gently.

"Lucas, it's Chance," I said through the door. "Can I come in?"

Wanda opened the door and pulled me in, then went back to sit by Giselle on the floor. Lucas sat with his back to the wall, while Giselle and Wanda were propped up against his bed. Shade sat in an antique-looking chair in front of a wooden desk.

"Hey, Chance," Lucas greeted me. His hand moved in something like a wave, but otherwise, he just sat there.

"I'm sorry, man," I said as I went to sit in front of him.

"Not your fault," he said. "The cops said it was a gas explosion. If Junkyard and Shade hadn't smelled the gas … I would've been dead too." He sighed. "I don't mean to sound ungrateful, but I wonder if that wouldn't have been better."

129

"No, Lucas," I said. "It wouldn't have been better. And yes, it was my fault."

"What do you mean?" he said, his face suddenly taking on some semblance of life.

"I mean my father was the one who arranged for the 'gas explosion' to happen. He did it to force me to come live with him. I knew he was going to try to do something, but I thought it was going to be something simple, like messing up my car or something. I never expected him to do … that."

Lucas shot to his feet, and I came up to face him. "I understand if you're mad at me, or if … you hate me. But I couldn't lie to you, or—" The rest was cut off as his fist connected with my cheek.

My head rocked to the left for a second, then I was facing him again. For all that I loved Lucas as the best friend a guy could want, and as brave as he was, he couldn't throw a punch worth a damn. I looked back at him, and his face was contorted with emotions I didn't dare name.

"That's for letting your dad kill my family," he yelled. I nodded. He threw a second punch, and even though I saw this one coming, I didn't try to block it. His fist connected, this time a little harder. I saw white for a second and staggered back.

"That's for giving him what he wanted!"

Wanda was on her feet and moving to get between us, but I held a hand out to try to stop her.

"No, he's right," I said.

"No, he isn't!" she said with something in her voice that made both of us stop and look at her. "Both of you are acting like idiots. Your father made his *own* choice. You didn't force him to do what he did. He made that decision on his own, and if anyone is going to pay for it, it doesn't need to be you, Chance. Stavros Fortunato did this, no one else. Stavros Fortunato pays for this. *No. One. Else.*"

I had seen the face of the Goddess in her compassion and in her wrath, and Wanda was definitely channeling the latter. Not in a figurative sense, either.

"She is right, *enkel,*" Hans's voice came from behind me. I turned to see him standing in the open door. He walked past me and put his hands on Lucas's shoulders. "Stop hitting your

130

friend. *Nein,* friend, it is not enough word. Lucas, *enkel,* he is your … you are *waffenbruder.*"

"Weapon brothers?" Lucas said, his expression showing as much concern as confusion.

Hans turned and gestured to include Wanda and Shade. "*Ja,* you've shed blood together; you are all brothers and sisters in arms. What, you think I am not hearing because I'm so old? I hear the stories you whisper to each other. The Goddess in you, Wanda. You, standing at your friend's side against *der Blutsauger* a few months ago. And *der Werwolf* in the fall before that. And you," he said turning to me. "You are always there for them. You even try to own the bad that is not yours, because you feel responsible for them. Lucas, I know we have lost so much, the family we were given by birth. But you must hold on to the family you still have, these, your brother and sisters. Give your anger to the one it belongs to, this Stavros."

Lucas stood there for a few moments, his fists still balled up and his arms quivering. Finally his head came up and he nodded.

"I'm sorry I hit you," he said in a tight voice. "But I'm still pissed you gave him what he wanted." I couldn't look him in the eye. Hans gave a curt nod, and headed for the door, muttering something about kids on the way out.

"I couldn't risk him going after Wanda or …" I let it trail off, not even able to imagine anything happening to Shade without my brain locking up. "Besides, he's not getting what he wants. Not by the time I'm through with him."

"So, how do we fuck up his world?" Lucas asked, his voice cold.

"I'm working on that," I said. "And you're going to be a big part of it. But there's something else I need your help with. Dulka's got a familiar, and he's got her on a recruiting drive. She's targeted a guy named Gilbert Vasquez." I pulled out the copy of the email I'd printed before I'd left my father's place and let everyone look it over.

"So, when you say 'recruiting drive,' you mean he's trying to get this guy to sell him his soul," Wanda said in a cold voice.

"And he's using the website I set up for him to do it," I said bitterly. "I'm not going to let him get away with that."

"How?" Giselle, quiet and all but forgotten up to then, asked. "How do you make it so this guy doesn't sell his soul to this Dulka? I mean, if he really wants to, he's going to do it no matter what." Wanda sat on the bed and Giselle moved so that she was leaning against it between her knees.

"Good question," I said. Wanda put her hands on Giselle's shoulders, her eyes distant. "We can't mess with his free will."

"We need to figure out who this guy is and what he wants first," Shade said. Her head was tilted forward, and her eyes were bright. "Maybe we can ask Collins to help us do that?"

"What about the circle?" Lucas asked. "The email said he was going to have to summon Dulka in a few days. Are there any supplies he'd need for setting it up that he can't get from your website? For that matter, if he ordered stuff from your website, what about the shipping address he used?"

"He'll need powdered chalk, dung of some kind, and some herbs, like hellebore and foxglove. And, for a summoning circle, he'll need a pentacle made of some metal other than silver. The chalk he can get at any hardware store. As far as his shipping address, he used a P.O. box, so that's a dead end."

"You can only get hellebore and foxglove at Spirit Garden," Wanda said. "And they only sell silver pentacles there. My mom and I can ask around there."

"One of our suppliers sells copper and pewter pentacles," Lucas added. "And not just the jewelry versions; they have the altar-sized disks. No one else in town sells those."

I nodded, suddenly feeling something stir in my chest at seeing my friends coming together again. For a couple of seconds, it was hard to speak, and I had to fight to get my voice to come without cracking.

"Okay," I said, my voice still a little thick. "Shade, can you talk to Collins for me? And you guys have the supply angle figured out. Lucas, you're going to get an email later tonight. You'll know what to do from there. And I'll see you tomorrow at the memorial service, even if I have to sneak out to do it."

"No," Lucas said. I did a double take at the firm tone in his voice, but he stepped forward and put his hands on my shoulders. "Don't push things with him. I don't *like* that you gave him what he wants, but I get why you did it. And if he says no, then don't risk pissing him off any more."

I nodded. "Okay," I said. "But I'll be there if I can."

"I know," Lucas said. "I'm surprised he even let you come over tonight. He *did* let you come over, right? Right?"

"Technically, no," I said. "He's not home on Friday nights, so I snuck out. But don't worry. I've got an inside man."

"Dude, don't push your luck," he said. "Get the hell out of here then. Shade, can you get him back there? Like, an hour ago?" Shade put her arms around me from behind and kissed my neck before she answered.

"I'll get him there before he even left," she said, and I could hear the smile in her voice.

"When did you turn into the rational one?" I asked as Shade grabbed her backpack and her helmet.

Lucas's face turned to stone and his voice was flat when he answered. "I'm not being rational, Chance. I'm being practical. I want your father to go down hard, and I'm not going to let anything get in the way of that. Not even you." He turned away and sat back down against the wall, and I let Shade pull me out into the hall.

"Remind me to never piss Lucas off," she said as she strapped her helmet on. She straddled the bike and looked over her shoulder at me as she started it.

"No shit," I said. "That boy's got his evil genius on."

I stood at the back of the throng of mourners, still a little surprised that my father had let me come. The black suit I wore was hot and confining, but I figured I still deserved a little extra suffering. The minister read the usual passages of comfort from the Bible, and I saw a few heads nodding as at least a few people seemed to find the solace the words offered. From where I was, I could see Lucas as he sat under the awning with his grandfather. Wanda and her family and a handful of other folks sat with him, and I wondered if their presence somehow made the grief easier to bear. Dr. Corwyn and Dee stood a few yards away, and I had seen at least one Sentinel lurking near another headstone about a hundred yards away. The goon with me today shifted uncomfortably beside me, but I didn't have any pity for him.

Elias Kotsakas was one of the few guys who had been with the old man from the beginning, and also one of the few who didn't have any compulsion spells laid on him. The only scars he had were on his fists, because he'd never even seen a fair fight up close. Where most of my father's hired muscle would have had a handgun under their left arm, Elias carried a micro-Uzi and three spare magazines for what he had once gleefully called 'crowd control.' I wondered if the thin Kevlar vest my father had insisted I wear under my suit today was more for protection from his enemies, or his friends.

The minister started the closing prayer, and I bowed my head. When he said the final "Amen," I looked over to see Elias with his head still up.

"I'm going to go talk to my friends," I said to him. "Stay here."

"I got orders to stick close to you," he said.

"You know why my father agreed to let me show up to this?" I asked, tilting my head toward the black limo where my father and Mike Cassavetes waited in air-conditioned comfort. He shrugged. "Mike told him it would help with the custody case because the press and the paparazzi will make him look like Father of the Freakin' Year. I think that guy over there has a telephoto lens. I'm sure the second I move, he's going to start snapping pictures of me. And of you, if you *act* like a goon and follow me around with your head up my ass. I'm sure Dad would love it if you made him actually *look* like a criminal." I watched the gears turn in his head for a few seconds.

"Don't go far," he finally said.

I gave him a dismissive wave and headed for Lucas. The guy with the long lens didn't even point it at me. The few photographers that were there were pretty much interested in what the Spartan was up to. I only became interesting if I was close to him. I headed for the two caskets and laid the pair of roses I was holding on them, then went to Lucas.

"I'm sorry, man," I said with my throat tight. He grabbed me in a fierce hug.

"Still not your fault," he said in my ear before he stepped back. "I got that email. It's done."

"Good. How are you holding up otherwise?"

"I have my moments," he said. "But … it could have been a lot worse. We didn't argue the last time we saw each other or say anything stupid."

Another mourner came up beside me, and I held my hand out. Something pressed against my palm when Lucas shook my hand, and he gave me a smile that didn't last long enough to reach his eyes before he turned to talk to them. I pocketed whatever he'd given me, then turned to his grandfather.

"He told me you saved his life," Hans said with a teary smile. "I thank God every day that you were there that night."

"If that lady hadn't hit him …" I said.

"*Ja,*" he said. "We forget the tiny miracles sometimes. But he won't forget that he owes you his life."

"I could live with that if it brought his parents back," I said.

"Nothing will," he said. "All you can do is give them justice."

"I hope that's enough." He nodded and shook my hand, then turned to the next mourner. Wanda gave me a tearful hug and held me tight for a few moments. I moved on to find myself face to face with a pair of gray eyes I would know anywhere. With her hair pulled up under the black hat and most of her face covered by a gauzy veil, I didn't recognize Shade until I was literally standing in front of her. Her eyes were red and I could see wet trails down her cheeks. Even without makeup, with her face a little blotchy from crying and her smile missing in action, she made my heart leap. I took her hands and cursed the black gloves she had on. I wanted to feel her skin on mine, the comfort of her touch.

Her face suddenly lit up, and her lips turned up a little at the edges.

"I'm so glad to see you," she said as the same words were leaving my mouth. Her smile got a little wider, and my world got a little brighter.

"Funerals suck," I said, and she nodded. "Almost as bad as living with my old man."

"How much longer are you stuck there?" she asked. "I miss talking to you, and seeing you. Wrestling in your backyard."

"I don't know," I said. "Too long, I know that. I miss you."

She ran her right hand along the glove on her left, and pressed a plastic baggie with something rectangular inside it into my hand.

"Got something for you. It isn't much, but it might help things go faster."

"Thank you," I whispered as I slipped it into my pocket.

"You're welcome," she said as she put her fingertips to her lips then pressed them to mine. "Your watchdog is coming this way."

I nodded, lips aching to kiss her for real, then turned and moved to intercept Elias. He nodded toward the car and fell in step beside me as I turned to go to the limo. As we went, I stuck my hand in my pocket and opened the baggie, then slipped whatever Lucas had handed me into it before closing it up again. Now the trick would be getting it past my father's paranoid security measures.

The driver got out and opened the door for me, and I slid into the back seat beside Cassavetes. Elias made for the black SUV behind it, and moments later we were on the road.

"Thank you for letting me go to the service, Dad," I managed to say without cringing or gagging.

"Shut up, son," my father snapped. I gave him a quick "Yes, sir" before lapsing into silence.

"We can spin this pretty easily," Mike was saying. "Grief-stricken son pays respects to his friend's family. Maybe send a wreath for the headstones."

"Deal with it," the old man said. "I've already wasted enough time on this good father bullshit. I swear, the boy's a bigger pain in the ass now than he was before I gave him to Dulka. And that son of a bitch Corwyn was there, too. Something unfortunate needs to happen to him real soon."

"I'm afraid that would only complicate things," Cassavetes said. "But once the custody case is settled, I'm sure he'll have an tragic accident."

"Fuck an accident," the old man snarled. "I want that fucker to pay for threatening me in front of my family. You got that?"

"Of course, sir. I'll see to it personally."

I sat there, ignored for the rest of the ride. While my father and Nick planned to get a shipment past customs, I slipped the baggie out of my pocket and stuck it between the seat cushions.

"Son, you didn't hear any of what we talked about," my father said as we pulled in the driveway to his McMansion. "I consoled you on your friend's loss."

"Yes, sir," I said. "Thank you." We got out and headed inside.

"Turn out your pockets, son," he said as soon as we were past the doors. I did it without hesitating. "Give me your jacket." It came off and I handed it to him. He searched through the pockets for a few moments, then tossed it on the floor and nodded to Nico, who stood ready with a bucket of ice water.

"Do we have to do that?" I asked.

"Yeah, we do," my father said with a chilly smile. "Corwyn was there. He might have put some kind of spell on you."

"Sir, if this is entirely necessary, may I suggest doing it outside or in the bathroom?" Jeremy said quickly. "The water runs into the carpet in the next room and mildews. The smell tends to permeate, and guests do remark on such things. Also, if pouring cold water over the lad removes spells, shall I summon Miss Lucinda to renew the compulsions?"

The old man turned to look at Jeremy, a thoughtful look on his face.

"Come to think of it, you're right, Jerry," he said, mangling the name. "Water doesn't dispel spells. But I want it done anyway. He was around Corwyn; this ought to make him think twice about getting chummy with him. Nico, get him outta those pants and that shirt before you douse him. They're dry-clean only. "

A few minutes later I was standing out on the back patio, shivering as cold water ran down my body. Nico threw me a towel, and tossed a pair of sweats and a t-shirt on one of the patio chairs. I got dressed as quickly as I could then followed him back into the house. Then all I could do was wait.

If the mansion was empty on Friday night, on Saturday it was packed. Kara's Lincoln Town Car left around seven, and several other cars pulled up around eight. Downstairs, I could hear men talking and laughing, and the occasional sound of a game of pool. The acrid smell of cigar smoke and the pungent odor of pot eventually overpowered the air conditioning. Around one, people started leaving, and by two, the downstairs was quiet. Kara's Lincoln pulled in half an hour later, and at a quarter to three, I grabbed a few things and slipped out of my bedroom.

Further down, I could hear Kara crying out in a steady rhythm. Stifling the urge to pour bleach in my ears, I padded toward the opposite end of the house. Years ago, the live-in staff were at the far end of the other wing. I padded past their quarters to the stairway that ran down between the kitchen and the supply rooms. Just outside the kitchen was the master key box, the thing I really needed. With one end of a paper clip folded into a makeshift tension wrench, I bent the tip of another paperclip to serve as a pick. After a few minutes of work, I worked the tumblers into place and the lock turned for me. All of the key hooks were labeled, so it was only a few seconds before I had the keyring for the limo in hand and was heading for the garage. The remote unlocked the doors for me from ten feet away, and I dug the baggie out from between the seat cushions. Then I locked it back up and jogged back into the kitchen.

One thing I'd learned working for Dulka was to always have an alibi, so after I put the keys back in the box and locked it up again, I raided the pantry and the refrigerator. Sure enough, as I padded back down the upstairs hall, one of the doors opened, and a bleary-eyed Hispanic woman poked her head out. I held up the bottle of Pepsi and snacks I'd liberated from the kitchen, then smiled at her and put a finger to my lips before I put my hands together in a pleading gesture. She rolled her eyes and waved me on before she closed the door.

Finally, in the safety of my room, I pulled the baggie out of my waistband and dared to actually look at it. The first thing out was the thumb drive Lucas had given me, then the folded-up note. I opened the note first. Shade's carefully done cursive strokes were covered by a Missouri driver's license and a bank card. The bank card was also taped to an index card that had a website and an account user name and password written on it. Her ID guy had come through for me. Then I read the note.

Dear Chance,

I can't tell you how much I miss you, baby. I'm going crazy not hearing your voice, and I can't wait to be in your arms again. Promise me you'll kiss me until I beg to come up for air.

I talked to Det. Collins. Herbert Vasquez is the youngest of three kids, and he's a junior at Prescott High School. His father was in the Army, and he lost both legs in Iraq. His older brother works for the DEA, and he's been missing in South America since April. Collins thinks Dulka may be promising him a way to find his brother. His address and phone number are on the back of the note. I hope this helps.

Come back to me soon, Chance. I miss you so much.

Love,
Shade

With a dozen things I wished I could say to Shade just then, I tucked the note into my waistband again and pulled out the thumb drive. For the first time since I'd been there, I got on the internet. The first thing I did was download a software security program and run it. Sure enough, the old man had planted a keystroke logger and some kind of program that would let him see what I was doing even while I was doing it. I killed both programs for the moment, but I didn't delete them. Then I plugged the thumb drive in.

Lucas had a list of all the things Gilbert had purchased. Everything he needed to cast the circle was on it, between what he'd ordered from my website and what he'd picked up in person at Spirit Garden and Mitternacht's. But Lucas had gone more than the extra mile. He'd researched the spell using the mountain of notes Dr. C had made me write down during the first weeks I'd been his apprentice, and he'd found the place and time where it would have to be cast. Not to be anything less than thorough, Wanda had also left a note.

Chance,
I figure Shade told you about Gilbert's dad and his brother. I talked to some people who know him, and I found out a little bit

139

more about him. His family has all served either in the military or law enforcement. His older sister is trying to go to nursing school, but between his father's medical bills and everything else, she's not going to be able to. Since his brother has been missing, the DEA has held his paycheck until he comes back or he's declared dead, so they can't touch that money. She's applying for scholarships but there's some pretty tough competition for them. I think it's a toss-up whether he's asking Dulka to help his sister get into nursing school, or if he's asking for his brother back. Either way, we think it's going to be hard to convince him not to go through with whatever deal he's being offered. Lucas thinks his father or his sister would be able to talk him out of this, but I'm not sure we should expose them to this.

The worst part about this is that Gilbert is a really good guy. Everyone who knows him says he'd do anything for his family. Including sell his soul, I guess. I don't know if any of this helps, but I thought you'd want to know as much as possible.

Blessed be,
Wanda

I closed out the program and leaned back in the chair. The more I knew about this whole thing, the worse it got. From what I'd read, coming from a family of cops and soldiers meant he came from a long line of heroes. It was probably a lot to live up to, and with his sister wanting to go to nursing school, I could see the pressure to either find his brother or step up and somehow save the day for her.

I stood up and ran my fingers through my hair as I paced the room. There weren't a lot of options open to me that weren't a huge roll of the dice, and if the numbers came up anything other than perfect, someone was going to end up losing their soul. I knew I couldn't let Gilbert make that sacrifice.

Worse yet, this didn't bring me any closer to understanding why my father and Dulka were working so hard to get me back. Dulka had a familiar now, and a willing one at that. Plus, there was McCain to consider. If I knew my old boss, Riker was as much there for Dulka's sake as for Lucinda's. What did they need with me? Was it simple revenge or was there a deeper

140

motive in place? Or was it a little of both? I really only had one way to tell.

I sat back down and logged into my email account, then put in the email addresses for Dr. C, Shade, Wanda, and Lucas. The message was simple:

Going to kick the hornets' nest and see what happens. Bring Hell down but leave the family out of this. Stay home for this. I hope to be back home soon.

I hit send, then deleted the email from the out box. Now all I could do was wait.

Chapter 9
~ A loyal man knows when to lie to you and when to do
exactly the opposite of what you tell him to. ~ Nick Cadmus,
Master mage

Demonic summoning spells are never bright and shiny. Which is why the best time to cast them is during the new moon, when the night sky is supposed to be darkest. Since Gilbert didn't have an ounce of magickal Talent as far as I knew, he was basically relying on tools, timing, brute force, and repetition to complete the spell. From where I sat, I could see the sweat pouring down his face in the light of the four black candles he'd placed around the circle. He'd been chanting for half an hour, slowly building energy and working himself into a trance state that would allow him to actually channel the magick he was trying to call up. His face was turned up to the sky, his aquiline nose in profile to me as he repeated the summoning spell over and over again with feverish intensity. By now, his dark hair was plastered to his skull, and his shirt was showing darker patches under his arms and around his neck and shoulders.

My vantage point was on a stone wall with an arched opening in the middle. What the building it belonged to used to be was lost to the past, but it was easy to climb in the dark and close enough to his circle that I could do what I needed to. My heart ached as I looked down at this kid with my mystic sight and saw the first black tendrils starting to creep into the pale gold of his aura. Streaks of pale blue were already laced into it, desperation and despair that had led him to this fateful moment deeply embedded in his psyche. His aura told me he was a good guy. Everything about him looked normal. He should have been worried about pimples and dates. He should have been obsessing over girls, movies, video games. Not demons. In all of the uncertainty that had filled my life the last few days, there was one thing I was sure of: Gilbert Vasquez didn't belong in that circle. If there was any place at all for him in the world I knew, it was on this side of things, fighting the darkness.

The power swirling around him grew, spinning into a vortex only I could see, drawing to a point thirty feet above his head. My left hand came up, ready to disrupt the spell, but I held myself back. No matter how badly I wanted to stop the spell, the only way I was going to settle this was to let him finish, and let Dulka show up.

In the middle of the circle, the copper brazier he'd lit flared to life with a burst of purple flame, and Gilbert reached for the black-handled ritual blade. In one smooth motion, he grabbed it and plunged it into the chalice, then stuck the dripping blade into the wooden pentacle in front of him.

A blue-black flame rose along the edge of the larger circle, traveling counterclockwise along its circumference. It was time for me to make my entrance. I gathered my feet under me and jumped off the wall. When my feet hit the ground, I let my momentum push me into a roll that brought me back to my feet only a couple of yards from the chalked outline of the circle. Two steps brought me right up to the edge, and I tossed a handful of salt into the air.

"*Circumvare!*" I called out as the circle's casting hit my own smaller circle. The flame split, leaving a trail between me and the inside of the circle, and at the same time sealing me off from the outside world. It continued on until it met the edge of Gilbert's carefully drawn summoner's circle.

"No!" Gilbert called out. "You'll ruin everything!"

"Your circle's fine, Gilbert," I said. His eyes went wide when he heard his name.

"How do you know …" he sputtered.

"Because I am great and powerful," I said.

"You're a meddling brat is what you are," Dulka's voice came from within the circle. Both Gilbert and I turned to look at the purple column of flame that had risen from the brazier. One blackened, cloven-hoofed foot slid into view, then the rest of Dulka's ugly self followed. His left horn was still broken, and his cheek bore a fresh set of criss-crossed scars from where I'd beaten him with his own broken horn. "It took you long enough to stick your nose in on this, though."

"What do you mean?" I asked.

Dulka let out a long, rumbling laugh. "I mean, you're right where I want you to be," he said. "Trying to save some stupid human's soul with a noble gesture."

"Hey!" Gilbert protested.

"Actually, I'm with the demon on that," I said to Gilbert. "You are being pretty stupid."

"I don't have any other choice!" he said. "If I can get Danny back and help Celia get into school, it's worth any trade!"

"Any trade?" Dulka asked with a smile. "Because your soul is only worth one of those. But if you can get me another soul ..."

"No!" Gilbert blurted. "Just my soul."

"Then choose," Dulka said. "Now."

"Wait!" I said. "Gilbert, you said it was worth any trade. If you believe that ..." I hesitated, hoping he was at least half the man I thought he was. "If you believe that, then I have a counter-offer. I'm offering my soul in place of yours." Both Gilbert and Dulka did a double take at that.

"You're making this so easy, boy," Dulka crowed. "I accept your offer. So, this just got a lot easier for you, Gil. You get one of the things you want, and you keep your soul. Or, you could have both and I get both your souls."

"Are you willing to trade someone else's soul for this?" I asked. "I know you're willing to sacrifice yourself, but are you ready to give someone else up in your place? Can you live with yourself if you do that?"

"You're just one guy," Gilbert said. "I don't know you. If it was up to you, I wouldn't get anything out of this. Well, I'm not walking away empty-handed. My family has been through enough that ... that ..." He faltered, and his eyes went to something outside the circle. I turned to see Shade standing at the edge of my circle, with Lucas and Wanda behind her.

"He's trying to save you from something worse than death," she said as she stepped forward. The circle stopped her cold, and she pressed against it. "Chance, if he gets you, he gets me, too. Please, let me in. I'm not letting you do this alone." A wordless cry escaped my throat at the sight of her, willing to pay the price of her soul.

"Your soul belongs to something else, girl," Dulka said. "As much as you'd like to play Juliet to his Romeo, you can't play this game.

"I can," Lucas said as he stepped through the shimmering barrier and came to my side.

"So can I," Wanda added. The barrier flared bright white as she passed it, and Dulka cringed back from the glow that permeated it. I put my hand to the barrier, pressing it against where Shade's palm lay. Tears ran down my face as I felt my heart lurch in my chest. She would have done it, I knew. Lucas and Wanda had, but she'd stepped forward first. As much as that meant to me, I was glad she was still on the other side. I turned to Lucas and Wanda.

"Guys, no, you can't," I said. "Please, I know what you're trying to do, but I can't let you do this."

"Lucky for you," Lucas said, "you can't stop us from doing it. Just promise me you won't be mad."

"I'm already … Hell, I can't be mad at you."

"We'll see if you say the same thing later on."

I growled in frustration and turned to Dulka. "Their souls aren't part of this," I said. "You already accepted my offer."

"But *he* hasn't accepted it," Dulka said, extending one taloned finger at Gilbert. "So, negotiations are still open. However, I do have a proposal for you, one that lets your friends walk away with their souls intact, and everyone has what they want. Well, almost everyone. You're still fucked." He made a gesture with his hand, and I felt like something was being pulled through me. I fell to my knees as blinding pain flared in my chest.

"Stop!" I yelled. "What are you doing?"

"Adding insult to injury, I think," Dulka said. "Salt in the wound, kicking a dead horse, pick your metaphor. See, it never occurred to you that you, as you are, are worthless to me. Your soul is broken, basically trash for the rubbish heap. It isn't *you* that I want. Frankly, I'm happy to be rid of you. But you have something that I do want … desperately." He drew the last word out, almost as if he was savoring it. He stretched his arm out and closed his fist, then pulled his hand back. Another wave of pain lanced through my chest, and I felt myself pulled toward the inner circle.

"Leave him alone!" Wanda yelled, and Dulka turned his face away. Some small part of my brain took a little too much pleasure in that, and I noted we were finally going to find out what Dulka really wanted.

"What?" I panted. "What are you after?"

"Nothing much," he said with a grim smile. "Just this." He made a gesture and I felt like my whole body split open. Then, there was a sense like something had come free, and I felt another presence nearby. I turned my head as I gasped for breath, then froze.

"No," I said. Hovering outside the circle was the Maxilla. With it under his control, he could rule Hell and Earth. I'd been played, and I never saw it coming. Dulka knew all along that I'd do this, that I would put my own soul on the line to save someone else's. He'd been counting on it. Even though I wasn't its Wielder, I was still the Page of Swords, the Seeker and guardian of it when it wasn't in the care of Steve Donovan. I was one of two people on Earth who could even pick it up. If he could keep it out of Steve's hands, then the good guys would be missing one of their most powerful weapons in whatever looming conflict that had made it choose a Wielder.

"You do realize that once I get your soul, which you've already freely offered and I've accepted, I still get this. It bonded to you the moment you first picked it up. 'No' isn't part of this bargain." Dulka laughed and gave me a broad grin. "Count yourself lucky, boy. The world is about to change, and when my Masters arrive to claim it, I'll rule at their left hand and you ... you will sit at my feet, exalted above all humans, privileged to serve Mammon through me."

"He still has to say yes," I said as I let Lucas and Wanda help me to my feet. I fought a cold chill as I struggled to straighten. If the Maxilla was bonded to me, and Dulka had my soul, there was a very real chance he could transfer that bond to himself. I fought the wave of despair that threatened to suck me down at the thought of a demon wielding the one weapon that might even be able to kill angels.

"Three souls," Dulka said, turning his attention to Gilbert. "Three people who never lifted a finger to help you before, when your family needed it the most. But now ... now they'll finally be doing something to benefit your family. It's someone else's turn to make the sacrifice."

Gilbert was shaking his head, and I could see the first doubts start to show in his eyes.

147

"Think about it, Gilbert," Wanda said. "Would you do this if your family was here to see you? Is this what your brother or your sister would want?"

"They'll never know!" Gilbert yelled. "They've sacrificed enough. It's my turn!"

"No, son," another voice came from the edge of the clearing. Gilbert let out an anguished sob as a man hobbled into the light. A pair of artificial legs supported him, but he also had two metal crutches to help keep him balanced. Slowly, he stepped forward, with a young woman beside him. Both of them looked like slightly different versions of Gilbert, the man with gray at his temples and in his mustache, the girl like a slightly narrower picture of him. Dulka cackled with glee, and I wanted so badly to punch him again.

"Poppa! No, you shouldn't be here!" Gilbert cried out.

"Yes, we should," the girl said. "I won't let you do this, Gil. You can't trade them for my school. I couldn't live with myself." As she spoke, his father hobbled toward my circle. When he reached the edge, he leaned on one crutch and grabbed Wanda by the arm, then yanked her out. Shade ran to her side and helped her to her feet as he pulled Lucas out by his shirt front. When he laid his hand on my arm, I shook my head.

"You can't pull me out," I said softly. "It's my circle. And I'd just come back in anyway."

"You don't understand, Celia," Gilbert was saying. "He can get Danny back. He can make sure you never have to worry about paying for nursing school, or if you even want to become a doctor. We've lost enough … too much. No one was there for us when Poppa lost his legs, or when Danny disappeared. All they want to do is make sure we still don't get anywhere."

"Then he can have my soul," his father said, and stepped into the circle. A moment later, Celia was at the edge, but her father had one hand on her shoulder as he shook his head. She shrugged his arm off and stepped in beside him, her eyes blazing. "This is what it means to sacrifice, Gilbert. No one pays our debts for us."

Time stood still for one eternal moment. I looked across the few feet between us, into Gilbert's eyes. Tears ran down his face, and his eyes went to his father, to his sister, then to me. Then he

148

looked at Lucas and Wanda, and finally his gaze turned to Dulka. He stood straight and wiped his eyes, then glanced back at us before he turned back again. Dulka was almost drooling in anticipation as he saw Gilbert's resolve harden.

"Demon, I've made my choice," he said. "I refuse." He stepped back, out of his circle, and it collapsed, leaving the main circle intact. I turned to Mr. Vasquez. In the distance, I could see lights in the woods. Either a dozen random bystanders had come to the park and brought flashlights with them, or a group of Sentinels was headed our way. Behind me, Dulka roared his outrage and rushed the edge of the circle, but it held against his assault.

"Go," I said as I pushed Mr. Vasquez toward the edge of the circle. "Talk to those people coming down the hill, and demand a trial."

"I don't understand," he said as he cleared the barrier.

"And I don't have time to explain. Just do what I told you to."

He nodded, then headed for Gilbert as Lucas and Wanda joined me in the smaller circle again. Dulka lurched back from the barrier, his fists suddenly smoking, and howled in pain. Shade hovered near the edge, her eyes gold and her teeth bared.

"Now what?" Wanda asked.

"Shouldn't he go away when the circle collapses?" Lucas asked.

"He was already here," I said. "Different summoning, different rules."

"So if it drops now?" Shade asked.

"Not even my father can control him until sunrise. Which means he'll probably go on a rampage and try to kill the old man."

"You know what we have to do," Lucas said as he shrugged my backpack off and set it on the ground. He gave the Maxilla a pointed look as he knelt and unzipped it.

"No," I said. "I won't kill him permanently if I don't have to. And how did you get my stuff?"

"I borrowed your car," he said as he pulled the LeMat out. "You did reload this thing, right?" He handed me my paintball gun, and I checked to see what it was loaded with. The white tape showed on top. Holy water and silver nitrate.

"Of course." The circle shuddered and Dulka hit it with a blast of Hellfire.

"So, we don't kill him all the way," Lucas said. "We just kill him a little."

"No!" I snapped. "My father will still have—"

"You can *fix* that!" Lucas snarled. "We have to send them a message tonight, or we'll never be free of their bullshit!"

I closed my eyes for a second and tried to find fault with his argument, but I couldn't. I handed Wanda the paintball gun.

"Stay behind Shade until you hear the signal."

"What's the signal?" Wanda asked as they stepped out of the circle.

"Screaming," I said. "Lots and lots of screaming." I turned to face Dulka. He'd gone quiet, and he was pacing the edge of the larger circle.

"Big words from the mewling mouths of children," he sneered. "You can't kill me with that thing. Your heart isn't pure, and your motive is pure vengeance. So here's what I think of your threats." He stopped and laughed, offering me his middle finger. Obviously, he'd missed the Evil Overlord List rule about cackling maniacally.

"I may not be able to kill you," I said as I jumped out of the circle and grabbed the Maxilla, then dropped the point and muscled it into a thrust as the circle dropped. His laughter stopped as the blade stabbed into the back of his right hand, and I saw it emerge on the other side. "But I can hurt you."

He looked at me in shock. "You stabbed me," he said.

I leaned forward and made sure he was focused on me. I only had seconds before the shock wore off.

"We have a message for you," I told him. "Don't fuck with us."

Lucas and Wanda stepped up beside me with Shade at their back.

"It's bad for your health," Lucas said as he raised the LeMat. I pulled the blade free, and Dulka screamed. Lucas pulled the trigger, and the first incendiary round caught Dulka in the chest. He staggered back as Lucas calmly thumbed the hammer back and pulled the trigger again, shooting him in the gut. Each shot staggered him, and Lucas stepped forward to deliver the next round. Wanda stayed next to me, her face sad as she watched Lucas fire again and again. When the hammer finally fell on an empty chamber, I walked forward and stood over Dulka's fading form.

"Wounds from the Maxilla," I said softly, "never heal. The blade has tasted your blood, and if you show back up on this plane again, it's going to want to finish the job. And so will I."

Beside me, Lucas pulled the hammer back and thumbed the lever down to fall on the twenty-gauge lower barrel.

"We might want to be back a ways before you pull the trigger on that one," I told him.

He nodded and we retreated to what I figured was a safe distance. For a moment, he just stood there, then he thumbed the hammer forward and shook his head.

"Let him suffer," he said.

"No," Wanda said as she took his hand and brought the gun up again. "It's not the right thing to do."

"What is the right thing?" Lucas asked incredulously.

"We're the good guys," she said. "We don't make people suffer longer than we have to." He nodded, and I turned away, my face suddenly hot. Behind me, the gun went off again, and the night lit up as Lucas put Dulka out of his misery and sent him screaming back to Hell.

Moments later, Sentinels came out of the woods with their *paramiir* in blade form. Carter, square jaw leading the way, walked up to me and scowled.

"Gunfire, demons, and explosions," he said with a trace of humor in his voice. "And you at the middle of it. Why am I not surprised?"

"This time, none of that was me," I said.

"What's the deal with the boy?" he said as more Sentinels entered the clearing. "His old man says he turned the demon down." Two Sentinels escorted Gilbert into the brighter light, and Dr. Corwyn and Gage emerged right behind them.

"He did," I said. "On his own. He also didn't technically summon the demon. It was already here."

"He cast the circle, he called its name," Carter said. "That was all he needed to do."

"His family has already been through enough," I said. "Don't do the extra crispy justice thing on him. I'll even vouch for him."

"Lucky for you, Corwyn already did, but I'll hold you to it, kid. The Council meets tomorrow night. Be there."

"I will be," I said.

Twenty minutes later, the fire was out and the world was once again calm, if a little scorched in places. Aversion runes hung in the area around the collapsed circle, deflecting any attention away from the area for the next few days. Lucas and I were standing at the edge of the clearing, though where I really wanted to be was halfway across the opening with Shade. An awkward silence was stretching between us, and I couldn't figure out how to be diplomatic, so I just forged ahead.

"I told you I didn't want his family involved," I said, letting a little heat creep into my voice.

"Why not?" Lucas said. "What he was doing affected their lives."

"Because I was afraid they'd go and put themselves in harm's way. And guess what, that's *exactly* what they did."

"And that's exactly why I *brought* them," he said, his own voice louder now. "Because that was the only thing that was *certain* to convince him to turn Dulka down."

"I almost had him there on my own. Now he's going to have to live with them seeing that for the rest of his life."

"And maybe he should!" Lucas yelled. "You had to live with your choices, no one gave you the easy out there. So excuse the hell out of me if I think this guy needs to face the music for his." He stared at me, his jaw set, eyes ablaze, and I was reminded again of a Chihuahua with an attitude. Still, he was wrong about one thing.

"No, Lucas, you're the one who had to live with my stupid decisions," I said.

"Stop it," he said, and he punched me in the chest. "Wanda was right. What your father did, that's all on him. The only thing I need to know ..." he stopped, his voice thick. "Is he going to pay for it? Or are you going to keep on taking the blame for him?"

Years of rage welled up in my chest, and I could feel it creeping into my aura. "My father has a lot to answer for," I said. "And I swear to you, he will." The rush of ethereal wind lifted a few strands of my hair, and I saw his flutter a little as well as my whole body tingled with the power of that promise. His eyes went wide at the sensation that a mage's promise left.

"Does that happen to you a lot?" he asked.

"Every time I make a promise," I told him. "A mage's oath is binding."

Wanda and Shade came over, their faces expressing varied degrees of "What the fuck?" Shade put her arm around my waist and gave me a level look.

"What did you just do?" Wanda asked.

"You felt that?"

"Baby, I think everyone within a mile of you felt it," Shade said with a shake of her head and a smile. "Now, answer the question, before an adult asks it." She nodded toward Carter and Dr. C, who were both headed our way with more demanding expressions clouding their brows. Gage was in tow, trying to look serious but mostly succeeding in looking lost.

"I promised Lucas I'd make my father pay for the things he's done."

"I'm coming with you," Shade said. "Try and stop me," she added before I could even think of protesting. I shook my head and held up one hand.

"Not stupid," I said. "I'll be glad to know you have my back."

"Always," she said, her voice bordering on a growl in its intensity. "And you have mine."

By then, Dr. C and Carter had made it to our little circle.

"What oath did you just make?" Carter demanded.

"I'm claiming the right to carry out justice against my father," I said. Dr. C's expression went from demanding to shocked, while Carter's turned thoughtful.

"Are you sure about this, Chance?" Dr. C asked. "If he kills you or beats you somehow, the Council can't step in, and he's off the hook for everything. You've already risked more than I would have liked."

"I'm sure. I made a promise to Lucas. I'm not going to break it."

153

"As the wronged party, we gave you the option of calling for justice," the Sentinel said. "Not the option to exercise it on your own."

"He can, however, challenge his father," Dr. C said quietly. "Procurso Judacatem, Trial by combat."

"The man isn't a mage," Carter said, sounding more disappointed than upset. "He can't be called to face the Procurso Judacatem."

"Technically, he's a warlock," Dr. C reminded him. "As such, Chance can challenge him like he could any other mage."

"He did summon a demon, and he does have access to focuses for releasing spells," I added.

Carter nodded and smiled. "It's an old tradition, and pretty much no one uses it anymore," he said, and held his *paramiir* sword out in front of him with his free hand on the blade. He nodded to me, and I placed my hand on the blade beside his. "But it's still valid. Chance Fortunato, the Council has found that you have been wronged by your father. You have chosen to forego the Council's justice and in its stead have exercised your right to Procurso Judacatem. You may challenge Stavros Fortunato to seek satisfaction by battle judgment. The Council agrees to abide by the outcome of this challenge, and will consider justice done."

"I understand," I said.

"Then the burden is yours. Settle this quickly, and do not let the sun set on your vengeance."

"Oh, I don't plan on letting the sun rise on it," I said.

"I approve," Carter said. "If he refuses to meet you honorably, your second can fight at your side. If you can find one, an impartial witness is recommended."

"I'll stand as witness," Gage said. I did a double take and frowned at him. Carter smiled and clapped a hand on his shoulder.

"You're way too happy about this," I told him.

"I thought the Hands of Death should have asked for your forgiveness for killing him, not your permission," he said.

"I have my reasons for keeping him alive," I said. He grunted at that, and I turned to Shade and Gage. "Let's go do some damage." I felt like a bad ass as we headed for the trail to the parking lot. Halfway there, I remembered I didn't have my keys.

Chapter 10
~ Barbarism with the trappings of civility, without the irritation of mutual consent. ~ 18th century pamphlet calling for the abolition of Procurso Judacatem

"So, who are you and what have you done with Winthrop Gage?" I asked as I pulled out of the parking lot. "I mean, I'm glad you're coming along … at least, I think I am, but a few days ago, I was lower than whale shit as far as you were concerned." He was quiet for a few minutes, and I looked over at him to make sure he was still awake and breathing.

"Less than a day after I met you, you fought a demon," he said slowly. "Since then, your mother has been arrested, your friend's family has been killed, and, if your sister's dreams are accurate, you've been beaten nearly senseless several times by your father." His voice was soft, every word seeming like it belonged to someone other than the guy I had met back in San Angelo. Hearing the last week described all at once made it sound more than a little overwhelming.

"Not my best week ever," I said.

He let out a strangled laugh. "And you're still an incorrigible wit," he said. "Tonight, I find out you put your own soul on the line to save a stranger. And that you fought another demon."

"I had some help with that," I said.

"I heard," he said. "Your friends gambled their own souls alongside you. Even after you told them to stay away." He fell silent for a few moments after that. "I don't know anyone who would do that for me."

"And all of this somehow adds up to 'Chance is a good guy'?" I asked.

"Good may be going a bit far," he said with a slow smile. "Dedicated is the word I'd use. You have endured hardship after hardship, some of it by choice and still you persevere. How can I do anything less than see my own task through to the end?"

"Even if it means following me into a war zone?" I asked.

"Even so. I am a Gage and I will not shame my family name. Besides, I don't think your father is going to be nearly as much of a challenge as a demon."

"He can surprise you," I said as we turned onto the road leading into the Pittsburgh district. As we did, my cell phone rang. I handed it to Gage and asked, "Whose name is on the screen?"

"It says Jeremy," he read back. I pushed the button to answer it.

"Put it on speaker," I said. Once Gage nodded, I spoke again. "Jeremy, what's up?"

"The young woman who works for that loathsome creature is here, along with her ... bodyguard," he said, his accent somehow even more proper than ever. "She seems quite agitated, and she's informed your father that you are not in the house. He's most upset, and I fear he's going to do something most unpleasant. He's already made threats against several people whom you care for, including your mother."

"Jeremy, get the hell out of there," I said. "Pack a bag if you can and *go.*"

"Tell him to take his passport," Gage said.

"Did you hear that, Jeremy?" I asked.

"I did, sir," he said, his voice sounding a little more distant, like he'd moved his mouth away from the phone. "May I ask why?"

"I'm on my way there right now. And if things go right, you may be unemployed come morning."

"Thank heavens, sir," he said. "And thank you."

"You're welcome," I told him. "I'm sorry it took me so long."

"Not at all, Master Chance. He'll no doubt have his men on alert. Do be careful, and, if you don't mind my saying, good hunting, sir." He disconnected the line, and I tossed the phone to Gage.

"Dial the first number," I said as I handed him a sheet of paper. Moments later, I heard the ringing of a phone as Gage put the call on the speaker.

"Who the hell is this?" my father's voice came over the line. "Who gave you this number?"

"Hi, *Dad,*" I said.

"Chance!" he bellowed. "You worthless little son of a bitch! I hope you said goodbye to your friends, that bitch you call a girlfriend, and that asshole Corwyn, because I'm gonna kill every last one of them unless you bring your ass back here right now!"

"Shut up and listen, old man," I growled. "I'm coming for you. I challenge you to trial by combat, Procurso Judacatem. Meet me at the gate, and you might walk away from this with just an ass beating."

"Fuck you!" he said. "I'm no wizard."

"No, you're a warlock," I said. "You summoned a demon and you made a deal with it. That's mage enough. If you're not at the gate in ten minutes, I'm gonna huff and I'm gonna puff and I'm gonna blow your house down." I ended the call and tossed the phone in the back seat.

"That was dramatic," Gage said. I shrugged.

"I've done better, but I couldn't come up with a good movie line," I said. "Do me a favor? Take the white-marked hopper off of the Ariakon, and put the one with the blue tape on instead."

"What are those?"

"Knock-out doses. Grab a couple of the red ones, too. They're a little more … explosive."

"You don't think he's going to meet you at the gate, do you?"

"Smart money isn't on that bet," I said. "Before we get there, I need to know. Are you just an observer here? Or can I count on you to fight?"

"Do your father's people know the difference? Or respect it?" he asked. I shook my head. "Then you can count on me to fight. Strictly in self-defense, of course."

"Of course," I said. "Then get that light spell of yours ready."

My father wasn't waiting for me at the gate. Lucinda and Ryker, however, were. Ryker took up an acre of driveway, and I was willing to bet that the blue sweat pants that he'd cut off at the knee on him would be a lot bigger on me. I didn't even want to think of the stress his tank top was under. Behind him, I had almost missed Lucinda, partly because she was in the shadow of my headlights. As Shade pulled up beside me and cast the bike's headlight on her, I realized that she was also wearing black. Just not very much of it. A black pleather bra and hot pants both rode low on their respective parts, while a pair of black hose covered her legs until they were swallowed up by the knee-high boots she wore. She had on a pair of matching half-gloves and a black leather hood with cat ears over the top half of her face. The most important accessory she wore was the belt around her hips, with the pouches that I would have bet the entirety of my non-existent fortune were full of focuses.

I stepped out of the car and stepped into the light with Shade on my left and Gage on my right. Ryker looked down at Lucinda, and she took a step forward.

"Okay," I said. "Looks like the old man is a no show. We can—"

"Kneel!" Lucinda barked as she waved a black riding crop at me. "*Pareo!*" The glyphs of the compulsion spell flared a faint red in my aura sight, but with Dulka banished, it was amazing that she had any power at all.

"*That's* your focus?" I said, pointing at the riding crop and laughing.

"*Pareo!*" she repeated. The compulsion hit my defenses with all the power of a gnat on a windshield. I let out an exasperated sigh.

"About that," I said. I brought my right hand up with my new wand in it. "*Compulsis negatis.*" The glyphs fizzled and disappeared, and Lucinda's eyes went wide. Her hand went for the belt, and I had a split second to react.

"*Obex!*" I said, and the black darts of energy she'd thrown at me sizzled against the invisible barrier that I'd erected between us. "Gage! Now!" Even as I said it, I closed my eyes.

"*Fotizei!*" he called out, and even with my eyes closed, I could see the flash of white. I heard two different voices cry out, and I opened my eyes. Lucinda and Ryker were both blinking and looking around as if trying to find something. The Ariakon came up as I walked forward and pulled the trigger three times. Lucinda made a confused-sounding noise before she hit the ground, and Ryker turned toward me with his teeth bared and a look of pure hate in his eyes. He started to move toward me, and I tried to bring the paintball gun to bear on him. I still had seven shots left; hopefully it would be enough to drop him. His fist drew back as his feet pushed him forward. Before I could pull the trigger even once, a dark form leapt in front of him. His right fist came forward in a blur, and the dark figure held up one hand.

His fist hit the open palm in front of it and stopped cold. For a moment, he just looked at his hand, his brows together. In the split second that things were still, the dark figure resolved into Shade's hybrid form, mostly human-shaped but with a lot of wolf showing. Her body was covered in fur, and two-inch-long claws tipped each finger. Her hair was a mane of black that fell down to the small of her back, and I could see every muscle flex as she held Ryker back. He grimaced and let out a grunt as he leaned forward, trying to overpower her. For a moment, it looked like he was making progress, but while his strength was beyond even human maximums, it was still no match for Shade's. She adjusted her stance and slowly straightened her left arm, pushing Ryker back until she was at full extension. He roared and swung with his left, but Shade was simply not there, ducking under the punch as she sprang back, crouched and then leaped straight up. Her feet came up as she reached the top of her arc, about shoulder height on Ryker, then shot forward to slam into his chest. He flew backward and hit the iron gate as Shade arched her back and did a handspring so that she landed on her feet beside me. The gate bent under the impact, then fell backward, its top hinge snapped.

Metal screeched in protest as Ryker tore himself free of the gate's decorative bars and got to his feet again. Shade shook her head as he staggered forward. With a yell, he took a couple of steps and leaped into the air, his fist back, knees drawn up under him, a perfect-looking flying punch. Shade jumped to meet him.

When they met, I expected traded punches or something. Instead, it was like they stopped in midair, then spun around somehow and just … fell. Ryker hit the ground with a sound like a slab of beef on a butcher's block, and Shade landed with her feet on either side of him. Her fist came down like a pile driver, and Ryker's arms and legs flailed once as he let out a wheezing sound. He gasped and retched as he struggled to get to his feet, but Shade seemed to be done fighting fair. She grabbed him by one wrist, planted her feet wide and twisted her body, sending him flying into the square stone column that supported one of the gates. As he staggered away from the shattered stone, she

161

grabbed him again and repeated the process with the other column. And he *still* tried to get up.

She let out a growl and walked over to him, grabbed him by the throat and proceeded to use his face like a punching bag for about a second. I didn't even want to try to count how many times she hit him. But when she let go of him and stepped back, he stood there for a moment, then his knees wobbled and went out from under him. As he sat there on his butt, he managed one more weak swing before he flopped onto his back.

"Dear Lord!" Gage said. "Did you kill him?"

I looked at him with my mystic sight, but his aura was strong, and the spells on him were still there, though fading. I looked over at the unconscious form of Lucinda, and saw something completely unexpected. Hovering over her were the two matrices I'd constructed the day she'd first cast the compulsion spells on me. One looked half-depleted, which explained how she'd been able to fuel Dulka's spell focuses even after he'd been banished. They must have transferred when she'd kissed me, since I'd been in the process of severing the two right when her lips had touched mine.

"The augments Dulka gave him should heal him, but he's not gonna be happy about it," I said. I grabbed my backpack from the back seat and walked forward, leaving Gage to follow or wait. As I passed Lucinda, I knelt and put my hand to her temple and whispered "*Vox probrum, aufero quod transfero volo.*" It was an old spell that let me pull my own energies off of someone else and bring them back to me. The tingle of magick spread up my forearm as the energy-filled lattices attached themselves to my aura again.

"I believe your father has refused your challenge," Gage said as he caught up to me.

"Yeah, I'm going to say that's a pretty solid no." I paused for a moment and took the chameleon charm off my pack and handed it to him. "That should keep you from drawing any serious fire, but stay under cover and stay behind me."

"You can count on it. And Chance ... *bonne chasse.*" I smiled at the French, the same benediction Jeremy had given me earlier. Up ahead I heard a single gunshot, then a man screamed. Gage hastily put the charm on and faded from sight.

Shade was waiting for me when I made it to the portico. One goon was laying crumpled by the door, one arm and one leg at decidedly unnatural angles. Off toward the garage, I could see an easy dozen cars. The old man must have put out the call for all hands on deck.

"Was he it?" I asked her.

She shook her head. "There was another one," she said, her voice deeper and rougher. "I think he's in Kansas by now."

"Well, knocking's out of the question," I said as I turned to face the door.

"Hey little pig, let me in," Shade growled.

I stuck my hand in my pocket and grabbed the TK wand. "Not by the hair of his chinny chin chins," I said and pointed the wand at the door. "*Ictus!*" The doors flew off the hinges with a *boom* and took the three goons behind them along for the ride. Shade leaped in and punched another guy who had been standing off to one side. I stepped through as a fifth goon came around the corner with a Taser in hand. I popped him with a knockout shot and he dropped. I heard the pop of a Taser being launched, and Shade stiffened beside me as the gun clicked and sent current through her. She snarled and yanked the wires loose as I put two shots into the goon at the top of the stairs who had tagged her. I headed into the house, the threshold not even slowing me down since the old man had made me a resident here days ago. When I got to the lower hallway, I turned right and saw half a dozen goons waiting for me.

"*Obex!*" I spat, and the shield went up. A trio of paired Taser leads sparked as they bounced off the shield. I dropped it as the other three men rushed forward, and sent a broad wave of telekinetic force their way. They tumbled like bowling pins, and Shade leaped into the middle of them before they could get back up.

"Chance, behind you!" I heard Gage say, and turned to fire a round from the Ariakon. The guy coming up behind me dodged to the side and raised his Taser, only to find himself blinded by a flash of brilliant light from Gage. I nailed him with the second knockout round and nodded a quick thanks to Gage's blurred outline before I turned back toward my objective. Ahead of me, Shade was pounding the last of the bigger group into submission.

163

She looked up after her fist slammed into the face of the last of them.

"You good?" I asked as I walked up to her. She nodded and let the guy drop to the floor.

"I don't hear any others except for whoever's in there," she said, pointing to the door into my father's study. I gave her a nod, then turned to face those doors. While I'd served Dulka, I'd hated them. Whenever I came here with my old boss, it was usually to get yelled at and to take a beating. Not tonight though. I was about to give my father a taste of his own medicine. But, being my father, he was a tricky bastard, and I'd learned from his example.

I took a calming breath and closed my eyes, then opened my Third Eye, the source of my mystic sight. When my eyelids lifted, the physical world was slightly out of focus, but the energies around me were clear as day to me. Four auras were on the other side of the door, with two in the middle of the room and two spread out to either side. One of the two in the middle had the reddish-black smear across it that I'd seen a hundred times before. If I had to guess, the old man was hiding behind one of his men. The other three were nothing pretty, either. Each of the goons' auras was stained with the dark red that bordered on the purple of violence, with the putrid green of greed running in streaks through them.

"Four inside," I said softly. "Two in the middle, the other two here." I pointed toward the two spread-out auras, and Shade nodded. "Gage, over there, beside the door. Stay down until we give you the all clear." There was a shifting blur on my left, and I waited while he moved.

"Chance, are you out there, boy?" my father's voice came from the other side of the door. On my right, Shade mimed taking a deep breath, and I smiled.

"I'm gonna huff, and I'm gonna puff," I said as I drew on the stored energy I'd taken from Lucinda.

"This is your last chance to—" the old man started to say.

"*ICTUS!*" I roared. The doors didn't come off the hinges. They exploded. The guy in front of the desk caught the residual energy from the blast and went sailing over it as I saw my father dive for the carpet. Chips of wood stuck in the front of the desk, the drapes, and anything softer than cherry wood. I raised my shield with a whispered command, then stepped into the room as the other two men were picking themselves up off the carpet.

"And I'm gonna blow your house down," I said. Shade went for the guy on the right, and I put two knockout rounds into the one on my left. The guy behind the desk stood up, and I saw a familiar face. Elias looked at me, then at Shade, before drawing a blade and rushing Shade. My shot went wide, and before I knew it, he had one hand around her neck and the blade at her throat. She stiffened as the point touched her skin, and her eyes rolled down to look at it.

"That's right, bitch, it's silver," he said as he transferred it to his other hand. His right hand came back up with a heavy revolver and he pointed it at her head. She whimpered for a second and her eyes went to the gun as her nostrils flared. "Oh, ya smell that, huh? Smell the silver in those bullets? Yeah, I blow your head off with these, your bitch ass stays dead."

My father came out from behind his desk, a smaller pistol in his hand, this one trained on me.

"Put the wand and the gun down, Chance," he said. "Now, or your girl's brains are my new wallpaper." I looked at Shade, who seemed to have her fear under a little better control. I focused my will on the revolver and let my breath out through my mouth.

"Do it, punk!" Elias said as he thumbed the hammer back.

"*Necto,*" I breathed. "It's okay, babe. He can't hurt you now," I whispered, knowing that of all the people in the room, only she could hear me. She nodded and shifted her feet slightly.

"Hell with it," my father said when I turned to him. "Kill the little cunt."

"*Capio!*" I snapped as Shade moved. The old man gasped as bands of telekinetic force closed around him and slammed his arms down to his side. Shade grabbed Elias by the wrists and twisted. There was a series of wet snaps as his right arm bent in places it was never supposed to, and he let out a high-pitched shriek as the gun and knife tumbled to the floor.

"*Rursus*! I said, and my father flew backward to slam into the wall. Shade bent forward and sent Elias flying across the room to slam into one of the bookshelves. As he fell headfirst onto the floor, she reached down and picked up the silvered dagger. With his right arm cradled to him, Elias pushed himself into a sitting position, then twisted his arm around for the butt of the pistol still holstered under his left arm. Shade tossed the dagger into the air, caught it by the point, then flung it across the room. It hit Elias in the shoulder and drove him back against the bookshelf. He let out a shrill scream that resounded through the house and didn't let up until he ran out of air. Then, after a sobbing breath, he screamed again. After a few seconds, I put the last two knockout rounds into him.

"Thank you," Shade said as she rolled her eyes and massaged her blistered fingertips.

"Any time," I said as I walked toward my father.

"What do you want?" my father said as I got closer. "Money? No, wait, I'll get the charges against your mother dropped. Whatever you want, I can get it for you, Chance. Be reasonable about this. We don't have to be enemies here."

"What I want," I said as I pulled him down to look me in the eye, "is to watch you burn in Hell. I want to watch you squirm in a jail cell. I want to see everything you made me build for you blow up and burn while you watch it happen. But you know what I really want? More than anything else in the world?"

"Whatever it is," he said quickly, "I can make it happen."

"I want you to give Lucas's parents back," I choked out, and he went pale.

"Son, I'm sorry about—" he said before I slammed my fist into his face. Blood gushed from his nose as his head rocked back.

"I am NOT your son!" I shouted at him. "You will NEVER call me that again. Swear it on what's left of your soul."

"I won't, I probise," he mumbled.

"Say it all," I yelled at him. "Every word of it. On your soul."

"I probise," he began haltingly, "on by soul ... I won't call you sund again." His eyes widened a bit as I felt the power of a mage-given promise rush through him. Evidently, Dr. C had been right about his summoning Dulka making him mage enough to count. I gestured and he flew back against the wall.

"You're about to lose a lot of money, old man," I said as I kicked his trash can aside and knelt beside the desk. I lifted the flap of carpet under it and exposed the safe set in the floor below. Then I pulled the list of info I'd stashed from my back pocket and looked up the combination.

"How did you …?" he asked as I spun the dial.

"I'm an apprentice mage with an good teacher," I said as the final number came around. "You'd be amazed at what I know now." I turned the handle and it came open with a soft click.

"Chance, please," my father said when I drew out the black cloth sacks in the safe. "Listen to me, you don't know what you're doing here. You can have half of my money, hell, take three-quarters! Just don't … don't do anything with those." I reached back into the safe and pulled out the bank books and credit cards, finally grabbing the stack of compact disks at the bottom. Each one had a series of names written on it, and if I was guessing right, blackmail info on each of the people named on the front. Dr. C and I had talked about these, and remarkably, he'd agreed with me about what to do with them. I turned and set them on the desk.

"Shade, can you hang onto those until we can get them into the right hands?" I said as I grabbed the bags and went to the fireplace in the wall to my right. I tossed the focus bags onto the grate, then went to the painting beside the mantle and swung it to the side. This combination was digital, so it went faster.

"Chance, wait!" my father cried out as the bolts clicked open. I looked over my shoulder at the old man and smiled. Jeremy had warned me about the trap inside. Once I had the door open about three inches, I slipped my hand inside and felt for the wire that was connected to a hook set into the door. Once it fell free, I opened it the rest of the way and looked inside. A metal plate had been set up to hold a grenade of some kind with a two-inch-high metal ring around the bottom. The pin had been straightened and pulled partway out, leaving only a fraction of an inch to go before it came free. I reached in and carefully pushed the pin back in, then pulled it out of the safe. The side read:

Grenade, Hand
Offensive, MK IIIA2

My father flinched as I set it on his desk, then I went back to the safe and pulled out the banded stacks of bills and the smaller black bag behind them. There was a stack of fake passports, but I left those for the cops.

"Take what you want, s—. Anything in there you need. Just leave me something to work with," the old bastard said, his voice now starting to rise in pitch.

"Everything you have," I said as I reached back into the safe and pressed against the back, "came from me." The false back fell forward, revealing the last bag of focuses, the most critical ones. Everyone who worked with him personally, except Elias and a few of his hand-picked cronies, had compulsion spells on them, and he kept those focuses separate.

"I'll get it all back," he said. "No matter what you do, or how much you destroy, Dulka will help me rebuild. If we make a deal, we don't have to part as enemies. You don't want that."

"Lucas sent Dulka back to Hell," I said as I tossed the focus bag onto the grate with the others and turned to face him. "Your contract with him is null and void, just like you asked me to do once. Remember? Well, now you get your wish. Your soul is yours again. And you already made an enemy of me when you killed my best friend's family. Cross me again, and I'll do more than destroy your life."

He let out a harsh laugh. "How can you do worse than that?" he asked.

"You can still walk and you have use of your arms," I said as I walked up to him. He went pale as I called up Hellfire. "And so far, you don't have any brain damage. Yet." He gulped and looked away from me.

"Chance, time is running short," Shade said as she looked at her cellphone. "Collins says the police are on their way. They'll be here in ten minutes." I nodded and turned toward the fireplace, my left hand blazing with Hellfire.

"*Miterre!*" I spat, and a ball of the blue-black flame streaked across the room. It hit the focuses and disrupted all of the spells at once. The result was more than a little spectacular. A multicolored shockwave slammed through the room and knocked us all staggering. My father dropped to the floor as the explosion of magick disrupted my TK spell for a moment, but Shade was on him in a heartbeat. Even Gage was visible for a moment before the chameleon charm reset.

"I swear, I'm gonna-urk!" he gurgled as Shade's hand closed around his neck.

"You won't do anything," she snarled in his face. "See, I have a monster inside me. Sometimes, the only thing that keeps it on the right side of a very thin line…is the feel of your son's arms around me." She tilted her head and bared her teeth at him for a moment. "If you hurt him, if you hurt *us* … I will rip your heart out of your chest and eat it in front of you. And if you're lucky…that will be the *first* thing I do to you." She let him go, and he fell to his knees, with his hand clutching at his neck.

"I'm going home now," I said as I tucked the money and other goodies in my pocket. "You will not bother me again. Or my friends. Or Mom or Dee. Between what's here, and the evidence on your computer, you're pretty much screwed." He smiled at that, and I turned to go.

"That computer is clean!" he cackled, his voice still rough. I kept going, and his laughter was suddenly cut short by the sound of a fist against flesh.

"His computer isn't clean, is it?" Shade asked when she and Gage caught up to me.

"Nope," I said. "I put the same keystroke logger on it that he put on the one in my room, then looked up every incriminating piece of business he had. Jeremy even scanned in his secret ledger. And if they talk to Jeremy … my father isn't going to see sunlight for a long time." Her hand found mine, and we walked to the car in silence from there. When we got to the gate, Gage headed for the Mustang, but I walked with Shade to her bike.

"We made quite a team tonight," she said as she put her arms around my neck.

"Yeah, we did," I said. A line from *Sex Metal Barbie* came to mind. "And you … you were the belle of the brawl. You kicked serious ass tonight." I looked into her eyes, and remembered the moment at the circle. My heart pounded against my ribs as I kissed her. "Shade, I realized something tonight. I guess it's been true for a long time, but ... I just couldn't put it in perspective until tonight. When you tried to step into the circle with me, I don't think I've ever felt so relieved or happy as when it stopped you."

Her gaze came up to meet mine, and I could see a dawning hurt in her eyes.

"Why?" she asked, her voice small.

169

"Because I'd rather die than let Dulka have your soul. Because ... I love you." Her smile lit up her eyes, and she kissed me deep.

"I've loved you for a long time," she said. "I think since the night you told me no." In the distance, sirens started to sound, and we both looked down the road.

"We're not done talking about this," I said as I stepped back, feeling the heat of her body fade.

"You can tell me you love me any time you want," she said.

"I do ... I will!" I said as I turned and went to the Mustang.

"The police are en route, and you two are exchanging emotional platitudes?" Gage said with a slight upward tug at his mouth. "You're hopeless, plebe, completely hopeless."

"Was that a joke?" I asked.

"A humorous observation," he corrected. "Nothing more."

Chapter 11
~ Ruthless men are weak men, my king. ~ Merlin

Dr. C's knock at the door brought me out of the doze that I'd slipped into. My head came up and I yawned. The sunlight coming through the west window was a lot closer to horizontal than I remembered it being the last time I'd checked. Off to my right, Dee was a quiet little puddle of cuteness on the bed, her own seemingly endless supply of energy exhausted for the moment. Her Sonic Screwdriver dangled from limp little fingers, and her book had fallen over. Junkyard was curled up beside her, and he gave me a sleepy look before he laid his head back down.

"When was the last time you ate? Or slept for that matter?" Dr. C said as he stepped into my temporary room.

"Not sure, but I think it was a day that ended with a y."

"You've been awful busy up here," he noted.

"I've been taking care of a few things," I said.

"What kind of things?" he asked. "And don't try telling me that it's better if I don't know. You're my apprentice. I'm accountable for what you do whether I know about it or not."

"A lot of my father's money just disappeared," I said as I looked back at the laptop. "Some of it went into savings accounts for my friends' and my sister's college funds. Some of it, I think, is going to randomly pay off some people's houses here in a couple of months. I think Celia Vasquez just got a grant to go to college, too. A lot of it is going to a bunch of charities. My father is about to be a very generous man."

"And none of this generosity is finding its way to you?" he asked.

"No, sir," I said. "It can't. All of this is because of what Dulka did for him ... what I did for him. A lot of people got hurt making him rich. I'll fix what I can, but I'm not going to turn a profit on other peoples' pain."

"The argument could be made that you got hurt in the process as well," he said.

"I also did a lot of the hurting. Kinda cancels it out for me."

"I'm proud of you, Chance," he said. "Officially, I can't condone stealing from your father, but I think playing Robin Hood is a worthy cause. And sometimes, the Council sets itself

171

above *cowan* law, so I can't say you're not following the example set for you by your elders. Speaking of said elders, though … it's time." I nodded and reached over to wake Dee up as he left the room.

"We're off to see the wizards," I said as she blinked at me with barely focused eyes. I could hear Dr. C calling for Gage downstairs.

"Is Mom gonna be there?" she asked, her voice a little slurred as she made the trip to full wakefulness. Junkyard got up and jumped off the bed as she sat up.

"No, Mom's not coming home until tomorrow at least," I told her as we walked to the door. "But she *is* coming home." Dee took my hand and followed me out to the Mustang.

We followed Dr. C's Range Rover to the old Joplin airport. It had been shut down sometime in the seventies, back when New Essex had formally annexed the city, and Joplin had become a district of its larger neighbor. He took the main road toward the old terminal, then took a left just before the main parking lot, which led to a road that eventually wound around to a hangar. He pulled to a stop and got out. I grabbed the Maxilla and slung it across my back, then Dee, Junkyard, and I followed him through the smaller door and found ourselves standing on the vast open floor. A semi-circle of men and women in robes faced us, and the Sentinels held three people off to the left. A larger knot of people milled around on the right. As soon as we came in the door, everyone looked at us.

"Chance Fortunato," a familiar voice boomed out. "You are summoned before the Council of the Magi. Come forth, and be recognized." I let go of Dee's hand and walked to the middle of the semi-circle, Junkyard at my side. "You've been a busy young man," Draeden said, his voice no longer as formal.

"Got a lot to do," I said.

"Indeed you do," Draeden said. "Your proctor has indicated he is ready to give his report. We will hear that first."

I felt a cold wave of dread fill my stomach. I still hadn't cast a spell without a focus, or shown him I could scribe and cast a spell. I was pretty sure throwing around a bolt of Hellfire wasn't going to count, either.

172

Gage came up beside me and cleared his throat, then bowed to the Council.

"Esteemed members of the Council, I'm honored to stand before you today, and I thank the Council for the trust placed in me with this assignment," he said. "In regards to Mister Fortunato's skills, I have seen him cast spells with foci, and I've seen and inspected the tools he has made himself, including the telekinesis wand he is so well-known for. If he would be so kind as to hand me the aforementioned wand, I would like to point out a few things." I dug it out of my pocket and handed it over. "First, I should like to point out that it was handmade with mostly mundane tools. It is the equivalent of taking a pile of junk and building a working car. It is crude, but effective. He has completed most of the tasks required of any apprentice in my presence. I have spoken to Sentinel Dearborn, and she attests to his ability to scribe a spell and cast it. I might add that the circumstances under which he did so required a great deal of improvisation."

"And can he cast a spell without a focus?" Master Moon demanded.

"I have seen him do so multiple times," Gage said without missing a beat. I stifled the urge to do a double take at that, and tried to keep my face from showing how surprised I was.

"Fortunato's moral character has been a cause for serious concern to this Council," Polter said. His voice seemed even more nasal in the open space of the hangar, and I could see his eyes gleam as he watched Gage. "You have spent several days with him. What concerns do you have about his behavior?"

"None, sir," Gage said. "He may be coarse, ill-mannered, and prone to ignorance, but I have seen nothing to indicate any reason to be concerned about his moral character. I dare say that, with considerable effort, he might actually make a good example of himself." A low murmur rippled along the arc of Council members at that.

"What is your recommendation for placement?" Draeden asked after a moment or two.

"Basic apprentice placement, with consideration for Sentinel training, and select remedial course work to fill in the unfortunate gaps in his training."

"Preposterous!" Polter bellowed. "This miscreant will *never* be a Sentinel."

"Perhaps we should let the boy graduate before we start deciding his future for him," Moon said. "Do you feel that he needs further monitoring, Apprentice Gage?"

Gage let out a little gasp and I could see his eyes go wide. "No, sir," he said quickly and shook his head. "The time I've spent with him has been more than sufficient."

"Very well then," Draeden said with a smile. "Thank you for your assistance, Apprentice Gage. I will see to it that your academic record is duly amended."

"It was a pleasure to be of service," Gage said before he bowed and backed away.

"Well, it's official now," Draeden said with a little extra gusto. "Apprentice Fortunato. How does it feel?"

"Exhausting," I said.

"I'm sure you're equal to the position. Wizard Corwyn has informed me that you wished to intercede on behalf of the three accused," he said and gestured toward where Gil stood with Lucinda and Ryker. The first two looked scared, but Ryker just looked miserable. He also looked a little smaller. All three of them were wearing the same clothes I'd last seen them in, though Lucinda had taken off her cat mask. At his motion, they were led to stand in the semi-circle beside me.

Yes, sir," I said. "All three of them are here because of things I did. Lucinda and Ryker were old customers of mine. They were addicted to what I was selling."

"It's no excuse," Polter said, his upper lip curled up in a derisive sneer. "No one was making them come back for more."

"With all *due* respect to Master Polter," I said, "he is wrong. Every spell I cast for someone was designed to erode their will by tapping into their soul and siphoning off a little bit at a time. While I was in servitude to Dulka, I weakened them to the point where they were more vulnerable to Dulka than a normal person would have been. Gilbert Vasquez found his way to them through a website I had set up while working for Dulka. Each of their transgressions are the result of my actions. Thus, their crimes are mine."

"You were cleared, and your father was held liable," Moon said. "What they did took place after that."

"And my father has been held accountable," I said. "But not until this morning. After they did the things they're accused of. This Council said justice was done when I challenged my father. I hold you to that pledge."

Draeden stepped forward, his brow lowered and his jaw clenched. I was guessing he didn't like this any more than Polter did.

"You assume a great deal," he said, his voice tight. "Primarily that the crimes these three committed are part of your past, and won't be taken up as new charges against you, since you insist on taking responsibility for them. While you make a strong argument, it isn't perfect. So, why risk it?"

"Because the Council's idea of justice is usually based on what's convenient, instead of what's right."

"A death sentence pains this Council to pass," Polter said. "But it is necessary to deter others from committing the same—"

"Do you think Gil Vasquez made his choices knowing you would try to kill him for them? He's a *cowan*, he wasn't raised as part of our world, he doesn't know our rules. And who do you think you're punishing if you kill him? Not him, he was ready to make that sacrifice. You're just taking one more thing from a family who's already lost too much."

"The problems of a cowan family are not our concern," Master Hardesty said, her lips pressed tight together as she finished.

"They Goddamn well should be," I blurted out. "Because Hell is on the move, and people like Gil and his family are going to be choosing sides by the thousand!"

The Council went silent at that, a first in my experience. Draeden held up a hand when Polter started to say something, his head tilted to the side as he eyed me.

"Explain," he said.

"Gil was bait," I said. "Dulka wasn't after his soul. He didn't even want *me* back. He was after the Maxilla. He let something slip once he thought he'd won. He said that the world was about to change, and that his Masters would be arriving to claim it."

"And you believed him?" Polter scoffed.

"He was trying to rub my face in it; he thought he'd won. And believe me, so did I. At that point, there was no way either of us saw me walking away." I tried not to roll my eyes as Polter made a rude sound.

"No, Andrew, the boy is right," Draeden said slowly. "Something big is coming. Something potentially earth shattering."

"We've seen no signs—"

"No signs?" Draeden cut him off. "This boy is a sign! The sword he carries is a sign unto itself! The Maxilla has not only called a new Seeker, it has called a Wielder. The last time both a Page and a Knight of Swords walked the world, we went to war on a scale mankind had never seen before."

"But they already defeated the vampire who tried to open Mammon's prison," Hardesty said.

"And yet the Red Count still tried to take the Maxilla to court his favor," Master Moon said.

"All of which goes to prove Apprentice Fortunato's point," Draeden said. "We can't demand that cowans adhere to our rules if they are not aware of them."

"Master Draeden, ignorance of the law is no excuse," Polter said.

"And yet we seek to keep the cowan world ignorant of our very existence," Draeden said. "We foster disbelief, and then punish people for breaking the laws of a world they didn't know existed. We can't let that stand any longer. Bring the young man forward."

A pair of Sentinels led Gil forward, and his father and sister followed them, stopping just outside the half circle. Gil was trying to stand as straight as he could, but his hands were shaking and his shirt was soaked with sweat. Behind him, his sister stood silently, her eyes streaming with silent tears. His father stood stoically, but his eyes weren't dry, either.

"Gilbert Vasquez," Draeden said, his voice stern. "You stand here accused and adjudged guilty of summoning a demon, an act that you knew was wrong. You placed your own soul in peril. To what end?"

"Wh-what?" Gil stammered.

"They want to know why," I said.

176

"I wanted my brother to come back, and my sister is trying to go to nursing school, but we don't have enough money to send her." His shoulders slumped when he finished, and he bowed his head. Draeden gestured to the Sentinels flanking him, and they went to his father and sister and gently ushered them forward to stand by Gilbert. Then Draeden stepped out of the curved line of Council members and went to them, eliciting a gasp from the rest of the Council.

"My father came back from war missing a leg," he said. "And two of my brothers didn't come back at all. If your son is lost, we will at least see to it that he is returned home and honored as he deserves. If he lives, we will find him and see him safely to you. As to your schooling, Miss Vasquez ..." He paused, his eyes focusing elsewhere for a moment.

"It's being seen to, Master Draeden," I said. He looked at me with raised eyebrows for a moment, then nodded to Celia Vasquez.

"Even so," he said. "But, you, Gilbert ... you put your own soul in danger. And you put the souls of others in similar peril. Your intentions may have been noble, but your methods were, at best, misguided. Very few find a way to penetrate the Veil that shrouds our world. Having done so, you must be taught the ways of the world you've uncovered." He stopped and looked over his shoulder at the rest of the Council, then focused his attention on Gilbert again. "I believe a few months under the care of Master Moon will be sufficient to put you on the right path. Mister Vasquez, I can only assume this meets with your approval."

"I don't have much choice, do I?" he asked, his voice brittle.

"You do have other choices, sir," Draeden said. "As did your son. None of the other options left open to him are pleasant. I assure you, he will return to you a better man for this."

"I understand," he said, then looked to his son. "You do what you have to do."

Draeden nodded and the Sentinels ushered Gil and his family away. Four more blue-robed mages brought Ryker and Lucinda forward. Ryker was visibly smaller than he'd been less than eighteen hours ago. His skin was starting to sag and his face was bruised and swollen to the point of being almost unrecognizable. Beside him, Lucinda was barefoot, but still in the black outfit she'd had on earlier. Her eyes darted left and right, and she clung to Ryker like a drowning woman.

"You two," Draeden said, his voice stern and piercing. "Your case is much more serious. Even though you may be below the age of consent, and from the cowan world, the extent and severity of what you have done cannot be overlooked." Lucinda whimpered, and Ryker put his hand out and shoved her behind him.

"Sir," I said.

"No, Chance," Draeden said. "You were in their position, and you made the choice to change. They have shown no such inclination. It will take more than just your pity to earn them clemency."

"No," another voice uttered, and I turned to Ryker in shock. He hadn't spoken once in the last week, and in the face of his silence, that one word hit like a bomb. His mouth moved for a moment before he could speak again, and every word came slowly, almost painfully.

"No pity for me. Don't deserve it. But, Lucy … please. Scared and lost."

"Add my voice to Apprentice Fortunato's," another, softer voice came from the gloom behind us. I turned to look, thinking it sounded familiar, and saw a plump figure with thinning brown hair step into the light. "Not in pity, but compassion."

"You always had a soft heart, Roland," Hardesty said. "And a soft head to match."

"To some of you, compassion is just an inconvenience," Roland Dandry said. The plump little mage gave me a quick nod as he walked past me and stood next to Ryker and Lucinda. "To others, it's a sign of weakness. But when a man you're supposed to despise puts himself in harm's way for you and asks nothing but a kind word in return? It makes you question things. It makes you ask why you're supposed to revere a group of people who would rather kill children than give them a chance to redeem themselves. It makes you wonder why the most powerful wizards in the nation won't risk the wrath of a demon, but one fugitive boy would. So, yes, I will do more than add my voice to the call for clemency here. I will take these two under my care and tutelage, if they will accept my offer."

Draeden smiled and turned back to the Council. "How does the Council say?" he asked. "In favor?" Eight hands came up, more than enough to decide the matter. He turned back to Lucinda and Ryker. "You have been offered a chance to redeem yourselves. I have my own reservations, but I will allow this offer if you will submit to the Horus Gaze, so that Mage Dandry knows your minds. Do you agree?"

Lucinda nodded quickly, but Ryker was slower to respond. "Don't deserve it," he said, the words coming a little faster now. "But I won't say no."

"Be gentle with yourself, young man," Dandry said as he stepped up to Ryker. "As gentle as you were with your friend. Now, look into my eyes, Ryker. See me, and let me See you."

Ryker's gaze locked onto Dandry's and, for a moment, I felt like the world paused. Ryker's face went slack, and his mouth opened a little. Dandry, on the other hand, looked like he was getting the worst end of things. His lower lip trembled and tears began to course down his face as he held the gaze. Then they both took a step back, and Ryker reached out to grab Dandry's shoulder and steady him.

"I've got you, sir," he said as Dandry shook his head and wiped tears from his cheeks. It was hard to tell in the swollen mass of Ryker's face, but his expression seemed to hold some affection to it.

"Thank you, son," Dandry said. "I promise you, I'll do better by you. Now, Lucinda, it's your turn."

She looked at Ryker but didn't move otherwise. Ryker put one big hand on her shoulder as he turned to her. "He's okay, Lucy," he said. "Trust him. You'll see."

She slowly stepped forward, but Draeden was at Dandry's side first.

"Roland, maybe you should wait ..." he said, but Dandry shook his head and squared his shoulders.

"No, Master Draeden," he said. "These two have endured worse things than this. I will do no less for them. Now, Lucinda, look into my eyes. See me, and let me See you."

Lucinda's expression mirrored Ryker's from earlier, except for the slight smile that tugged at the corners of her mouth. At first, Dandry's face looked saddened like before, but then his jaw

179

clenched and he took a deep breath. When they pulled back a moment later, it was Lucinda who burst into tears.

"I'm sorry!" she said as Dandry took her in his arms. "I felt it … at the end … how mad you were. I'm sorry! Please, don't be mad!"

"No, child," he said, this time with steel in his voice. "You misunderstand. I'm not angry at you. Not at you." Lucinda looked up at him and he continued. "I'm angry at the people who hurt you."

"Mage Dandry," Draeden said after a moment. "You've Seen these two, and you know their minds, as they know yours. Is it still your wish to vouch for them?"

"Yes, even more than before."

"Ryker and Lucinda, what do you—"

"Yeah!"

"Definitely!"

Draeden nodded. "So be it. You will still be watched closely." He gestured and the Sentinels led the three of them out. As they passed me, Dandry looked at me and smiled, and I felt as if the world was not only a little better off for people like Dandry walking around in it, but also like things were a little more … right.

"Is there any *other* business for the Council?" Draeden surveyed the room.

"It looks like that's everything," Moon said with a smile.

"Thank God," Hardesty said.

"Then our business here is done. We open this circle."

"Let it remain unbroken," came the reply.

Dee and Dr. Corwyn broke from the crowd as Draeden came up to me. He looked at Dee and then gave me a broad smile that reminded me of a shark.

"So, it looks as though you won't be the only Fortunato attending the Franklin Academy," he said.

"That's up to her and Mom," I said. "But why would you send her?"

"Isn't it obvious?" Draeden laughed. "Corwyn gave her an iron-cored wand, and she still knocked a grown man off his feet. You, young lady, are going to be a powerful mage someday."

180

"I can be anything I *want* to be when I grow up," Dee said with her chin thrust forward.

Draeden shook his head. "I guess the attitude is genetic," he said as he walked away.

The rest of the Council was already halfway to the other side of the hangar, and the crowd inside was headed for the doors closer to us. Gage called my name out and trotted over before we could join the throng.

"I wanted to give you your telekinesis rod back, and say goodbye."

"Leaving already?" I asked.

"A week and a half in the same state with you is stressful enough," he said as he handed my TK rod over. "Closer proximity to you than that warrants hazard pay."

"And here I thought we were just starting to get to know each other." I turned the rod over in my hands, then asked the question that was on my mind. "Why did you tell them I'd cast a spell without a focus?"

"Because you did," he said.

I had to admit, he had the whole enigmatic thing down better than I did, but I had a steady glare that very few people could resist. "No, I didn't," I said. "I was there for every spell I cast since you got here. I think I would know."

"You'd think you would," he said as he plucked the rod out of my hands. With a casual twist, he pulled the butt cap free and turned it over to let flakes of magnetite pour onto his palm.

"What did you do to my TK rod?" I demanded, my face getting hot.

"Relax, I didn't *do* anything to it," he said as he poured the magnetite back into the rod. "I noticed it was broken right before you went to your father's. I replaced the core and put the cap back on, but I never got the opportunity to tell you about it before you left. I'd completely forgotten about it until the next time I saw you, and by the time I could address the situation, you'd already cast a spell to shield yourself. It was all rather sudden."

"So, all last night, I was casting TK spells on my own?" I asked.

"Indeed you were. As such, congratulations are in order on being granted full Apprentice status. I only ask one thing; that you do not dishonor the Academy." The condescending tone was gone, and for the first time, he spoke to me like an equal. He stuck his hand out, and I took it.

"I won't disappoint you," I said as we shook hands. He smiled, and it finally reached his eyes.

"I know," he said. "Good luck." He turned and headed for the far side of the hangar, and I went to join Dr. C and Dee by the door. As I got to the slanting rectangle of light near the door, I felt a familiar shift in my perceptions and heard a bell ring. My vision shifted as well, and I saw a sapling on a spit of sand in a creek.

Dr. Corwyn caught me as I staggered. He helped me get my feet back under me, then looked closely at me. I shook my head to clear it, but the afterimage was too clear in my mind.

"Chance, what is it?" he asked, his face etched with concern.

"My vision ..." I said. "Take Dee home. I know what I need to do."

Chapter 12
~ Rely little on prophecy and visions, for they do not instruct
you in your actions; they only remind you that you are on the
right path. ~ Oracle of Delphi

Maybe it was two days without sleep and almost as long without a decent meal, but there was no moment more perfect than the Missouri sunset unfolding around me. The sky was a pale blue fading to orange and red along the horizon. On my left, the trees that grew alongside the road were a wall of brown, gray and green, with shafts of light slanting through them to dapple the white gravel road. On my right, an open field was a pallet of pale green with a thousand different colors of flowers in bloom. Fairies and pixies flitted into sight and dropped back below the foliage on both sides of the road, and the first buzz of frogs and insects started to rise into the air. A breeze ruffled through my hair, dispelling the worst of the heat and bringing me the scents of clover and wildflowers. It was a perfect time and place.

I'd been here before, but the last time had been at night. Then, I didn't have the time to appreciate how pretty it was out here, and I certainly didn't have the light. The road forked, and I followed it to the left, like I had on my birthday, and like I had been doing in my dreams for the past few weeks. The sun started to dip below the horizon, the sky above me turned from blue to turquoise, and the fading light turned the clouds crimson. Laughter rang out from up the road, and I felt a moment of concern. Having visions probably wasn't a good thing with strangers around. A few steps later, the concern dissolved as I came to the edge of a campsite and saw a familiar silver Mustang parked off the road.

"What are you guys doing here?" I asked. Shade, Lucas, and Wanda looked at me from where they sat at the concrete picnic table, and I could see the same question in their eyes. Lucas's eyes were red and puffy, and Shade looked more than a little lost, her gaze going from Lucas to me and back.

"I think," Wanda said absently, her gaze not quite focused on me, "we were waiting for you."

"But how did you …?" I asked, not exactly sure what I wanted to say.

"Wanda called us," Shade said, her voice tinged with concern. "She said there was someplace we needed to be. It's like she's been in a trance since I picked her up."

"She led us straight here," Lucas added. "And then, she stopped."

"It wasn't time," Wanda said. "It still isn't. Almost, though." Looking at her, I hesitated to say her gaze was vacant. It was like she was seeing more than we were, focusing on things we couldn't see.

"Time for what?" I asked. I knew why I was here, but why had my friends and my girlfriend been called here?

"Magick and wonder," Wanda said with a smile as the sun dipped below the horizon, and the last light of day faded. True dark seemed to settle around us like a blanket, then hundreds of bright green points of light rose from the ground around us as fireflies took flight. The pale blue and white glow of pixies and fairies slowly descended around us, adding their own buzz and high-pitched giggles to the night sounds. They hovered in place for a moment or two, then moved in unison, creating a swirling pattern that bent on itself, then back the other way, forming something completely new and beautiful before bursting apart and reforming into something else entirely. We watched in awe as Nature danced to some unheard tune before us. After a minute, everything paused, and a path opened in the glowing mass, leading down toward the creek. A few pixies darted down it, chasing each other and giggling. Wanda turned to us and nodded her head toward the path with a knowing smile before she started walking. I followed her and felt a growing certainty that this was exactly what was supposed to be happening. We followed the glowing trail down to the creek, where fireflies hovered over the water, showing a way for us.

The creek bed was shallow where we stepped, and our path led across fallen logs or stones that made for a dry path most of the way. Then we were standing at the edge of the circle of saplings that marked the Maxilla's resting place. The circle of stones was still there but the runes were faded, and a circle of mushrooms made a fairy ring around Mr. Chomsky's staff, which still stood upright where I'd planted it. A vine spiraled its way up the length of it, and fae darted around the top. We all

184

stepped into the ring of saplings in unison, and it seemed like the world stopped just inside that circle.

Fireflies and fae circled the top of the staff, and I went to it. That it was still standing upright was amazing in its own right. When I got close, I could see a small green nodule near the top, and as I looked closer, I realized it wasn't from the vine. This little green bud had emerged from the staff itself. I stared at it in wonder then reached out and gently touched one finger to the base of it. It was real, living and warm from the sun's heat. As I stared at the bud, awestruck … it opened.

It was as if I was watching the Universe itself being born as the little green leaf unfurled, seeing something unimaginably huge mirrored in a tiny leaf. The change in perspective made me feel like I was falling, but also like I was floating, and a hundred things all seemed to be happening at the same time in my brain.

The Vision I'd been waiting for wasn't just mine. It was being given to all four of us, a glimpse of what could be.

Both separately and together, you have put your feet on the path of a powerful Destiny, I heard/knew. We were all hearing that, and yet, I knew it was meant as much for me specifically as it was for everyone else. I could feel all four of us as we stood in separate spaces that all seemed to touch for the moment. We could all see a shimmering path stretched out in front of us, every inch of it an image of what might be if we kept on the same path, hundreds of thousands of possibilities laid out in crystal clarity.

It is not an easy path. You will find the way contested if you persist. I knew that pain and suffering, lonely days and faded hope were down that path, but even the thought of doing things any other way was like looking into a pit of regret. Who I was at the end of that path was someone I actually wanted to be. Other roads looked comfortable, but again, regret always seemed to follow alongside the easy way. And I was okay with that. I'd never been very good at normal.

The world seemed to rush past me, and suddenly I was standing alone in the clearing. There was a tension in the air, like I was expecting something to happen, though I had no clue what that something was. But when She walked into the circle, I was certain I'd been waiting there all my life for her to show up. Whoever she was.

"Who am I?" she asked for me. "Perhaps I am Fate. Mayhap I am Destiny. To some I might be the Future."

"I don't believe in Fate," I said.

"I don't require your belief to exist," she said with a smile as she took a step closer. Her features shifted, and she looked younger. "But then, what you don't believe in ... is what I'm not."

"What you're not?" I said.

"Set in stone," she said. Her hand came up and she pressed it against my chest. I could feel the pressure, but not just on my skin, like her hand was passing through me. "I'm only as real as maybe. Your Destiny, your Future, is always in flux. All I can show you is what will probably happen. And that means only the really big things, those with the most momentum." She stepped back and pulled her hand away from my body, her face lined at the corners of her eyes and mouth, streaks of gray in her hair.

"Why are you telling me this?" I asked her. The clearing was gone, and we floated in some empty, dark place. I sensed movement just beyond the blackness, and didn't quite hear a rush of sound in the distance.

"So you will understand what you're seeing, and what you aren't," a little girl Destiny said from beside me. "And, most importantly, why you're seeing it."

"Why is ... that important?" I asked, trying to get around saying why twice in one sentence.

"When you took up the Page of Swords after Sydney died, you made the choice to become the Maxilla's guardian, and thus the Seeker later on. *You* became the Page of Swords because you *chose* that Fate, and thus the *wyrd* became yours. That was ..." she paused, now a young woman, "a small thing compared to what lies before you. You must understand this, Chance Fortunato, even if only for this brief moment. The futures I will show to you, you must consent to. The belief that Fate is set in stone, that the Future is fixed and beyond our control, it is the great lie mortals tell themselves to avoid this simple truth: All great Destinies, the ones that matter, the Fates that are the hardest but most worthwhile … all of those Destinies are chosen."

"What about the shitty ones?" I asked bitterly.

"Fate has no hand in what mortals do to each other," she said with a lingering sadness. "Those futures can be changed, like you changed yours. But that is what lies behind you; it leads to what lies before you. Are you ready to See?"

"Show me," I said.

Fear not. I opened my eyes to the sight of the Milky Way stretched across the night sky. The sounds of water over stone reached my ears, with a chorus of insects and frogs in the background. Two words resonated in my memory, like the pronouncement of Titans.

Fear not.

I had no idea what it meant. Vague memories of speaking to a woman … mists that dissipated even as I tried to recall them. All I was left with was the impression that something was going to happen. Those memories solidified on closer inspection. Suddenly, fear was the only emotion my brain had room for. The seals on Mammon's prison were weakened, and getting weaker by the day. The Emperor of the deepest pit of the Abyss, imprisoned for millennia, was stirring and all the horrific beasts that had been imprisoned with him were not slumbering as deeply as they once did.

Worse yet, the plan to awaken and free him wasn't exactly his own. Someone else had plans for the Emperor of Hell. And I was supposed to stop it. No … I was supposed to *help* stop it. I wasn't alone; I had three allies lying on the ground next to me. They weren't the only ones I could call on if I needed help. And, I had a magick sword. Even Mammon would think twice about facing off against the Maxilla.

"Wow," I heard Lucas say from somewhere off to my right. "I feel … weird."

"I feel … peaceful," Wanda said.

Shade crawled over to me and laid her head in the hollow of my shoulder, so that I could wrap my left arm around her, but she was still looking up at the sky.

"What about you?" I asked softly.

187

For a few moments, she was silent, then she took a deep breath. "It's … complicated," she finally said. "I just hope I'm worth it to you in the end."

"I could say pretty much the same thing," I said. "Being with me is going to be rough."

"I'm used to that," she said with a chuckle. "No matter what, if you love me, it's all worth it. And I don't plan on loving anyone else but you."

I kissed the top of her head, then looked back up at the stars. My thoughts came back to the little leaf growing from the top of Mr. Chomsky's staff. One image from my vision came back to me. I was going to come back here someday. And where Mr. Chomsky's staff stood right then, I remembered seeing a tree.

As the stars drifted overhead, I felt the first tears slide down the sides of my face. Ryker and Lucinda were in good hands, and some of the damage I'd done was being mended. Every spell I'd ever cast for my father and Dulka was undone, every person I'd enslaved for them was free. And Dulka was back in Hell, which meant even my father had a shot at redemption. I'd made a promise the night my mom brought me home, to make things right. Over the past couple of days, I'd started to make good on those promises.

Now, to face the threat of Mammon, there was me, a sixteen-year-old apprentice, ready to stand in the way of his return. Because someone thought *that* was a good idea. But in spite of the long odds, I still felt like I had a shot at stopping him. For the first time in a long time, I had hope.

As the stars began to fade in the east, we got up and headed for our vehicles.

"Get them home safe," I told Shade as Wanda and Lucas climbed into her silver Mustang.

"You want a ride back to your car?" she asked.

I shook my head. "I need to leave the same way I came in," I said. I leaned forward and kissed her, then rubbed my cheek against hers. "I've loved you since forever," I whispered in her ear. "And I don't plan on stopping…ever." She smiled as she pulled back and touched my cheek.

"I'm never going to get tired of hearing you say that," she said before she gave me a quick kiss and got in her car. I watched her car pull away, then started the long trek to my own car. The sky was gray by the time I reached it, and I saw the red blinking light on my phone that meant I'd missed a call. A familiar number showed on the screen when I slid it open, and I hit the call button as I turned the key in the Mustang's ignition.

"Hey, everything's cool," I said as soon as the call picked up on the other end. "Come by my house to get your stuff."

Three hours later, I pulled into the driveway at home. Dee was a limp, blanket covered bundle in my back seat. I got out and opened the trunk to retrieve the Maxilla, then leaned into the back to pull my little sister to me. Briefly, I wondered what our neighbors might think, assuming any of them were home to see. I pushed the door closed and allowed myself a smile at what I must look like, a teenage boy carrying a limp girl into the house with a big ass sword strapped across his back.

I laid Dee down on the couch as gently as I could, and winced as I heard a motorcycle engine and a throaty V8 out front. Dee stirred for a moment, then quieted when I told her everything was okay. Once I was fairly sure she was asleep, I headed for the door and yanked it open. Six feet of Nazirite stood on the other side, his right hand drawn back like he was about to start pounding on my door. In the four months or so that I'd known Steve Donovan, he had never *once* come anywhere close to being subtle or quiet. Now was no exception. Frustrated in his attempt to pound my door into submission, he smiled and opened his mouth to speak. My right hand came up and I covered his mouth, then put the forefinger of my left hand over my lips and pushed him back.

Even though he was as strong as Samson, he offered me no resistance as I pushed him off the miniscule front porch and onto the sidewalk that led to our door. Over his shoulder, I could see T-Bone, chuckling as he leaned against his blue Torino.

"Mm-mm rffmmhrrr," Steve said into my palm.

"Yeah, it's good to see you, too," I said, even though I had no idea what he'd actually been trying to say. "My sister's asleep, so use your inside voice. No, wait, that's still too loud. Use *my* inside voice." I pulled my hand away.

"But if I use your inside voice, what are you going to use?" he asked, actually pitching his voice soft enough that I wasn't afraid he'd wake anyone up.

"Interpretive dance," I said as I unslung the Maxilla. I heard footsteps on the grass as T-Bone came up.

"We were just about shittin' bricks when that thing up and disappeared," the gun-wielding Hand of Death said after we exchanged greetings.

"How'd you end up with it?" Donovan asked.

"I'm still connected to it," I said. "Dulka used that connection to summon it."

"Makes sense," T-Bone said. "Anything happens to Wonder Boy here, you take over as its guardian again 'til you find the next Wielder."

"Yeah, about that," I said. "Seems like we didn't exactly save the day as much as we thought when we killed Etienne. Even though we disrupted the spell, there was already some damage done. The bonds on Mammon's prison are breaking."

"That's some serious shit," T-Bone said as Steve frowned at me in confusion. "How long before they go completely?"

"I don't know," I said. "Dr. Corwyn figures that if they're left alone, it could be decades, maybe even a century or two. I'm not giving good odds on that, though."

"Does the Council know about this?"

"They will."

T-Bone nodded and turned back to Steve. "Come on, kid," he said as he headed back to his car. "We got us a lot of work to do." Steve and I clasped hands before he turned and went back to his motorcycle, then both vehicles were pulling away, headed back to the secluded farm where Steve was being trained by the Hands of Death.

I sat down on the front step, suddenly feeling a little lighter. The Maxilla was back in the right hands, and the right people knew what they needed to. Behind me, I heard Junkyard paw the screen door open, and a moment later, he was sitting beside me. He looked at me with big, puppy eyes, and I put my arm across his shoulders and rubbed at the place behind his ear that he liked. I scratched at an itch on my shoulder as I waited for Dr. C to bring Mom home and tried to enjoy the calm moment. There would be a lot of hugging and excitement soon enough, but for now, I could sit and be still. My eyes closed on their own, and I saw the image that had been taunting my memory. Black wings, and a circle. It meant something, but I couldn't make sense of it, or of the words rattling around at the edge of my thoughts.

The sound of Dr. Corwin's Range Rover pulling into the driveway pulled me out of the quiet space I'd built in my head. Junkyard barked a greeting, and a moment later, I heard Dee's happy squeal. She came barreling out the front door as Mom got out of the truck, and wrapped her in a flying hug.

The moment of calm was gone, the image so much mental static in my head. Maybe I didn't get a summer vacation. Hell, I barely got two minutes to myself. Then again, I was an Apprentice Mage. It was pretty much a given that things weren't going to be easy. I wrapped Mom in a hug of my own and let those problems wait. For now, this was enough.

For now, I could ignore the thunder on the horizon. But I couldn't forget; there was a storm coming and there was no getting out of its way.

Dear Reader,

Welcome back to Chance's world. This book came as something of a surprise to me, since I had opriginally only planned on having entries for the fall and spring semesters of each year. But then, a couple of summers ago while I was in San Angelo, I found myself wondering about Chance's summer. Of course, he can't have a boring summer! At least, not this summer. So, Vision Quest was born of a conglomeration of ideas.

Of course, a lot happened in this story, and we'll be seeing the repercussions from this one for some time to come.

As always, I welcome your opinions in the form of reviews, so please, let me know where I can improve! I don't take reviews personally, and I always look for patterns of concerns. I always appreciate your feedback. Also, if you want to make sure you are always notified of any new releases, you can follow my author page on Amazon.

And, the best for last, thank you for reading Chance's latest adventure. I wouldn't be able to keep writing without you, so I want you, dear reader, to know how much I appreciate your support as an independent author. My readers are my heroes.

Stay awesome, and check the next pages for more great books from my fellow authors at Irrational Worlds!

Ben Reeder
September, 2015

Wake Up Call by EM Ervin

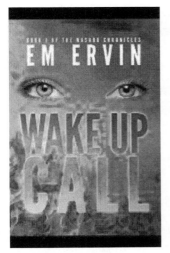

Jo is your average, everyday seventeen year old girl.

Wait, no she's not. Not by a longshot.

She is a girl with a secret. Possessed of powers no one would believe even if they knew that she had them. The ability to create illusions at thought is a dangerous weapon in the most responsible of hands, and Jo's aren't exactly squeaky clean.

Ever the trouble magnet, Jo is accustomed to finding more than her fair share of problems - most of which she brings on herself. The rebellious daughter of a senator and a diplomat, she has a rap sheet and has been kicked out of nearly every prestigious private school on the Eastern Seaboard.

This time, she's vowed to make an actual effort. Not to fit in - that'd be impossible - but to just not get kicked out.

Of course, this would be the school that turns out to be the favorite hunting grounds of a homicidal ghost.

What could possibly happen?

On The Matter Of The Red Hand by JM Guillen

In the distant world of Cæstre, a city teeters on the edge of tainted oblivion.

Thom never quite got accustomed to the visions that came like molten gold in his blood- but then the visions were just part of the job. As a Judicar, his oaths to the city bring him nothing but problems, but this time it's a problem that may get him killed.

Or worse.

Thom's alchemical visions lead him to the door of a madman- Santiago Il Ladren. Santiago is a monster, rumored to have his enemies creatively tortured to death- that is, the ones that don't simply vanish.

It is possible that Santiago will have Thom skinned alive, just for asking the wrong questions.

Soon, the mystery takes a sharp turn. Thom is lost in a labyrinth of misty streets and knife wielding thugs, looking to leave him all too dead. There is a missing girl- and it happens that Santiago is her brother. Thom stumbles through dark alleyways and only finds more mysteries, and beatings from unknown men.

Then things take a darker turn.

Soon it becomes obvious that someone is dealing with secrets that are forbidden and depraved. Every step Thom takes is another down a twisted road that leads to forgotten alchemies and experiments in horror, hidden in plain sight. Finally, lost within strange shadows, Thom is confronted with stark, horrifying truths that he never wanted to face.

Unfortunately, Thom may have learned these truths a touch too late.

The Herald of Autumn by JM Guillen

There are things unseen in the world of men, strange things that live in the secret cracks between places.

Fortunately for the children of men, there is one who protects us from the darkness that we cannot see.

Every year, with the death of summer, Tommy Maple, the Herald of Autumn, awakens to again wander the land. Wherever he goes, red and golden leaves follow him, and he hunts the twisted creatures in the darkness.

This Autumn, however, is different from those in the past.

Tommy awakens to the taunting of a mysterious and elusive worker-of-wonders. Soon, a sinister tale unfolds- a story made from the whispering of forgotten legends that ends with a dark revelation.

A story that Tommy has always been part of, even though he didn't know it.

Far from the eyes of men is an ancient abomination, hidden from even from the Facility. As ever, Tommy pokes where he should not, and soon the hunter is the one that is hunted, chased through a misbegotten wood by a creature who seems to be little more than darkness and feckless hunger.

The behemoth is pure horror, and can unmake everything Tommy is.

As the Herald faces a foe unlike any other, will he fall to the darkness that haunts our world? Will the shadows of a lost age devour him, causing him to be reborn as one of the world's sorrows? Or can he trust the wonder-worker, a creature spun from little more than trickery, malevolence and deceit?

Coming soon:
Aberrant Vectors (Dossiers of Asset 108) by JM Guillen

November 17,1999
San Francisco, California

Few things are worse than a system undergoing a cold boot...

Michael Bishop is an Asset of the Facility, but tonight is his night off. His expectation is to have a few drinks with his friend Wyatt Guthrie, perhaps go out and have a night on the town.

But the Facility has made other arrangements.

Before he realizes what has happened, Asset 108 has been dispatched to a carnage-filled interior location, lit only with flickering and lurid light. As Michael drifts through the shadows, encountering stuttering and broken Facility technology, he attempts to figure out why he has been dispatched here and what his mission is.

Yet before he can, he is fighting for his life.

Soon, with his personal gear malfunctioning, Bishop is standing against foes familiar to him, foes that have been transformed into inhuman abominations. With time running out, he finds his way to his cadre, and they fight their way to the depths of the mysterious Spire. There, they discover remnants of a lost, broken, carnage-filled world.

As Michael and his cadre stands against the inhabitants of an entire world of bloody ruin, he is forced to face a painful truth.

It is possible that this dossier will be his last...

Made in the USA
San Bernardino, CA
18 April 2016